True View

True View

James George

iUniverse, Inc.
Bloomington

True View

iUniverse books may be ordered through booksellers or by contacting:

iUniverse
1663 Liberty Drive
Bloomington, IN 47403
www.iuniverse.com
1-800-Authors (1-800-288-4677)

ISBN: 978-1-4759-4746-5 (sc)
ISBN: 978-1-4759-4747-2 (e)
ISBN: 978-1-4759-4748-9 (hc)

Printed in the United States of America

iUniverse rev. date: 10/2/2012

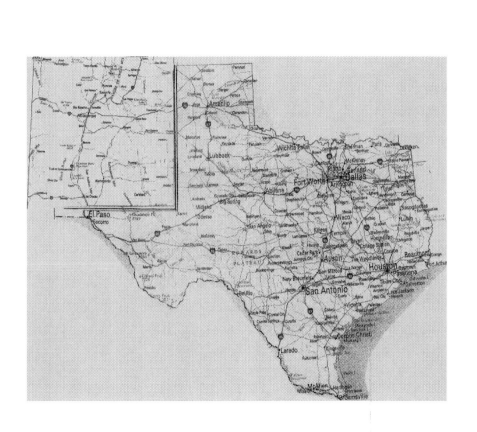

One

"Tower, I have a lock on radar and closing in. Cloud coverage is hampering my ability to gain a visual. Will close to within five hundred meters and report." A last-known conversation archived at Kinross Air Force Base.

"Target appears to be cylinder shaped with protrusions on two sides. Target appears to be an aircraft. Target appears to be sitting on land but surrounded by water. Target is lying on a lake bed. Stray thought of 'Superior' comes to mind. Stick to facts and write it down." I continue to think of the last project and am wondering if the UFO disclosure was ever made of the 1953 Lake Superior crash of the F-89.

I have to shake it off and concentrate on this audience.

"We do not perform magic, conjure up the supernatural, or delve into the occult. We use a manual created from science and years of research and repeated application. Remote viewing is a science; it's not mindreading. Questions, anyone?"

Good, no hands up.

"Thank you for listening, and enjoy your lunch. Thanks for inviting me today."

Walking past rows of tables, I get smiles and small waves. These people were once the world's greatest geniuses, but old age has taken a toll. They attend the meetings but are not really excited about them anymore. Being a member rocks my world. It's a good break from my day-to-day routine.

I was recommended to the Mensa group by Teacher, a well-known expert in the remote viewing world. I studied under him for four years while I was also teaching mathematics and computer science at Texas Tech. I grew tired of the academic world and wanted to see if I could make a living as a remote viewer.

I applied for employment with the government at the federal building here in Lubbock six years ago. I was granted an interview with an intelligence group but was rejected; my skill as a viewer was not understood, much less needed. However, a few days later I was contacted by another agency that ultimately trained me and put me to work.

The drive home is short. When I arrive at my house, my dogs—Bruno, an extra-large miniature schnauzer, and Rocco, who is just extra large—really need to go outside. Nothing more devoted than those two. Out the back door they go. I need to check my e-mail for my next assignment.

I fire up the computer and hear a voice: "Welcome." There it is on the screen: a list of current targets. Even though each is no more than a series of numbers, looking into them will lead to multiple descriptors. Common numbers will lead to unknown places and events.

I smile and think, *What a way to make a living.*

My computer sounds off with an incoming message. *Beep,* "Time to go to work." That is the phrase I have chosen to hear when they have a high-priority job for me. The subject line is blank, a signal that something is wrong. Normally there would be a series of numbers. I decide it is best not to open the e-mail. *Hmm, wonder what that's about.*

There goes the work phone. They rarely call. Communication is routinely done via e-mail. Maybe they are calling to tell me about the e-mail I just got. At least they could have waited for me to finish my lunch.

I see that familiar number. Not sure whether or not I want to answer. These guys make common feds look like amateurs.

If I don't answer, there will be a knock at the door.

"Hello?" No response. Wrong number, maybe? I'm concerned; I've been told to follow agency instructions if this happens. I prepare to leave immediately.

Apparently protocol has been compromised. I keep a go-bag ready for just such an occurrence. When it happens, all I need for basic survival is immediately in my hands.

I grab the bag from the closet and leave the house, walking casually. The dogs are still outside; they should have enough food and water until I get back. Better get the all-clear soon.

2

Nothing in the neighborhood appears unusual. It's the middle of the day; typically there's not much going on then. Everyone around here is either at school or work.

I walk two blocks to my local minimarket and go up to the deli to check out the menu.

At the end of the counter to my right I see two well-dressed men, definitely out of place. No ball caps, straw hats, or boots. I don't know them, but I'm pretty sure they know me.

"Ashlee?" one of them says. I don't respond.

"Ashlee?" They move quickly toward me, and one of them grabs my arm. "It's us, stop," he whispers, leaning into me.

I turn.

They're both over six feet tall, one wearing a gray suit and the other a faded black one. They are clean-cut and look serious.

The one in gray looks like he's pushing sixty. His hair is almost the same color as his suit. Chiseled face with a little slump in the shoulders.

The other looks younger, more alert, probably early forties. He has thick black hair, tan-colored skin, dark brown eyes. Funny—we have the same hair and skin color, but I have my dad's blue eyes.

"What?" I ask, playing it cool.

"You did well," the younger agent says, stepping close.

"Let's go," he says, pointing outside to a Suburban. I walk casually in the direction indicated, wishing they had a less obvious vehicle. Not like anyone will notice a big black Suburban with blacked-out windows.

We pull off in the opposite direction of the federal building downtown on Texas Avenue, where I assumed we'd go.

According to the older one, my phone and computer had been hacked.

"How is that possible?" I ask. "Aren't we the best of the best?"

They are silent. To say I'm a little worried would be an understatement.

We're approaching the end of the city limits. All I see are dry, dusty fields. It hasn't rained in West Texas in months. All the crops are dead or dying.

"What are we doing out here?"

"Stay quiet; you'll be briefed shortly," the younger one tells me. I stay quiet.

After a few minutes riding in silence, they introduce themselves. "My name is Agent Chris Jenkins," says the older of the two. "This is my partner, Agent Raul Cortez. We were sent to escort you to a secure location."

"Which office are you from? Abilene?" I ask.

"Amarillo. We'll drive you around until we get further instructions," Jenkins, the driver says.

"Why? I'm just a pencil pusher."

"An operation has begun, and you are to participate. Your skill is needed."

"For what? I work from home, not in the field."

"Your security clearance has just exceeded your pay grade," Jenkins says, looking at me in the rearview mirror.

I didn't know there was one higher. I was assigned a security clearance after completing training with the NSA, CIA, and FBI. Those took nearly a year, and then I had further training with a task group to learn the ins and outs of federal operations.

Having a PhD in mathematics and computer science from the University of Texas was only a part of what landed me this job. Having completed all of the advanced levels of remote viewing training was the kicker.

We are somewhere southeast of town, traveling across an abandoned farm—one of many in this dry part of the state. Flat, but with acres of dried-up cotton fields. Dust stirring in every direction. My watch shows it to be close to 3:00 p.m.

There are no buildings anywhere on the horizon. Just good old Texas prairie—flat, dirty, and full of cactus, cotton, and wide-open skies.

Cortez produces a small black keypad from the glove box. He keeps his back to me, and I hear him punching in a code. I count six numbers with random electronic tones to reduce the possibility of others identifying the digits.

About twenty yards in front of us, the ground begins to open. At first it seems there is a crack forming, but it continues to expand and grow in length. The ground begins to lift. Not one cactus or mesquite bush slides away. An opening twenty-five feet long and twenty feet wide appears.

Jenkins slowly drives forward. As we approach the opening, I see a ramp leading down into the earth. The ground that appeared to open is really two large metal plates with hydraulic lifts on the bottom. We begin the descent.

I grab the door handle—locked! They both snicker.

My heart is racing, and I begin to sweat.

We travel down the ramp, and as we do, the opening above us closes. Now I'm terrified!

When the doors close, lights come on.

We come to rest in a room with gray walls similar to a large garage.

Jenkins instructs me: "Get out and follow us."

Without having another option, I get out. About five yards in front of the Suburban is a gray metal outline of a door.

Jenkins opens it and steps inside, leaving the door slightly ajar. Cortez stays with me.

I can hear Jenkins talking to someone inside, and I recognize the voice. It's Senior Agent Daniel Strepp—not technically my "boss," but he's the guy I most often answer to.

After a few minutes, Jenkins comes back out and ushers me inside with Cortez at my heels. The room is about twenty by forty and filled with high-tech electronic equipment, as well as lots of standard-issue government desks, all of them unoccupied.

Senior Agent Strepp steps over to me and holds out his hand. I shake it tentatively, feeling uneasy and waiting for an explanation as to what's going on and why I'm here.

"Ashlee! It's nice to see you again. It's been too long since we've met face-to-face. Sorry for the cloak-and-dagger routine, but your talent is needed."

"We've had secret assignments before," I remind him. "But this is way out of the norm, especially for me."

Strepp stops smiling. He takes a piece of paper from a desk near him, frowns heavily, and takes a deep breath. He stares at the paper a moment, raises his eyes, and looks directly at me. I have seen him serious before, but this is extreme.

He turns to the desk, sits down behind it, and gestures for me to sit in the chair opposite.

I scan the room. Track lighting in the ceiling is turned off, but the desk lamps are on. There are large screens along the wall. The room reminds me of something from a sci-fi movie.

He begins to fill me in on the reason for all the drama.

"Some of our friendlier foreign intelligence agencies have been tracking a suspected terrorist across Asia and into South America. They had him into Mexico but lost him somewhere in Mexico City. We're fairly sure that the suspect has entered Texas through Laredo. We don't know where he's from, and he managed to avoid a full-face photo at the customs office in Laredo, so facial recognition is out. We think he may have a contact in the Southwest. We have lost track of him, but since so many others are interested, we intend to find him and discover his intentions."

Though he probably knows more, he doesn't give me any other details. He knows better. Target must not be known to me. Just knowing he is from another country is pushing it.

"Why all the secrecy? Why are we out here, swallowed up by the desert?"

He gives no explanation. The room is quiet.

Why are all the screens and computers off? Where are all the personnel needed to man this room? I wonder. I want to say something to him, but considering our location, what I have been told, and the silence in the room, I decide to wait for him to make the next move.

"You can't go home. Is the pack you brought prepared as you were taught?"

That was not the way to break the silence. My pack only has personal items I would need for a weekend away. They told me to have a go-bag ready, like a sailor's overboard bag. I never took the sailor example seriously though. Oops. He is aware the bag has none of the tools necessary to perform my job. "If you're planning a long working vacation for me, I'll need more than my toothbrush and dental floss," I say.

Strepp opens a desk drawer and hands me a three-inch binder and says, "Courtesy of your Teacher."

"Official US document" reads the cover. I open it; it's a duplicate of my manual.

"When did you see Teacher? Where was he?"

"It's been a while. Check the manual."

I look at the bottom of the front page and see the date, 1986. My heart sinks. Using an outdated manual to find a person today is like handing me a Commodore 64 and asking me to surf the web.

Daniel says, "Keep reading, whose name is listed?"

I read through all the official government mumbo jumbo and find a name. "Teacher!"

"He thought you might need it."

I thumb through the manual. Mostly the same as mine: index, terms, multiple pages of instructions, and a glossary. Printed on standard government-grade paper, words are fading and several pages are beginning to separate from the binder.

Daniel reaches into his drawer again; this time he hands me what looks like a high-tech laptop.

"Courtesy of Uncle Sam, it has a GPS tracking device inside. The satellite connection allows Internet and global tracking of your location."

He knows my background, so he's aware that I'm familiar with the technology. When attending initial orientation in Washington, DC, I was shown all the latest and greatest technology. What a long way from kindergarten in 1981.

"Ashlee, I know you'll need your standard supplies: pencils, paper, ruler, et cetera ... I assumed your backpack wouldn't be equipped with the tools of the trade. You are to go strictly old school with this assignment. It's okay; you'll find all your tools in your new desk."

It's been a long time since I used only the basics. My setup at home has software with sketching abilities.

He hands me a blank card with a magnetic strip on the back.

"This is for purchasing necessities and to draw cash." He smiles slightly. "We'll be monitoring the usage."

Then he reaches into his jacket pocket and hands me a cell phone.

"Thanks, how many minutes are available?" I say, smiling back at him. "And what about my house? Are you going to pull that out of your desk, too?"

"Your house is parked at Reese Airfield," he says. He reaches into his pants pocket and pulls out a set of keys that he hands to me.

Confused, I start to challenge him. "This is all great, but what about my dogs? I just left them out in the yard. They can't be left unattended for very long. And what about Eric, what do I tell—"

Before I can finish, he says to me, "A dog sitter will go by your house twice a day. Eric received a phone message from you saying you had to go out of town to visit an ill relative and will see him soon."

Okay, now I'm lost. They want me to leave all that I know and hold dear behind?

Strepp takes a notepad and pen from his pocket, scribbles something down, and tears out a page and hands it to me.

I look at it. Numbers. I stuff it in my pocket.

"Now it's time for you to go to work. While you're working this case, I'll be in constant contact by the phone I gave you. You will use my first name only."

Before I can respond, he stands and signals for Jenkins and Cortez. They walk over to me, pointing to the door. We exit the room silently and walk to the Suburban. Jenkins opens the back door for me, and I climb in. This time, however, Daniel is with us, riding shotgun.

Cortez sits in the back with me and uses the keypad again. The ceiling opens. Sunlight, after all this drama, is appreciated.

As we back out of the open door and ascend up to the desert floor, I welcome the sight of the endless horizon in the west. The sky is full of empty white clouds drifting by.

We head west, back toward Lubbock, past the city-limit sign, past the exit to my house. We bypass the city using Loop 289 and exiting on

Nineteenth westbound. Right on CR 1300, then exit onto Fourth Street, and we arrive at Reese Technology Center; formally Reese Air Force Base.

Reese Air Force Base is no longer used by the air force but has been leased out to various companies needing immediate runways.

We travel on a two-lane service road with very well-marked exits leading to runway accesses and maintenance buildings.

As we approach the center of the field, I can see a pickup truck with an RV attached. I can't believe it—a big-block diesel dually. Dad has one on the ranch. I drove that beast many times on the ranch and to town, but never towing anything of this size. This one looks new; they start and drive much easier than the one on the ranch. I've never towed anything the size of that trailer, though.

We park alongside, and Daniel steps out. "Come on out and get a look at your new home. The keys are in your pocket," he says with a grin.

Without saying another word he turns, walks back to the Suburban, and gets in. They drive another hundred yards down the runway and stop. Daniel exits and walks toward a small unmarked jet. He climbs the stairs and enters, never looking back. The door shuts, and the sound of the engine starting up and the jet racing down the runway disturbs the otherwise peaceful surroundings.

I turn away as the plane roars out of sight.

Are they serious? This is my new home? "You've got to be kidding me!"

The Suburban turns around and returns to where I'm standing. It pulls up, and the window comes down. "Call us anytime, 24-7, no limitations, no questions asked," Jenkins tells me as he hands me both his and Cortez's business cards.

"Does this thing come with instructions?" I ask as Jenkins closes the window.

"Look on the counter in your new kitchen!"

These guys are good.

The window closes, and they drive away. As my aunt once said, "Cops take you out, show you a good time, and leave without so much as a good-bye kiss." "Way more information than I needed," I told her.

I reach into my jeans pocket and pull out the keys. Looks like two are for the Chevy truck, so the two small round ones must be to my new home. Great, time to check it out.

I walk over to the trailer, insert one of the small keys into the door, and turn it. When I hear the lock release, I open the door and step in.

Having not been in one of these before, I'm quite surprised. Looks like a fully furnished small apartment. I enter the trailer in the kitchen area; every appliance I'll ever need. I turn to the right, climb three small steps, and open the door to a bedroom/bathroom area. All the essentials are here, though in a much smaller version than I'm used to. Towels and washcloths are hanging from the miniature racks, all blue. Definitely decorated by a man, but that's okay, I like blue. I continue to the bedroom area and open the closet to find it full of clothes, all my size, and a backpack. The bathroom has all the same toiletries as in my house. I'm no longer surprised. Funny, they know I don't use hairspray but don't know I use nonfluoride toothpaste.

I step outside and make sure to relock the door before I walk around to the truck's driver side. I unlock the door and climb in. Not bad—big, wide leather seat and four doors. I'm thinking if I run out of space in the trailer, I can use this as a second living room.

If I were looking for quality, I would be impressed.

I put the key in the ignition and turn it. It starts immediately.

The phone is vibrating. I reach into my pants pocket and pull it out. The caller ID shows no name, just a number. I should have known. I answer, and it's Jenkins, I can feel his smile.

"You're to take the rig to an RV park in Post, Texas. Put in for the night and wait for instructions."

"Sure, Jenkins, think I'll do just that. I'm an expert at driving my five-door hatchback. What makes you think I can drive this monstrosity? With all the planning you've done of my new life, did it cross your mind to teach me how to drive this beast?" Now I'm grinning back.

"Come on, Ashlee, we know about the ranch. But if you need help, there are instructions in the glove box. You're parked in the middle of an abandoned airfield. Knock yourself out."

I hang up and step out of the truck. Looking around, I see no one. I look up to the sky and let out a scream. Not one of those frightened-out-of-your-mind screams, but more like an if-I-could-get-my-hands-on-you-I'd-wring-your-neck scream.

I climb back in and find a set of instructions titled "Operating the Truck with Tow." I take it that means with a small house attached. I thumb through it. Seems simple enough.

While it is warming up, I step out and walk around the entire rig. No flat tires, the trailer is attached to whatever that contraption is in the bed of the truck, and I don't have to pee. All's good.

I step back in, release the emergency brake, take the shifter in hand, slip it into drive, and off I go!

Turning to the right into a large, empty parking lot, I push slightly on the accelerator. I feel the power and torque of the big diesel engine. I check in the rearview mirror and the backup camera monitor. There is a trailer following. All good.

What were they thinking, giving me this rig? The truck bed alone is longer than my car.

I'm up to about 40 mph, time to try the brakes. I hit the pedal. Too hard! The truck comes to a quick stop, and there's a loud noise—grinding, metal on metal. Something must be broken; Daniel is going to be pissed, and a huge repair bill will be coming my way!

I come to a complete stop and set the brake. I climb back out and walk warily to the rear.

With some trepidation I check everything out, and to my surprise, everything seems to be okay.

"What could all that noise have been?"

The phone rings. It's the nameless number again. "Jenkins, this is not the time!"

"Good job!" he says. "That noise was you applying the brake too quickly. Remember, you're at about twenty-five thousand pounds; it'll take a while for all that to stop. Keep it slow and easy."

Confused, I look around. No Suburban.

"Okay, how did you know?"

"We can watch you anytime and anywhere. You were told that. Keep practicing, and get to Post. The name of the park is written on a piece of paper attached to the driver-side visor."

He hangs up. I'm totally freaking out. My home and all that I have is gone. I'm taken to that scary-ass place in the desert, dropped off at an abandoned airfield, and told to drive this behemoth. Most of all, they want me to find the person who is the reason for all this. I'll find him, all right, and I'll wring his neck when I do!

I'm well educated, a trained remote viewer, and employed by the elite. Now I'm supposed to move equipment I know nothing about to an RV park miles away? When it comes to contract renewal, I'm going to be presenting a few facts to back a hefty pay raise.

I reenter the truck, shift, and push the gas. The truck is doing fine, and after a dozen or so laps around the parking lot, I'm finally ready to go. It's nearing 6:00 p.m., and traffic will still be a little thick.

I need to clear my mind. Concentrate more. Let go of the morning and move onto the rest of the day. Get my new home to a small town in the middle of West Texas. My mom thinks I live a boring life. Mom, an African American woman who married a tall West Texas rancher she met at the University of Texas. She was a literature major, and he, agricultural business. Her life was never boring after they moved to the family ranch and became the talk of the small community south of Midland. Mom's parents are professors at the university, and Dad's are generations of ranchers. West Texas ranching is hard work at best, and nobody expected her to hang in there. Many years later, the community was proven wrong. They live a quiet life on the ranch. I wish I were there now.

I follow the service road along the runway and soon come to a stop sign. No traffic. Good. Have to see if I can get this fifty feet of rig to turn into one lane.

Take a deep breath. Move out slowly, wait until the front end matches my lane, and stay true to course. Did it! Not so bad.

I make it on to Texas Highway 114 and see the signs for Loop 129. It is late evening; maybe traffic has begun thinning.

Coming to the entrance road, I see the southbound ramp. Going about 20 mph, I ease up onto the ramp and push for more speed. I get up to 45 mph and merge into the right-hand lane. I tell myself "good job," but subconsciously, I'm terrified.

Then the unexpected—car horns, and not one, many! I look into my rearview mirror and see a line forming behind me.

Okay, I know the posted speed is 60 mph on the loop, but come on! I stay the course. If only they knew!

I maintain 45 mph and stay in my lane until I see an exit sign for Highway 84 South, Post.

I turn on the blinker and begin to ease onto the exit ramp, horns still blaring around me. I find the button on the door panel and open the window. Once down, I extend my hand out the window and start waving like crazy as a plea for forgiveness. Man, if they only knew what I don't know about driving this thing.

I continue on 84 south for thirty miles to Post. It's an oilfield town that has a unique history. Post is the crossroads of US routes 84 and 380. It was founded by Charles W. Post, the breakfast cereal manufacturer. He did not move the cereal operation there but went on to ranching and oil exploration.

Good thing it has four lanes; I can travel at forty-five and get the feel of this rig. I meet another rig much like the one I'm driving heading toward me in the northbound lanes, and he waves. *What's he waving at me for?* I wonder. *Is something wrong?* Or maybe he's just waving because now I'm one of them, an RVer. *What irony,* I think. *An RVer in an RV!*

Holding the steering wheel with one hand, I reach for the envelope from the visor. Now off to the park.

What have I gotten myself into? keeps running through my head.

My instructions are simple enough. Go to Post RV Park on County Road 185, one mile from the city limits, on the left off Highway 84, can't miss the sign.

Great, got to make a lane change. Turn signal on, look in mirrors and over my shoulder, hold my breath, and proceed to the left.

Nearing Post, I see the sign for the park. Signal again to the left, watch for oncoming traffic, and ease over. Good so far.

I turn onto County Road 185, a narrow paved road. Just as I think I'm clear, I feel a bump. The trailer missed the road and now is bouncing around! I swerve and somehow manage to get all ten tires back on the pavement.

My heart feels as if I just ran three miles, and sweat is pouring off me. I tell myself to pull it together. I take a deep breath. About a mile later I see the entrance to the park, another narrow road. I stop.

I'm sweating more. Driving straight was a cakewalk; turning is a different story. If I make it without taking out the sign, I'll be amazed. "Here goes."

Easing forward, I turn in. Ahead is a white cinder block building, small but with a large white sign reading Office. An old man comes out, watching me with a serious expression. I don't know who is more worried, him or me. I ease the rig slowly on and feel the right rear tire leave the narrow road; there's that bouncing again. I turn the truck slightly to the left and am now squared up.

The old man is thin, about five foot nine, with thick gray hair and a well-weathered face. Standing with his hands on his hips, he's keeping a sharp eye on me.

I pull closer. As I come to a stop, I hit the brake too hard again. The trailer lunges and pushes me forward. I stop, but not without a lot of noise and grinding metal.

He looks at me harshly; at this moment I'm not sure if I'm more afraid of this rig or him. I roll down the window. "Hi, I'm Ashlee," I say, and I give my best West Texas grin. It doesn't work. So much for southern charm.

He steps up to my window and introduces himself as Jim, owner and manager.

I'm still smiling.

"Afternoon, Ashlee, jest git it? No one teach you how to drive that thing?" Jim says with a West Texas drawl, looking both me and the rig up and down,

Lying won't work. "Why do you ask?" I say with a bigger grin.

Jim doesn't say another word. He glares at me. I thought Agent Strepp was tough.

"Put it in park, set the brake, and come into the office." Clearly irritated, he turns away and heads inside.

I do what he says and follow him.

"Pull-through or back-in?"

I try hard to act like I know the answer. But I'm speechless.

His left eyebrow is cocked nearly to his hairline as he explains, "Okay, some of the lots you have to back your rig in, particularly if you're staying long-term. Pull-throughs are for those here short-term or just overnight."

"Back-in," I say. He grunts and shakes his head.

Jim looks at a chart of the park layout on the wall. "Sorry, out of back-ins."

My lucky day. Whether he was lying or just trying to help, I don't know or care.

"Daily, weekly, or monthly?" he says, pointing to a site number.

"Good question." I put my hands on my hips, not sure of the answer myself. "Let's try daily."

"Fill this out," he says, pulling a receipt book out from behind the counter and handing it to me.

I see the usual: name, address, phone number—easy stuff. Then it asks vehicle and RV info. He is staring again and is making me feel uneasy. I have to get with the program. He's beginning to make me feel like I don't have an ounce of intelligence. I always figured I could do that on my own.

"You don't know your vehicle info?"

"You're right; I just picked it up." I mumble, hoping he won't hear. I leave the office to get the needed information and to think. I walk around the rig, making note of plate numbers and the model of the truck and trailer. I can't help but wonder why they have sent me out here with this fancy truck and expensive trailer.

I return to the office and finish filling out the form. He looks at it, checking my information with something behind his counter. "Looks like you'll be staying with us for a month. Cash or credit card, no checks," he says, smiling broadly. Well, guess that question has been answered.

I hand him the card Daniel gave me, but he doesn't even look at it. Transaction completed. I step sideways to his front and center, wanting him to look at me. He ignores me.

Still looking down at the paperwork, Jim asks the big one. "Can you drive forward through this park and not destroy everything in your path?"

I look at the ground, at a loss for words. What do I tell this park Nazi?

"What's the park policy?"

"You drove it here; you park it," he says with a chuckle.

We walk outside. Jim gets in a golf cart parked next to the office. "Follow me, but keep your distance."

I get into the truck. He pulls out first, looking over his shoulder at me.

I don't know who is more afraid. I begin to roll, noting the park speed limit is 5 mph. Works for me! We head through the park. There are many different shapes and sizes of RVs. I'm wondering who all these people are.

We go up one row and down another. Is he doing this on purpose, letting me get some practice in? We finally approach the assigned site; I begin to brake as he turns into it.

I follow, ever so slowly. He signals for me to stop.

Standing in the middle of the site, he signals for me to move closer. Hope he has insurance.

I ease forward. Jim is continuously looking to each side of my rig, gesturing for me to keep coming.

I follow his instructions, and he finally signals me to stop. I look in each rearview mirror; truck and trailer are straight.

"You know that you have to unhook, right?" Jim says, walking toward me.

Unhook? He must be kidding. I'm more nervous than the first day at college. Walking up and down hallways totally confused, wondering if I am in the right building. Professors trying to help, but I'm so stressed I can't read my schedule.

I set the brake and exit. "What exactly do you mean, 'unhook'?"

Jim gives me that glare again. "Fifty bucks."

"To unhook and set up?"

"It's not for standing around and chewing the fat."

"Can it go on the card? I don't have any cash."

He sighs deeply and slowly nods his head.

For the next thirty minutes I watch him unhooking the trailer, dropping stands, and hooking up electrical cords and hoses that look like they belong in a garden. Had I needed to do all that myself, it would have taken me hours, if I had been able to sort it all out from the instruction manuals. Think I'll throw in another of Daniel's fifties.

I thank him and reach out to shake his hand, but he just turns, hops back on his golf cart, and leaves. I think he was unhappy with the extra work.

The phone rings and I tremble, startled by the noise. I answer and hear Jenkins laughing loudly.

"How's it going?"

What a prick. "I'm fine, at the designated park."

"We know; we've been watching the show, remember?"

I hear Cortez chuckling in the background. These two must be getting ready to retire and are practicing for their next job as comedians.

"All you need is inside the trailer," Jenkins tells me in a more serious tone. "Now you should get started. Daniel will be calling."

I hang up and enter the trailer.

Once inside, I'm surprised. It's a lot bigger than I remembered it. Jim has extended the three slide-outs, creating a lot more room. A desk is along one wall to my left as I enter.

I sit down at the desk, take a deep breath, and begin to think. Jenkins was right; this job is way over my pay grade.

Finally it hits me, anxiety sweeping through me. I've left my home, neighborhood, friends, dogs—everything. Now I'm in an RV park in Post, Texas. What a first day with this assignment.

Breathing becomes difficult. I'm feeling dizzy, and sweat is pouring down my back. I'm scared.

I move to a recliner in the living area. I catch my breath and finally begin to relax enough to focus.

Even though I know they are constantly watching and listening, I feel totally alone.

What have I gotten into?

I stand and take some deep breaths, regaining control of my emotions. I walk to the kitchen and look around in the fridge and cabinets. They've been fully stocked. They must have plans for me to be here for a while. This adds to my worries.

Suddenly I remember the manual. Where did I leave it? Did I bring it in? I go out to the truck. I don't remember where I put it during all the confusion. Frantically looking, I find it in the front seat. I grab it, thinking there's no way I can do my part without it. There are many years of training in this one book.

"Those bastards!" I say as I'm closing the truck door and I glance at the monitor for the backup camera. "That's how they did it; they hacked it!"

I go back inside, still muttering to myself at how long it took me to figure them out.

I sit at the desk and begin looking through the manual. It's laid out basically the same as mine and will work for now. Teacher's name is written on it with a bar code attached. These were archived many years ago and remain property of the government. As a manual for remote viewing, can't get more authentic than that.

I pull out the piece of paper Daniel handed me. Six numbers, nothing unusual. Why move me here? What is so important that I had to be uprooted? It's been a long day; I'm tired, and he didn't say to start right now. I'm going to eat some dinner, get some sleep, and start early in the morning.

Two

My alarm is sounding; six a.m. I was pleasantly surprised at how comfortable the queen-size bed was, and I slept quite well. It's time to find out if my five-foot-ten-inch body will fit in the miniature shower. I head for the stall, which is in its own little corner of the bedroom. I open up the glass door and find there won't be a problem at all. Nice. When I'm done, I check out the clothes in the closest and choose a pullover shirt and jeans. Both are just my size, too—spooky. As I enter the kitchen, I search the cupboards for coffee-making equipment and ingredients. After a few minutes getting acquainted with the coffeepot, I get the brew started. While I wait for it, I grab juice from the fridge and sit down at the desk. I can get used to this kind of camping. Back at the ranch it was sleeping bags, a pop-up tent, and an open fire. Dad was right; the grass is greener.

Upon opening the laptop, I see the newest version of my sketching program. Damn! I've been waiting to get my hands on it, but it hasn't been released to the public yet. How did they get it? What a time for me to go back to basics. Sure hope Daniel will let me keep the laptop when I finish this assignment. I log into my secure e-mail, anticipating instructions from Daniel.

In the desk drawer I find pencils, paper, and a ruler. Low tech as they may seem, these are essential tools of my trade. They haven't left anything to chance; they must be trying to eliminate the possibility of being traced or hacked.

No room for error. Where to begin? After all these years, I still get nervous at this point in the process.

My hands are sweating, making it difficult to hold the pencil that I'm nervously tapping. I can't seem to sit still; I'm jittery. All this must stop! Teacher wouldn't approve. I can almost hear him saying "Ashlee, focus" in that way he has of quietly reprimanding me.

Why did Daniel give me details? You should never know the target's true identity; that's standard practice in the viewing profession. It keeps it unpolluted.

He knows better than anyone the risk of telling me details. Knowledge can be deadly.

It's time to get to it. Enough of racking my brain; my gut is telling me this may be more important than previous assignments.

The computer sounds off with a familiar tone. Commonly it would be Daniel, but not this time. It's a virus alert. I rush to close the program. Not in time! The screen goes blank. What now? Have I been hacked again? Where do I run this time? I have not been given any new protocols.

As my mind is racing, the phone rings. "Hello?" I breathe a sigh of relief. Of course, it's Daniel.

"Stay there. The computer systems have been compromised again." I can feel concern in his voice.

"Don't worry," he tells me, "you're in a safe place."

Why do I doubt that?

My mind continues to race. What is going on in cyberspace? Why would I doubt Daniel? Why do I feel so vulnerable? The butterflies begin in the pit of my stomach. I'm like a fish out of water; I'm really out of my element. Fear is creeping in.

Daniel assures me I'm safe. I need to begin my job now. Someone will be in contact with me soon.

Click. He hangs up. I begin to think of an escape in case he is wrong and things aren't safe. If they can breach our computers despite all of our state-of-the-art technology, hacking a cell phone would be nothing. Who is doing all this?

I step outside to catch my breath, noting my new surroundings: the hills, mesas, open ranges. Remarkably, the terrain has changed in the relatively short drive to Post—and me with no horse or four-wheeler. I wish I had the dogs with me; they'd love to chase whatever they could find out there.

A big black-and-silver motor home slowly passes in front of me, being led by Jim in his golf cart. Back to reality. I head back inside, and the aroma of freshly brewed coffee hits me as I open the door. A cup of hot coffee will help me settle down. I fix myself a cup, not even surprised to find my favorite flavor of creamer in the fridge. I settle down at the desk and pick up my paper and pencil. Time to get to work.

I center myself in the chair, feet flat on the floor, and take deep breaths in and out. I gather my thoughts and feelings and write the numbers on the paper: 011211/80101.

Stage one begins.

Holding pencil to paper, never letting the lead leave the page, I scribble a configuration not familiar to most, but having multiple meanings to a trained viewer. Sketches are frantically generated from my thoughts of air, space, land, structures, and humans. These are common; why all the hype?

Then another thought: death—lots of it, and soon. My pencil stops.

I write "break, not ready" and step away for a moment.

Documenting the word *break* followed by the reason for it is part of the technique to keep track of your thought processes throughout the session.

My mind still racing, I think back to an old case where agents had involved themselves with an investigation and gotten too close to the bad guys. Both agents and bad guys are now dead. What is this all about? I have to calm down and let go of all that has happened in the past, including earlier today.

Clearing my mind of the old case and regaining focus on the present situation, I return to the desk. Pencil in hand, I note "break over" and continue writing.

I move through all the required methods to document what I'm seeing, finding many people and lots of chaos. Multiple locations come to mind; I need to focus harder. No, there are many people and only one location. I'm castling—what we call generating stray thoughts in the industry. Even the best have this problem. Descriptors of buildings, people, weather, destruction—these may be correct but do not necessarily apply at this early stage. They may, however, apply later. I write them on a separate page. I need to do the basics first. Okay, the basics; I need to sketch.

"Break; find pencil."

Where did I put that pencil?

I must have put it back in the drawer. That's odd; it's not there or on top of the desk. It must have rolled under the desk.

I look under the chair and then under the desk, and I see something that doesn't seem to belong. When I look closer, I see an object the size of a tiny button attached to the underside of the desktop. Is this how Jenkins knows? Or is this how the bad guys know? Or am I losing it?

I don't know much, but one thing is for sure—this was placed there. Do I remove it or call in? Either way, whoever put it there will know it's been found.

I grab the phone, step outside, walk about ten paces from the trailer, and speed-dial Daniel. No answer.

I know that I'm not going back in there. What should I do? This wasn't covered.

I dial again. Come on, Daniel, answer! After five or six rings, he picks up. I don't know if I'm relieved or if I should panic.

"Why are you calling? I know I said we'd be in constant contact, but we should keep the phone use to a minimum. They shouldn't be able to be monitored, but we don't know yet who we are dealing with. Try to keep it for emergencies only," he tells me, sounding irritated.

"Daniel, I know you guys bugged my laptop and hacked into the backup camera in the truck, but I found something suspicious under the desk."

Silence; then "Stay right where you are; agents are on the way."

Okay, now how did he know where I was standing? There must be more cameras on the outside of the trailer.

Not ten minutes pass before I see an old Buick heading my way. It pulls up to me, and I see Jenkins and Cortez inside. They exit the car, both dressed in T-shirts and jeans. They seem relaxed as they listen to me.

I tell them where the device is located. Cortez goes inside. He comes out with a cup of coffee in one hand and the bug in the other. "Good coffee; French vanilla creamer, my favorite." Not a word about the bug.

Cortez walks to the rear of the car and opens the trunk. I step over and watch him, curious as to what he is doing. He opens a briefcase; various electronic gadgets are inside. He selects a handheld device and heads toward the trailer. "Here, hold this," he says as he hands me his cup.

After about ten minutes, he comes back out and walks toward me.

"All clear," he says, not mentioning if anything else was found.

"Was I right; is it a listening device?" I ask, handing him back his coffee.

"Yes." He doesn't elaborate. I still don't know if it was a device from the good guys or the bad guys. And who *are* the bad guys?

Cortez tosses out the cold coffee and hands the cup back to me. He puts the bug in his pocket and the device back into the case in the trunk.

"Don't worry; Cortez is good at what he does. You're fine now," Jenkins says.

Why don't I believe them? I know they're not supposed to give me details, but maybe I need for them to forego that for my personal safety. Where are these two staying for them to get here so fast?

Without saying anything else, they get back in their car to leave. On cue, the phone rings.

"What now, Daniel?" I'm angry, and I hope my tone lets him know.

I hear him hesitate. "Ashlee, relax. It's common for those we chase to want to find us; you must remain calm."

Again I don't know whom to trust, but I will have to figure it out fast.

"Fine," I say, "but you tell those two they had better not venture too far." He reassures me he will and hangs up.

As I watch Jenkins and Cortez drive away, the feeling of being alone and vulnerable once again creeps back.

Back inside the trailer, I put the cup in the sink and realize that even while camping there is still housework to do. Some things never change.

Oh well, time to resume the task at hand.

"Break over."

I look at the ideograms and gestalts I made in stage one. An ideogram is a symbol or word used to represent a perception; a gestalt is similar, only using more words. *Focus,* I tell myself, and I clear my mind of all of today's events. Forget events that turned my life upside down? Not a chance. Pencil flying across the paper, I sketch what I can and jot down words for what I view but can't draw: flat, black, manmade, hot, structures, persons, objects.

Feelings at the target: I'm at a service center, feeling the need to fly. I hate airports and flying—way overrated. I note the feelings, leaving out my personal feeling about flying. Feelings at the target site are known as aesthetic impact—an emotional response viewers have when they realize they have established a relationship with the target. You are not on target unless you have an AI.

I take a few minutes to get all my pages in order. Each page needs to be numbered correctly for my analyst to have proper documentation of my thought processes. After all these years, I still have to use discipline to do the process correctly. I remind myself constantly that all my work has to be understandable to the analyst.

Time to sketch. I take a plain sheet of paper, remembering to let the scenario I see be true and not add to it. I let my hand lead the pencil.

A long, flat surface, not a road; both large and small buildings along each side. There are objects on top of the surface. I find myself unable to concentrate.

"Break; food."

I've been at it for a couple of hours; maybe this is a good time to take a break and get something to eat.

I note the time, put down the pencil, and stand up. With a deep breath, I clear my mind of the target and release what I have viewed.

I browse through the cabinets and fridge to see what kind of food they have for me to eat. It's well stocked: vegetables for a salad, sandwich makings, soda—much the same as in my fridge at home. Sure hope they thought to clean it out, or I'll have a real mess on my hands if and when I get to see my house again.

I make a sandwich and take a seat in the recliner at the rear of the trailer. I find the remote and turn on the TV. Life at these RV parks isn't so bad; no wonder so many folks do this when they retire. Who knew?

Flipping through the channels, I find the local afternoon news. I'm not usually a news buff, but today it may be a good idea to see what's going on.

What the hell? There's a Lubbock news van here in Post. State troopers and feds are everywhere.

I watch anxiously; Post is only a mile away. I have been so consumed by my task that I haven't heard any sirens.

A reporter is standing in front of a Motel 8 along Highway 84 downtown. There is an ambulance in the background with a body being loaded into it. Then I see a Buick next to where the reporter is standing. It looks just like the one that Jenkins and Cortez were driving!

Oh my God! What's happening? My heart begins double-timing, and my mind is racing.

"Authorities say two men were found dead in their room," a reporter is saying. "The cause of death appears to be multiple stab wounds to the throat." I'm stunned beyond words or thought.

"Identities are not known. The case is being handled by the FBI."

I drop my sandwich. I'm shaking, my mouth is dry, and I'm dizzy. If someone can do that to two armed federal officers, what chance do I have? I want to run, but my legs refuse to move. Even if I could, where would I run?

Who can I trust? My thoughts are interrupted by the ringing of the phone. My heart is in my throat. What do I do? What if it's not Daniel?

I rush to pick up the phone. I push Talk but don't say anything—a moment of quiet ensues.

"You've seen the news," Daniel says, breaking the silence. It's a statement, not a question. Is there anything they don't know? "Ashlee, don't leave the trailer. In the next twenty minutes, there will be an agent with you. Try to remain calm; I know you're scared."

"I'll give you that twenty minutes, but after that I'm gone."

"You will stay put!" he yells.

I repeat myself and hang up. Time is dragging. I stare at my watch, willing the minutes by. Time, a paradox, is so important now, but in my work it means nothing.

Fifteen minutes have gone by, so I decide to grab my work tools, leave the trailer, and wait the last five minutes in the truck. I step in and put the key in the ignition. Nothing. I keep trying. No use; it still isn't starting. Maybe I'm not doing something right. I keep trying, stupid truck!

I'm concentrating so hard I don't notice the man standing at the truck door, staring at me. It's all I can do not to pee my pants when I catch a glimpse of him.

He is speaking.

I'm so afraid! I don't understand what he is saying! All I can think of is that I'm about to die. Who will tell Eric? What will happen to my dogs?

"Ashlee Sutton! Dammit, stop! Daniel sent me!" He grabs the door handle.

I sit shaking, staring at him. My comprehension slowly comes back as reality sets in. Just like the other agents, he is about six feet, obviously cut from the same cloth as Jenkins and Cortez. I have never seen him before. I don't trust him, not after everything that has happened.

He reaches inside his jacket and pulls out a black wallet. He opens it and shows me his federal ID through the window.

"Ashlee, Daniel sent me. Get a grip."

I relax enough so that I can unlock the door and get out of the truck, hoping I'm making a wise choice.

"You better?" he asks, looking at me.

"Yes." He introduces himself as Agent Chad Byrnes, and we shake hands. He has soft but muscular hands. He's well dressed, but different from the others. His eyes are blue with a green tint; he has a serious look, but deep inside there appears to be kindness.

Gathering my pencil, paper, and ruler from the seat of the truck, I reluctantly invite him into the trailer.

We go inside and sit in the two recliners at the rear of the room. Agent Byrnes hasn't said anything else yet; he's still sizing me up, I guess, just like I am him.

"Would you like something to drink? Soda? I could make some coffee."

"No thanks."

"I saw the local news. I just can't believe they are gone! They were both just here!"

"Yes, it's terrible. I knew Jenkins, and he was up for retirement next month. I hadn't met Cortez. Next time Daniel or any one of us tells you to stand down, do it!"

"I waited long enough. Running was my first instinct, but in reality I had no idea where I'd go. I figured going home wasn't an option."

"Did you really think we would let you drive away? Did you not notice the truck wouldn't start? Were you not told we are always here?"

I'm thinking he is way too serious. He must be bucking for Daniel's job.

"You're kidding! You controlled my truck? What if there was an emergency? What if I just needed to get out of the park for a while?"

"Not unless we allow it," he says sternly.

He tells me his partner's name is Agent Angie Smithers and she will be joining us later. He will be the agent in charge of the mission. He lets me know that I am not to call Daniel without him being notified first. Information viewed was to be seen by him first and then relayed to Daniel.

"Why all the additional steps?" I ask.

"Quality control of the information to keep the chain of evidence. The same as with any case."

"What about my phone? Daniel said he would be in constant contact."

"He is, but while we are in the field, you go through me for everything. Understand?" He does not waver.

By now I'm fuming. Not unless we allow it? I want to scream at this guy, but evidently that would be a mistake.

"I understand you're the best at what you do," he says, changing the subject and softening his tone somewhat.

"No, Teacher is the best."

"Daniel really trusts your work, and he is the best at what he does."

"I wouldn't know if Daniel is the best at what he does. He has never told me what he does or who he works for."

He grins. "Nice try."

I hear a car pull up and the engine stop. A moment later, there is a knock at the door.

Chad gets up, walks to the door, and opens it. A woman enters; she is my height and similar in build—slim and about five feet ten; kind of short for an agent. She's fair skinned, well dressed, and has brown hair. She is all business, no play.

She walks over to me, extends her hand, and introduces herself as Agent Angie Smithers. We shake hands. "Just call me Angie; I'm Chad's partner. We'll only use first names while we're on this assignment. Keeps radio communications easier and more anonymous."

"I guess you already know my name. And probably a whole lot more."

She grins and nods.

Chad sits in the other recliner while Angie makes herself at home on the sofa.

"Do they know who killed Jenkins and Cortez? Not that we were close friends, but we were supposed to work this case together."

Neither of them answers.

"Whoever killed them, are they after me, too?" I ask.

"You're still alive," Chad says. "Evidence enough that they didn't give away your location."

I have no reply. Is he saying I was the target or they were? Either way, I'm not good with any of this.

Chad continues. "They let someone get too close and dropped their guard. Basically, they erred, and in our business, that's the reward."

"Too close. Who got too close? Again, who would want to kill them?"

Neither Chad nor Angie answer. They just sit quietly for a moment. I can see the wheels turning in their heads.

Angie speaks up. "It is not a matter of who, but how. How did their assailant get that close to be able to kill them, knowing they were armed?"

Chad is staring at me again. "Enough chatter. Time for you to do your job. We'll be close by."

Yeah, just like the other two were. I'm not worried.

They leave. I get back to work.

Three

It's time to create a matrix. With a ruler I draw a line lengthwise across a blank piece of paper. I divide the matrix into eight columns, and each column is labeled with a term: *stages, site picture, stray cats, aesthetic impact*—the rest are left blank for now. This is the guts of how to begin describing the target. I number the page.

A description of a man begins to form. Medium build, medium height, brown hair, intelligent, dangerous. Danger is the feeling at the target, the aesthetic impact. Now I know I'm on target. I write in the stray cat column "white male." It's not that it doesn't apply, but I'm guessing; this cannot be a guessing game. Stick with the descriptors. A stray cat is nothing more than the viewer's perception—not necessarily wrong, but possibly off target. It is documented to be used later.

Another description comes to mind: slim, short black hair, and smooth face. I command myself to move to him, looking at his face. He is Asian, and he is looking me in the eyes. Not uncommon. I write "Asian" in the stray cat column. Too soon, need more facts. A viewer is taught early on to give herself commands at targets to more fully examine the site.

I begin viewing the long, flat surface again. I tell myself to move five hundred feet above the surface and describe it. The runway has many structures along it, possibly for storage. Aircraft hangars—stray cat. Stick with descriptors. Time to write a quick mini summary.

A mini summary is the documenting of information gathered from castling; it allows the viewer to clear her mind of possibly useless data. It's sort of like emptying the recycle bin on your desktop. The mini summary is to be added to the final summary, which is then submitted to an analyst.

Mini Summary #1—Target area appears to be an airport. Flat surfaces running north and south with no markings indicating traffic lanes. Adjacent asphalt road connects and leads to a large structure. Structure has bay doors as well as standard-size doorway entrances. A windsock sits along the runway on the far side so it can be seen in any direction. Private Property signs displayed at a small building at what appears to be an entrance road.

The phone rings. "Break for phone."

What is it this time? He knows I need at least a couple of hours to complete my task.

"How's it going?" Daniel asks as soon as I answer.

"Not much yet; what's the rush?"

"Chad is on the way to pick you up. He'll be there in a minute. Secure the inside of the trailer and be ready to leave."

"Where am I going? It's getting late; it'll be dark in a few hours, and I haven't finished."

"Do it now!"

I rush around the trailer, quickly washing up the dishes and stowing them back in the cupboard, making sure nothing will fall from the counters when we're rolling. I take another walk-through and mentally note the arrangement of the inside of the trailer—all good and secure. I pack up my work supplies in my go-bag. I step outside, and as if on cue, a black sedan with Chad at the wheel is already there.

"Angie will be traveling with you," Chad tells me, opening the driver's window as Angie gets out of the car. She is out of her usual dress clothes, wearing a pullover and jeans. She's dressed for a cool spring night in West Texas.

"Hope she knows how to hook up in the dark," I tell him sarcastically. "Where are we going?"

Chad doesn't respond, just rolls up the window and speeds away. He really likes being in control a little too much. Guess he's not traveling with us.

"We're going to Houston."

She's sure not dressed for Houston weather.

"Why? I was just getting started."

"It'll take about eight hours to get there. You can work on the way."

"I commonly work alone in a quiet, nonmoving place."

"I have instructions for you to work on the way," she repeats.

Bewildered, I glare at her. "You've got to be joking!"

Next thing I know, she is in the truck, cranking the engine, backing up to the trailer, lining up to the hitch on her first try. She begins unhooking from the park's facilities. For a fed, she is not afraid to get her hands dirty. "Do you know how to operate the slides?" she asks.

The what? I tell her no.

"Never mind, I'll do it," she says impatiently. "Take your stuff and wait in the truck."

Minutes later, Angie is in the driver's seat. "You did pretty well at stowing everything," she tells me. "Next time, though, make sure all the inside doors are closed so they don't bang around when we turn a corner." She checks all the mirrors, puts the truck in drive, eases forward, and stops.

I hear that metal sound in the rear of the truck again. Why isn't *her* phone ringing with a laughing fed on the other end?

"What's wrong? Why'd we stop?"

"Nothing, old trick of the trade to ensure that the kingpin is set in the hitch."

"Wow, so that explains it. I'm impressed." I smile and say, "I'll have to give that a try next time I'm at the ranch and they need a hand hauling cattle. Daddy will be proud."

Moving again, we slowly maneuver through the park, past the office; it's closed now for the night, and all appears quiet.

As we slow to make the turn onto the road, I think I see a shadow of a person stepping out of the dark on my side. The shadow steps right up to my window. My heart races to the point where I fear it may explode. I want to speak but can't; my eyes are bulging. After all that's happened already, I'm about to pass out.

Thankfully, it's just the park manager, Mister Friendly himself. He yells through the window, "Y'all come back now!" I think he's serious. He waves.

Angie rolls down my window. "Sure thing, Jim, see you soon."

I stare at her, "Really? You know this guy?"

"It's a small world, Ashlee; get used to it."

We finally hit Highway 84 and head south. I know I need to work up some more information. I've got to get my mind off the events of the day.

I think for a second. I've never done this before—work a target in a moving vehicle. It's kind of exciting.

"Is there anything in here I can use to put my tools on?"

"Reach in the backseat. There's a small lap tray; use it to work on."

I look back and retrieve the tray.

I begin by laying out my supplies. I note, "Break over; working target in moving vehicle." That should get my analyst's attention.

The truck is remarkably quiet, and the ride is smooth even though we are hauling a small house behind us. Surprisingly, I have no problem continuing, but I'll need to use the laptop to organize my notes. I'll get to it later.

Using my left hand, I run my fingers over the ideograms.

A site picture begins to emerge, possibly a target, just a perception; I won't know until more information is documented.

I use my matrix to describe a runway and hangars; I begin to sketch again. The sketch appears to be a runway about ten thousand feet in length with a hangar on the north side. The main runway is north/south. Returning to the matrix, I note that gestalts were manmade. Focusing in on the largest structure, I tell myself to move to the top of it. I put my right hand on the surface of the structure and find it to be hard and smooth. It's steel. Looking in both directions, I see that it seems to be painted silver. It appears to be rounded and has no openings, not even for ventilation, but does have several antennas. I tell myself to go inside. It's massive and appears to have a concrete floor. There is one aircraft. I need more descriptors. Need to verify what has been viewed by using all of my senses and determine if it's the correct target.

I need a break.

"Break; food/sleep."

I glance out the window. We are clearing Abilene.

In my field it's well known that you can leave a target at any time and go back to it in the future.

"Can we stop for a minute and maybe grab a bite to eat?" I ask.

Angie looks at me with that serious look she does so well. "Okay, but only for a few minutes."

We stop at a small truck stop on the right just as Highway 84 leaves the city limits. We turn right into the parking lot and stop in front. Once inside we find a small deli and restrooms to the left—just what I was hoping for.

I wish I could call Eric; he has to be worried by now. Marriage is our hottest topic. We have been together since college, and he is my closest confidant. The first thing that attracted me to him was his height; at six

James George

feet two he was one of the few men at UT who was taller than me. He's a tall, lean Texan with deep blue eyes and sandy brown hair. Eric knows my occupation and how different it is from most jobs.

My parents worship him. Ever since we met and I brought him home to meet them, it's been as though he can do no wrong. Now that he works for the US Department of Agriculture in Lubbock, we talk a lot about getting married. I've got to get home to him soon.

I have a haunting question running through my mind: *What have I gotten into? What am I going to get into?*

I grab a sandwich and a bottle of water. At the counter I realize I have no cash, and I use the card that Daniel gave me. Once again, I have no trouble; the card slides right through.

I ask Angie, "Can we stand here for a while, while I eat?"

"No time; eat on the way."

I guess she doesn't know the word *please.*

"I'm not familiar with this route; we normally go through Sweetwater."

"South of Abilene heading for Brady, then Austin."

"Austin? I thought we were going to Houston?"

"I'm using back roads to reach I-10 at Columbus. Leave the driving to me."

I dig in to my sandwich. It looks good, and I'm really hungry. I figure we are about six hours out of Houston. I haven't been there in a few years—too much city for me.

"When you're done eating, get back to work."

"It's the middle of the night, and I'm tired; I need a long break."

We get back in the truck, and Angie sits looking out the windshield for a minute before she starts it up and slips it into drive. I wonder what she is thinking.

We travel for about thirty minutes. I finish eating and reach for the radio.

Angie looks at me, and I expect her to slap my hand away.

"Blues or rock if you can find any."

I smile and think she is human after all. I find an alternative rock station coming out of Abilene, set the dial, and adjust the volume.

The next several miles are good. I'm fighting sleep but eventually nod off.

When I open my eyes, I see the Austin city limit sign.

We exit onto Highway 71 heading for I-10. Two more hours and we'll be in Houston. I nod off again.

I wake up to the motion of the rig coming to a stop. We are at a gas station in Columbus, the intersection of I-10 and Highway 71.

Angie gets out without a word. Through the side mirrors I see her reach into her left front pocket and pull out a cell phone.

I decide to get out so I can stretch and pick up another bottle of water. As we walk toward the store, I hear her repeatedly saying, "Yes, sir. Yes, sir."

I'm guessing it's Daniel. I cannot picture Angie "yes siring" anyone else.

"Ashlee!" Angie shouts. "We're leaving! Get in."

I head back to the truck; no point in debating it. I hear the urgency in Angie's voice. We get in, and she pulls away from the service station in a hurry.

We travel east on I-10. Only an hour and a half to go to Houston.

"What's happening?"

Angie looks concerned. "The One Forty-Seventh Texas Air National Guard Squadron based at Ellington Field was hit at approximately two a.m., about an hour ago. A drone base, a hangar with twenty-four drones, was destroyed."

"Where is that?" I ask, trying to think of which theater our forces may be in.

"Houston."

I can't believe it. Is that the place I was viewing?

"Any causalities?" I ask.

"Eleven dead and many wounded."

"Seems someone breached the security line near the hangars, entered, and used explosives inside, which set off more explosives."

I'm not sure what to think. My specialty is to find people, so now what kind of person am I looking for? And why is she giving up so much information? She has been so secretive till now.

"What about suspects? Were there any witnesses?"

"No. It's being investigated by military intelligence and the FBI."

"Is that where we're going?"

She doesn't answer.

I ask again, and she hesitates for a minute before speaking.

"We were going to the federal building downtown to have you continue your work and then have field agents follow up on your findings."

"Where are we going now?"

"Daniel wants us to put down for a short time in Sealy. He doesn't want you to come into Houston. We are to wait for further instructions, and you are to keep working."

I don't know where Sealy is, but I guess I'm going to find out.

About thirty minutes from Columbus, we come to the city limit sign for Sealy. There is a road sign for TX 36; we take the feeder road to it. We turn right toward Rosenberg.

I want to ask where this old highway goes, but I keep my mouth shut. Angie has been deep in thought since Columbus. Her actions have me worried.

We exit onto an unmarked county road and travel another mile or so. Ahead is a white wood-frame house, probably an old farm.

Pulling up to the house, Angie uses the truck headlights to sweep the area around the property before stopping and cutting the engine.

"Get out, and follow me."

"Okay, but where are we, and whose house is this?"

"No more questions; just do as you're asked."

It's dark, and as we walk up to the front door, it opens. Someone is standing in the doorway.

No way am I going in there after yesterday's unbelievable happenings. Step into a blacked-out house with who knows who running around? My feet are itching to take off, and I turn to run.

"It's okay," Angie tells me, and she grabs me by the arm.

I turn around, and the person begins to walk toward us. With a sigh of relief, I see that it's Chad, trying to look confident but noticeably shaken by the latest event. So this is where he went when he left us this morning. We walk in, and the lights come on.

Angie breaks the silence. "All clear, and Daniel has been notified."

I'm sweating again. Less than forty-eight hours ago, I was snug in my home back in Lubbock, asleep in my bed with Rocco and Bruno lying next to me, Eric just a phone call away.

Now I'm in some farmhouse on an unmarked county road and Houston has been hit by some unknown terrorist. At any time I will wake up from this nightmare. What is it they are expecting from me?

Angie goes back out to the truck, and I hear it start. It sounds like the rig is moving to the rear of the house. I'm in no position to ask questions and have come to realize they won't answer anyway. I guess it's time for me to cowboy up and stand up for myself.

Chad and I enter a room that appears to be a living room but now contains a large table with chairs scattered around.

"Have a seat," Chad says invitingly, pointing to one of the chairs.

I grab one next to the wall near the door leading to a kitchen and pull it up to the table.

In the kitchen, the back door opens. It's Angie. She enters the living room and walks over to Chad.

"Have you heard any more news about Houston?" I ask.

"No," Chad answers.

Both turn to me, Chad with a serious look.

"When are you going to be ready to finish the task?" Chad asks.

"I need about four hours of sleep, and then I'll get on with it."

He agrees. I'm shocked he didn't want it now.

Nothing more is said. Angie grabs a flashlight, and we leave the house through the kitchen. We walk toward the trailer, which she has parked about fifteen feet from the back of the house. I hear a low hum coming from the rear of the trailer and ask Angie about it. "It's the generator; I turned it on when I parked. We've got to have the power on." Once inside, she faces the door and points. "Watch and learn."

Above the door, there's a black panel with eight buttons on it. They are marked Left Rear, Right Rear, and Left Front. They are also marked Open and Close.

She pushes Open for each, and the trailer expands; all three slides ease outward.

"Same procedure to close," she says.

Angie walks to the living room, stands in front of the couch, reaches just under the front cushion, and pulls up. It opens, and she pulls out bedding. I had been wondering how the sleeping arrangements were going to work since there was only one bed.

She makes up the sofa and lies down without saying a word.

I sit at the desk, once more setting out paper, pencil, and ruler so I'll be ready to go in the morning. Now for some much-needed sleep.

I turn to Angie. "I take it we'll be resting for a while?"

"Yes, it's been a long night."

"Good, I'm turning in for a few hours; then I'll get back at it."

We leave it at that.

I start to set the alarm on my watch but figure those two have no intentions of letting me sleep beyond that four-hour mark. I have to admit that I like having them this close.

After stretching out, it doesn't take long for me to relax and fade off to sleep.

Much too soon, I get the feeling that someone is in the room. With half-opened eyes, I see Chad standing next to the bed.

He's clean shaven, without a wrinkle in his suit, and still lacking a smile. It's evident he's in charge.

"Get up; there's food ready." He leaves the bedroom and goes back outside.

I get up and stumble around. 8:55 a.m. I'm not a morning person, and being unfamiliar with my environment isn't helping.

The bathroom in this rig is really quite nice. As I face the doorway leading to the kitchen, the shower is on my right, and on the left is a small compartment that contains the toilet. I'm getting used to taking a shower in here. After showering, I dress in a pair of jeans and a short-sleeved blouse. I find some lace-up boots in the closet that fit me perfectly.

I go to the house and find everyone already gathered in the kitchen.

Chad and Angie are eating at the table.

I grab a plate and dig in. This is the first hot meal I've had since I left home. Wonder who cooked? I don't really care; it's good: bacon, eggs, and toast.

"I'm curious. How do you guys know so much of my personal habits?" I ask Angie.

"Better eat up, long work day ahead." Angie grins but doesn't answer the question.

I eat my breakfast but can't fight the urge to ask. "When do I get to call home?" I look at them both, wondering which of them will let me make a call. I feel like a teenage girl trying to convince my parents to let me call a boy they have never met. I hated that then and hate it even more so now.

"When do I get a phone call? Someone has to take care of my dogs and look after my house."

"Eric has been called, and someone is feeding your dogs," Angie answers.

"I want to make that phone call."

She gives me the same answer, but there's a smile there too.

All three of us are gridlocked into silence. I'm not going to give up.

Now I'm pissed. I've had enough of these two. "Call Daniel; tell him what I want," I say loudly.

"Listen," Chad says, "silence and secrecy are our only advantage now; you will have your call later."

I pick up my breakfast and head for the living room, trying not to stomp my feet like a mad little girl.

Walking into the room not quite in a rage, but so mad I can barely see, I bump into someone solid standing right in the doorway. I almost drop my plate. I want to scream and am fighting tears—not from fear, but because I have taken all I can from these guys.

In front of me is a tall, solidly built white man. He's well dressed and smiling. I take it they have a cookie cutter and when they need an agent, they just make one.

He excuses himself as he steps back, attempting to be somewhat friendly.

I set the plate down, turn to him, and introduce myself, just like Mother taught me. "I'm Ashlee Sutton."

"Hello, I'm Joseph," he says, extending his right hand. We shake hands. He excuses himself again and leaves the room, heading toward the kitchen.

There's a TV. I turn it on and return to my breakfast. The airways are flooded with the Houston attack.

There are no aerial photos. The military has declared it a no-fly zone. Then I recognize my target!

There is a film crew near the entrance to the base. Near the gate is a hangar like the one I saw. I'm sure of it. The hangar door is open, and inside is an aircraft with a long wingspan.

On the side of the hangar, large black letters read NASA.

So I had been nearing the true site! My intention was to walk through the various hangars. But with all the interruptions and traveling halfway across Texas, I had not been able to maintain the target.

What is going on and who is involved?

I hear them talking in the other room, so I turn off the TV and take my plate back to the kitchen. They stop talking.

I smell coffee. Scanning the counter, I find it next to the sink. Jackpot. I pour a cup for myself and then turn to the others, smile broadly, and say, "Anybody?"

"Bring you and your coffee to the table; time to talk," Chad says.

I sit with them, not sure what to expect. I don't trust them and am sure they feel the same about me.

"Daniel needs your findings—a complete report."

"Okay," I tell him, "that's what I do. I'll get right to it, but understand I will call home today."

Nobody says a word.

I get up and excuse myself, leave the house, and return to the trailer and add some creamer to my cup. I set the coffee down on the desk and take a moment for myself. Before sitting down, I plant my feet shoulder width apart, close my eyes, center myself, and take a few deep breaths. I use mental imagery of my feet planted firmly on the earth to reverse my negative thoughts. I do this for about a minute. Relaxing around these guys is not easy. I'm also having a tough time pushing aside the Houston incident. After a few minutes, I'm relaxed enough to begin.

Feeling better and mentally relaxed, I sit at the desk, pencil in hand. I begin. I write today's date and time and "011211/80102."

Four

The numbers are used like a library filing system: date, number of times viewed, and tracking number. Mostly they are used to stimulate thought.

With the pencil never leaving the paper, making what would look to you like scribbles, an ideogram is born. Stage two: gestalts. Describe with basic words: *manmade structure, a man,* and *danger.* Stage three: sketch out flat, brown, dusty, gray terrain. Draw one large structure with four large openings. Then some smaller buildings. These structures sit atop a hot, flat, manmade surface.

I must use strong mental discipline not to write down what it is until I go into stage four. The matrix will tell all. I take ruler in hand and draw a line lengthwise and begin labeling the columns.

A knock on the door interrupts me. I write "Break; answer door," noting the date and time.

I don't open it. "Who is it?" I ask.

"Joseph. We need to talk to you; come to the kitchen." I hear him walk away.

I leave the trailer and head to the kitchen, where I find them all sitting around the table.

"Angie and I have to run into Houston," Chad tells me. "Joseph will be here. We'll be back."

What am I supposed to say? They are actually acting as if they care whether I know or not. "Okay." I walk over to the coffeepot, pour myself a cup, and wonder where the creamer is hidden.

"No more than four hours," Chad tells Joseph, and he gets up to leave. Turning to me, he asks, "Is there anything we can get you, Ashlee?"

I look at him, not sure what to say. Why the concern now?

"No, nothing, but thanks all the same." Since I have his attention, I throw it at him again. "Can I call Eric?"

Chad doesn't answer at first. "It'll be discussed with Daniel, and I'll get back with you," he finally tells me.

Chad and Angie leave the house and drive off in the sedan.

Joseph and I sit at the table as I finish my coffee. He's looking me over—that fed thing, sizing me up.

"How are you moving along with the viewing?" he asks.

I don't answer. Only Daniel will see my work—standard protocol. I'm uncomfortable with the question.

"I read a book about viewing and met another viewer a year ago," he tells me. "I just find it fascinating."

"You've still got a long way to go," I tell him.

He changes the subject, talking instead about the Houston attack.

I ask him if I can I see aerial photos of Ellington Field. "I could use it for feedback."

Feedback is critical for a viewer. Unfortunately, most of the time it comes long after the assignment has been completed, sometimes years. A few months ago I read in the paper about a small aircraft that had been located in Arizona and was linked to a pilot who was found in Colorado. I had been tasked to locate the pilot of that plane, who had been missing for twenty years. After completing the job, the analyst doubted my findings of there being two locations but forwarded them to the project manager anyway. My dowsing skills are not to be taken lightly.

He tells me he'd have to okay it with Daniel first.

This guy is so much easier to get along with than Chad.

I finish up and leave the kitchen. I head back to *mi casa*, sit at the desk, pull out the cell phone, and look at the dial pad. Should I or not?

I dial Eric's number and hold the phone next to my ear. Surely they don't have his number.

Before any ringing begins, there's a message. Daniel's voice informs me that the number is blocked from this phone. Oh well, I had to try.

There's a knock at the door. It's Joseph. "We're leaving," he tells me through the door.

I open the door. "Leaving? Where? I was told four hours, and it's only been two." He has that serious look again.

I pack up quickly and throw my backpack into the truck. Joseph is standing in front of the cab and begins walking around the trailer. He steps inside, and I watch all the slides move inward.

He walks past me. "Where are we going?" I ask again.

Still no answer. We get into the truck, and Joseph cranks it up. Whoever dreamed this would be a standard skill of an agent?

I can't stop wondering what is going on. Is this the norm for these guys?

Without another word, the rig is rolling back down the unmarked county road. We come to a two-lane blacktop road with no signs. I believe it's Texas 36. We turn to the left.

The sun is to our left at a slight angle; we're traveling southeast. If I remember my Texas geography correctly, we're headed toward Freeport. The Texas coastline: flat, lots of refineries, and not much to see.

"Take it we're going to the coast?" I ask Joseph. He's being very quiet.

Steadily looking out the windshield, he finally answers. "Yep."

More syllables than I got from the others on the road. Then he looks at me intently.

"Time to do your job," he says.

"I'm new at doing it the way everybody else wants." I say. "Not once in all those years of class and practice did anyone ever mention moving vehicles, feds, and being scared out of your mind." Again no reply.

I give in, reach into my backpack, and find my tools. I need something to use as a desk. Where is that tray?

"Where did that tray go?" I ask Joseph.

"Look on the backseat," he says

I look on the backseat and find it; it'll do.

I look up and note the passing signs: Highway 36 and Rosenberg city limits—basically Southwest Houston these days.

I put the paper and pencil to work and follow all the steps to continue from a long break.

Immediately I'm on the target. I'm viewing what appears to be flat, natural ground with a long, black surface. Buildings stand nearby. The words *runway* and *hangars* are running through my mind. I document them as stray cats; I'll be coming back to them later. I give myself a command to move one thousand feet above the target. It is, without a doubt, a rural area, with what appears at first to be a small town. There are people about, clear skies, and lots of sunshine. There appears to be a railroad a short distance to the west of the complex. No other buildings in any direction, and only one road in and out. This is a well-maintained and well-controlled area.

Time to use one of the P6 tools. Symbolic sketch would work. It would help me determine what kind of facility is there.

Starting with a blank paper, I number it and mark the letter *N* at the top, for *north*. With north in mind I draw a line down the length of the page. I mark the line with *X*'s. I draw two lines east and west, keeping the lines separate. I then repeat the same going north and south. I note on the sketch, "blacktop, may be roadway." The same large building comes to view. I mark four lines representing corners and a curved line over them to represent a roof. Next I see four large openings, and I mark those as well. Not sure of their use yet. I use triangles to represent smaller buildings; I'll get back to those later. I tell myself to move 2,500 feet to the east. I view one of the openings in the large building. What appears to be an aircraft sits inside the open bay door. I now label the large building a hangar.

Viewing the target site repeatedly may not be telling you that you are on target, only that you are on the right track. You may need to pursue another avenue in the same vicinity. Don't dwell on it; move on. I'm having some difficulty focusing. My concentration is wavering. I tell myself to disregard the current target site. I sit erect and mentally put aside the last site viewed. Then a new one comes around. I view what appears to be a burning building and people lying around. Others are running. Have I mentally strayed from the true target site, or does this one also apply?

Joseph's cell phone rings.

"Break."

Joseph answers. After listening for a moment, he turns pale.

We're coming to the city limits of West Columbia. At the intersection of Texas Highway 35, we turn right. The sign reads "Bay City 30 miles." we are traveling away from Houston and Freeport.

"What's wrong?"

"There was another hit in Houston—the reserve center on Old Spanish Trail. A large explosive was set off; it leveled one building and damaged three others."

I don't tell him what I had just viewed. But it's immediate feedback on what I had viewed, no waiting years this time. I enter another mini summary of the site as well as the feedback.

We're about halfway between West Columbia and Bay City and turn left onto another unmarked county road. It's marshy with lots of trees. We travel about half a mile and stop at a brick house, well into the woods.

Joseph starts to get out. I push my work into my backpack.

"Wait here," he says. He doesn't have to tell me twice. I lock the doors after he gets out. Joseph goes inside and, within a minute, opens the front door and signals for me to come in.

I really want to go home. These guys are playing with something more dangerous than I can even imagine. Joseph signals again and gives me a stern look. He starts toward me, and I unlock my door.

I get out and walk up to the door; Chad and Angie are there. I thought they would be in Houston, chasing the bad guys.

The house is okay—old, but okay. There are three bedrooms, two baths, and furniture from the '70s—lime green stuff, but still in good shape—lots of portraits hanging on the walls; big family.

"Guess these people aren't home today?" I ask Chad. I smile at him but don't get one in return.

"They won't need it anymore," he tells me. Now there's a pleasant thought.

Chad and Joseph talk briefly. Joseph leaves and goes to the truck. I see it through the window parked on the east side, again just outside the kitchen door.

Fifteen minutes go by before he comes back and tells Chad, "We're all set up for the night."

The three grab chairs in the living room. "Go to your house and do some work," Chad says, then, "We have matters to discuss."

Yes, Daddy. I'll be a good girl and go to my room.

I really didn't want to hear them anyway. Time to figure out this target. I go into my new little home, take out my tools, and place them on top of the desk.

"Break over."

I go over the last effort on the symbolic sketch. Run my fingers over the lines. Like ideograms, impressions can be found by touch. Nothing. I may have lost the site picture, or I'm losing concentration.

I step back, take a deep breath, and mentally set aside the day's events. Focus is mandatory to maintain control. The whole point is to stay within a structured procedure. It gives you tangible guidelines and documentation for a paying client. I always have to remind myself of that, especially since I don't work with a monitor very often. Once a project goes to the analyst, he or she needs all the written information to put together the report. Lots of paperwork—too much, it seems at times.

I step back up to the sketch and take pencil in hand. I need to use a couple more P6 tools, but I'm not ready yet to determine location. This is not a guessing game; I have seen that lives are at stake. P6 tools can be anything from a sketch to as little as a line on paper. The viewer taps along these sketches or lines using a pencil, pen, or just fingers, tapping or tracing to determine locations or time lines.

As I relax, I have another mental picture. A male, midfifties, medium height, black hair, fair skin, possibly Asian. This is the second time I've seen him; he must be part of the target. I go back to the P4 matrix and review descriptors. He was first viewed standing on a flat, narrow surface. This time he was viewed standing and looking upward. There is a multistory building in front of him. "More descriptors," I say out loud. I tell myself to stand next to him. I do so; the texture of the flat surface is concrete and it's about sixty inches wide. He is wearing a black Astros baseball cap, a long-sleeved gray pullover, and jeans. I look at the flat surface and see he is wearing gray tennis shoes. There is a blue backpack slung over his right shoulder. He is looking up at the side of a building. I tell myself to step back ten paces and move up one hundred feet. When I do, I can read the lettering on the side of the building: "Texas Children's Hospital." I must stop and tell someone!

No, wait. What am I going to say? What if he's not the one we're looking for? I watch as he enters the double glass doors—must be the main entrance. Should I alert the feds, or is it still too early?

"Break."

I leave my trailer and go to the house to find Chad. He is sitting at a table in the living room. I motion for him to meet me in the kitchen. "Daniel needs to know what I just viewed."

Chad appears concerned even though I have not yet told him the details.

Chad punches Daniel's number into his phone and hands it to me. I tell Daniel what I viewed. This is outside of protocols, but current events have changed many things.

Daniel asks a fair question: "Did the person do anything alarming?"

He's right. Did I just stray from the true site picture? Am I losing it because of all that is happening? Anxiety is racing through my body.

I tell Daniel that I viewed both of the events in Houston while they were happening and the feedback proved them accurate. He knows what

I am talking about. Feedback is our confirmation that a viewer either hit or didn't. I'm usually 95 percent correct.

"Relax," Daniel tells me, "I'll notify local authorities."

I don't relax.

I return Chad's phone to him and go back out to my desk. I'm stressed out and exhausted. I need to lie down and rest for a while.

It takes about thirty minutes to finally regain myself; it's very quiet in the trailer. I go to the small living room and turn on the TV to watch the evening news. I get more feedback.

Local authorities and FBI are at the Texas Children's Hospital. I hear one word repeated over and over: *Bomb.*

The reporter says that someone planted a bomb in the cafeteria and set it off; there are an unknown number of causalities. They further add that investigators have positively linked this attack to the Ellington Field incident.

I go back to the house. The three others are sitting there, not speaking.

Chad's phone rings, and I literally jump to my feet. Surprised I didn't hit the ceiling. Get a grip.

Chad hands me the phone. "Hospital security found a backpack sitting in the corner of the cafeteria," Daniel tells me. "We believe the use of a radio by responding officers triggered a detonator. The bomb went off."

I'm dumbfounded. Who is this guy?

Daniel knows better than to tell me, but I ask, "What kind of animal am I looking for?"

He doesn't answer for a moment, and then he says, "Good job, Ashlee, but it's time to get back to work."

He knows better than to pollute the target. Any suggestion of target facts or details given to me will lead to false perceptions. False perceptions could lead us on a wild-goose chase.

He did have one other item of note. He told me that another viewer was involved up until this morning. That viewer opted out when the danger level became too much.

Thanks. Even the Lone Ranger had a partner.

I hand the phone back to Chad, and they talk momentarily.

I have one question for Chad. "For the project's sake, are the reserve center and hospital close?"

"Yes, very close, considering the size of Houston. Why?"

He heard Daniel and me talking, but I can't tell him any more of what was documented, though I can give him a clue. "Has this guy's means of transportation been determined?"

"Not yet, why?"

"Sometimes it's difficult to follow a person using multiple forms of transportation. If a true site picture is made, I can determine the means of travel." He gives me the damndest gaze. "Sorry, didn't mean to go over your head."

As I'm leaving the house, Chad calls out, "Meet us in the living room at eight a.m. with your gear; we're leaving in the morning." I guess we're putting down for the night. Good thing; I can use a full night's sleep—first one since we started this ride.

In the morning, I pack up, once again rinsing out the few dishes I used and stowing everything that'll move around. I even remember to close the doors. I put my gear in the truck, and Joseph asks if I'm ready—as if I can say no. Besides, I wasn't given the choice to opt out.

Even though it's morning, it's already humid and warm. As we are prepping the rig, I realize the difference in humidity between here and Lubbock. I'll take the desert anytime.

"Where to this time?" I ask once we get underway.

"It's all about the trade winds." Trade winds? Are we going sailing?

"Are we talking airborne danger?"

"Yes, there is a nuclear plant near Bay City."

We're going south on Highway 35, heading to Bay City. "You did say Bay City?"

"Don't worry." He grins at me. "If it goes off now, you won't feel a thing."

"That's not funny."

We come to a crossroads in town and turn right on Highway 36, going west to someplace named Needville—yet another town in Texas I've never heard of.

"Where are we going?" I ask again.

Joseph continues looking forward. "About three hours down the road. In the meantime, you need to get to work."

We come to a city limit sign for Wharton. Another crossroads: IH59 left to Houston or right to Corpus Christi.

He turns left. The next city is Victoria, but then again, with these guys, who knows.

Joseph's phone rings, and he answers. "Yes, sir. Yes, sir. No, sir." He doesn't look well.

He looks at me, pale and unsure.

"What is it?" I ask him.

"A man was seen crossing the perimeter near the visitor center at the Bay City nuclear plant. The nuclear security team was dispatched; two of them intercepted the intruder on the far west side near the Colorado River. He was seen at the riverbank holding a gun on two fishermen in a bass boat. He killed the fishermen and went downriver toward the gulf in their boat."

I asked, "Is this on video? Surely the nuclear plant monitors everything."

"Yes," he said, "that's why we know so many details."

"Did anyone get an ID on this guy?"

"No, he had on a hood and mask."

We're both in shock. Earlier we were concerned about airborne chemicals, possibly from the Bay City nuclear plant. Thank goodness he didn't hit it.

"So they think he went downriver? How far can he go with that boat?"

"He can make it to Palacios in about an hour. Once there, he can stash the boat in the turning basin. It's about a half mile into town from there. The town is too small to have a bus terminal, but there's probably a convenience store with a Greyhound stop where he can get a ticket."

Who is this guy? Or is there more than one?

We continue south. We arrive in Victoria and come to the intersection with Highway 87. We turn right, and the signs indicate we're going to San Antonio. I really wanted to do this tour of Texas, but on my own terms.

Not much to look at here; mesquite and cows, and plenty of each.

I grab my backpack and use Joseph's briefcase as a work space. I have to keep trying; the death toll is worsening.

I lay out the necessities on the briefcase.

"Break over."

I begin a fresh ideogram page, clearing my mind of any events or details I may have overheard. After all, this is not psychic work; it's mental discipline applied to paper. Teacher always reminded us of that. "I am not psychic," he would say. "This is a discipline; use your mind and the protocol. Apply it to paper; write it down no matter what." It's true, this is not a fortune-telling gig. All that I and others do is a science—a science of the mind.

Begin again: 011211/80103. My pencil flies along, scribbling out lines and loops. But now I'm caught off guard. Once I stop the pencil, I see an outline of a face. I'm not sure if it's female or male. That will be determined by the time I do the matrix.

I go through the P2 stage. I document *smooth, white,* and *soft*; gestalts are biological.

Stage 3: sketch out a face. Like the ideogram, collar-length hair and eyes belonging to one likely to be of Asian descent. I'm feeling fear, darkness, death, hatred, and evil-mindedness. I get the shivers.

Now I can move into stage 4. Matrix time. I line the paper and create the columns. Lots of descriptors that indicate a male. I write all these in columns and need to write a mini summary.

> **Mini Summary #2**—Person viewed appears to be Asian, medium build, black hair, tan skin, no apparent scars, blue pullover shirt, jeans, black ball cap, and gray tennis shoes. While viewing the person's description I felt death.

Definitely an aesthetic impact, and not a good one.

I try not to let it worry me. Aesthetic impact occurs when the viewer has an emotion associated with the site. The emotion tells the viewer what is being felt at, or associated with, the target.

Joseph tells me we're stopping. I should quit.

I document "break."

We're approaching someplace called La Vernia.

Once in town, we turn left onto Crews Street, travel about three blocks past the Baptist church, and arrive at the corner of Crews and Kingsdale. We travel across Kingsdale and enter a driveway. A small white house is on the right. I see a black sedan parked outside. The feds must be here.

The house sits in view of any traffic or people coming in from the highway. Open fields on two sides. No sneaking up on this one.

"Sit tight," Joseph orders me once we're stopped. He goes in first and then signals from the door for me to come on.

Chad and Angie are inside. The feeling in the room is somber. Everyone is in shock after the events of the past few days.

"Have you worked up any more facts?" Chad asks. This time I don't question the fact that protocols are not being followed; I just tell him what I had.

He calls Daniel and puts me on the line.

I tell Daniel of my viewing of the male and give him a description. Daniel remains very quiet. I stand there with the phone in my ear, waiting. He finally speaks. "Ashlee, you're on target. Now don't lose focus and stray from the true target."

I remind him that I have done this more times than I can remember. Number one rule: if your mind strays while working a target, put down the pencil and walk if off. Then come back and continue.

"You're dead on; your feedback is all positive," he tells me to offer encouragement. "Let's figure this out before more are hurt or killed."

"Yes, sir," I tell him. "I'm on it; I'll give it my all."

He asks to speak to Chad, and I hand him the phone and walk into the kitchen.

Looking out a window above the sink, I see Joseph moving and setting up the trailer. There are no close neighbors on either side of the house.

I relax, leaning on the counter just short of the sink, and tell myself, "Relax your mind."

I feel like my feet leave the floor. It's a soothing feeling, and I look out at the open field. My mind is at ease, but then I see the man described in my session. He is in a building filled with people, waiting at a counter. Using my mental abilities, I tell myself to back up ten feet. He is waiting and anxious. The room is wide, with rows of items for sale. A double glass door leads to a parking lot. There is a hallway with doors labeled Men and Women. I move outside to the parking lot and see two rows of gas pumps marked Texaco. Back inside I stand behind the counter and read the vendor license. There's an address: 1111 Henderson at Hwy 32, Palacios, Texas. I look out the front window and see a bus pull up. The male is at the counter; I hear him ask the clerk for a ticket to San Antonio. I continue watching as he walks out of the store and boards the bus. My next image is an endless field. Gripping the countertop behind me, I become tense.

It's not uncommon for a viewer to continue a session after taking corrective measures to stop. The real discipline is to make sure to put all that is seen on paper in the appropriate order. Then it can be used by the analyst.

I quickly leave the house and go back to the trailer to retrieve my backpack. Once back inside, I ask Chad to follow me. We sit at the kitchen table. I've got to let Daniel know about the bus and the possibility that the suspect is heading to San Antonio.

After giving Chad a recap of what I saw, I ask him to call Daniel. I must document this while it's still fresh in my mind.

Chad looks at me with surprise and disbelief, fumbling with the phone, glancing at me repeatedly.

I'm dedicated to writing down as many descriptors as possible. I don't hear the conversation. It is time to find him. I know it's not going to be easy. Is he on a bus, or was the bus a decoy?

"Let's load," Chad says when he hangs up,

"Where to this time?"

No answer.

All the drama about whether or not they believe me and when to call in, and now no answer at all to my question. I have to bring this up; it's just not acceptable.

I need time. "Stop, just stop! I need thirty minutes; you know I have to write all this down." My voice is shrill, just short of a scream.

Glaring at me, Chad says, "Thirty minutes, and then we're gone." He is pissed.

Time flies when you're dedicated to making sure everything you can possibly think of is written down. You become so involved trying to hold on to all the details and writing that you lose where you are in the present. Time is up as I list the last descriptor.

Chad and Angie are gathering gear. He tells us to mount up. Time to leave the house.

I wrap it up, stuff away my notes, and exit through the kitchen door. Where is Joseph? Is he in the trailer or the truck?

Chad and Angie are in the sedan. Joseph exits the trailer and signals to me, pointing toward the truck. I get in the passenger side, and Joseph starts the truck, not saying a word. We leave the way we came in, on Crews Street. Joseph turns left as Chad's right-turn signal flashes. We're on Highway 87 heading into San Antonio, it is midafternoon, and traffic is going to suck.

Joseph is really quiet, and I wonder why we went in opposite directions. Should I ask? Maybe later. He is concentrating on driving the rig in traffic.

We exit south, onto loop 410. Traffic is starting to thicken, but Joseph pushes onward. I take it he's a city driver; he doesn't seem fazed by the cars whizzing by him. We make the loop and plow into major traffic at I-10 westbound. Slowly we creep, bumper to bumper, Joseph not saying a word.

After about twenty minutes, we break out of San Antonio city limits heading toward Kerrville.

People pay good money for a setup like this; truck and trailer together must run about one hundred thousand. I had no idea that they can run a steady 70 mph. Why do all those snowbirds drive so slowly?

I hear a phone ring, and Joseph doesn't answer his. What did I do with mine? I check my pack. It's Eric!

"Ashlee is that you?" What can I say? My hands are shaking, and my palms are sweating.

"Hi, Eric," I say, trying to find my tongue. I clear my throat and close my eyes. I'm relieved to hear his voice, but how did he get this number?

"Don't worry about the dogs; they're taken care of."

"You have no idea how badly I want to be home."

"Your uncle called and explained everything."

My uncle? I only have one uncle, Ted, in Amarillo. We haven't spoken in years.

"What exactly did my uncle have to say?"

"He told me your great-aunt had passed away in Cuero and had already been cremated. Since no one else was able to travel, and you were in Las Vegas at the remote viewer conference, there wasn't anyone to retrieve her ashes. I was happy to do it; you know how I feel about your parents. By the way, where am I supposed to take these ashes?"

"I'm not sure; I'll give Mom a call and ask. Oh, Eric, I can't thank you enough. You could have said no."

So that's how they got him away from Lubbock and are keeping him out of harm's way. I couldn't have done better myself. I hope he doesn't feel my grin through the phone.

"I miss you."

"I miss you too; I should be back in a few days."

This is a tough call; I am trembling and trying to keep my composure.

"I've got to go; I'll call the minute I get a chance."

"By the way," I ask, "did you call my cell number?"

"Of course. Why?"

"No reason, I just didn't remember if I had forwarded my calls."

"Okay. Drive safe and come home soon."

I assure him I will, and we hang up.

Maybe my real question should be, why did you take so long to call? With all that's going on, I won't press the matter, but I definitely will later!

I can't believe it. He dialed my cell number and the call was routed to this phone. I left my phone at home. They could not have set the call forwarding without it, could they? Besides, other people call me; where are those calls?

A dead aunt and selected calls being forwarded. Okay, I give up; they win.

This joyride across Texas is beginning to bother me. Why is it I can determine the whereabouts of the bad guy and then we happen to be on the same route? Who is really following whom?

Five

Joseph's pocket is ringing; he is so tuned in to driving that it rings several times before he snaps to and answers.

It's evident he is new to all this. His mannerisms are not natural, and he is out of the loop as compared to the others. He reminds me of the burros back at the ranch. If one is a different color than the others, it's not allowed in the circle at night. After enough time goes by, it is finally accepted and allowed in.

He gives the usual "yes, sir" and disconnects. "Time to go back to work," he says, turning to me.

The last sign read "Kerrville 20 Miles." Maybe we'll stop there; I could use a room with a desk that's not moving.

Joseph signals for a right turn onto the exit for FM 1341, Cypress Creek Road. We take the exit and follow the feeder road for a short distance and go back under I-10. About a hundred yards down, we turn right onto a dirt road and follow it to small house with a tin roof. We can see a thousand yards in any direction.

"How is the team able to drive straight onto these hideaways?" I ask him. "Aren't you worried about being followed? We know he has intel too."

"Our people are keeping close watch on us by satellite, and we are being directed to the next safe location."

Figures; they use technology to follow a car but can't follow a person who is using mass transit.

The sedan is already there when we pull up. How do they do that?

Joseph exits and goes inside, and I wait until I get my signal to follow.

"No time to chat; we need info fast," Chad tells me when he meets me at the door.

Joseph heads outside to get my house/office ready. Better than working in the truck.

Once inside, I close my eyes and relax for a moment to clear my mind.

I begin using the ideogram from the last session, where I saw the Asian man boarding a bus. Again I see facial features and experience a feeling of danger. Staying focused, I write down what I am viewing. It appears to be a woman. I must maintain mental discipline. I begin sketching on a blank piece of paper. Narrow jaw, small forehead, shoulder-length black hair, small nose, and narrow eyes. Her eyes seem to be able to look right through me. I number this page and add it to the growing stack. I then get more details of the site picture. I again see the man that I saw at the bus station. I make notes in my matrix of descriptors for two different people—one male, one female.

Continuing, I grip the pencil, and images flow but seem to become a little scrambled. This is new. I apply more discipline. I'm filling columns with a lot of descriptors of him, but where is he? And who is the woman? Are they together? I'm using stray cats and castling; I must stop. Refocus. Back to the last location I viewed, and forget the woman for now.

I tell myself to move five hundred feet above the target. I do so and see many buildings. I then return to my last position and observe. When I do, I see the Asian man again, right in my face. I tell myself to step back fifteen paces so as to observe more details. There he is, dressed the same as before and looking up at an angle. Apparently he is trying to read something written on a wall. I look up as well and see a list of destinations. He is at a bus station. I tell myself to stand next to him. Once there, I look around. It's not a large station: a single room with just one person standing behind a counter—a young male, early twenties. The Asian male approaches the counter, and I follow him. He talks with the clerk. I hear it as a whisper, but I can make out the words "El Paso." I do not detect a foreign accent. I view his ticket as it's being written out: Kerrville to El Paso, 7:30 today's date.

I close out the viewing and write as fast as humanly possible. When I finish, I push the paper into the pack and head to the house at a run. Bursting through the front door of the house, I call out "Chad!"

"What?" he yells back.

"The suspect is at the bus station in Kerrville," I quickly explain. "He's got a ticket to El Paso; the bus leaves in less than an hour."

Chad closes the door behind him and dials on his phone. He tells Daniel what I told him. Sure hope I'm right; sometimes a viewer can become fixated on something or someone and stray from the target.

"Authorities and our field agents are en route; you'd better be right," Chad says when he finishes the call.

I'm very confident. I've viewed a lot in the last few days and the feedback has all been positive. This is the guy I saw at the children's hospital.

"Come sit down and relax," Chad says.

Come sit and relax? Are we going to hold hands and tell scary stories? I have a feeling that is totally unfamiliar to me, a feeling that someone is watching. We sit in uncomfortable silence for what seems like hours but is probably only thirty minutes until Chad's phone rings.

I sit anxiously, literally on the edge of my seat, while Chad is on the phone. He is clenching his jaw and about to squeeze the phone to pieces. Memo to self: don't piss this guy off.

He tells the person on the other end thanks and hangs up. He is glaring at me.

"He wasn't there; Daniel will talk to you later."

I lean back on the sofa. All three of them in the room are staring at me. I feel like a fool. I was sure it was him.

"The only clue was that the clerk spoke with someone just before we got there that was Asian, but this person had a Texas accent."

I decide it's time to defend myself and my trade. I stand and say, "I told you he did not have a foreign accent."

"Are you sure?" Chad says, standing up as well.

"Absolutely." I remind him of my percentage of accuracy and years of working with the agency. "So get off my ass," I say.

Chad steps forward, looking me in the eye. I take it this is where one gets her ass kicked.

"About time you grew a pair." He smiles. "I'll call in that fact."

Chad walks out of the room, and I sit back down muttering to myself. "What were you thinking?" That guy eats way too much red meat. Oh well, Chad's not my problem. I need to find out where the bad guy went after he left the station.

I excuse myself from the others and go back to the rig, where I sort through all the data I've compiled. There are pages and pages by now. This is where I would normally have the target sited, documented, and forwarded to the project manager or analyst. This time I don't even know who the target is.

I need to clear my mind and emotions.

There is a technique called centering. Relatively easy thing—sit still, close your mind, take slow, deep breaths, and let go of the emotion. This job calls for a strong-minded person; emotions can blur your sight.

A knock sounds at the door. It's Chad. "Are you up for more work?"

"Sure, but only for an hour or so."

He's a pro and has been around viewers before. Even though he wants to ask, "Where is this guy?" He doesn't; that would pollute the target.

"Break over."

I run the fingers of my left hand over the sketch of the man. I draw another ideogram. This is common; if you feel you need to draw an ideogram, do it. Writing gestalts: *curvy, black, hot and sunny, going, coming,* and *standing.* These are normal for gestalts and seem to be part of the session. "Write everything down," the echo of Teacher says in my mind. I begin filling the columns; descriptors are flowing. Then that blurred vision thing happens again; what is that?

I focus, trying to put together a location. I sketch out a roadway—four lanes coming and going, blacktop, sunny day, curvy roads leading to it. Using the sketch, I feel along the lines. A letter and then numbers—I-10 displayed on a small blue sign. I command myself to move fifty feet above the sign. There it is, Interstate 10: two lanes to San Antonio and two lanes to El Paso. About fifty yards away is a man with a backpack, thumb out. I command myself to move next to him and observe. There it is again; I can't see clearly. Headache, right in the forehead. I must stop.

"Break."

I write all that I can remember.

Time to talk to Chad. I return to the house. No Chad or Angie, just Joseph.

"Where did they go?" I ask.

"To help with the manhunt. Seems your information was verified and found to be accurate."

I look at him and wonder if they are looking for the terrorist or trying to prove me wrong. This whole venture has been way out of the norm for me. Spy games are not for me.

"Who verified it?" I ask.

Last I heard, there were no other viewers involved, especially any of those I usually work with.

"I don't know. Chad got the word."

"Call Daniel; I have something to tell him." Let's see how much stroke this rookie has.

Joseph dials out, begins talking, and ducks his head so I can't see his face. Just as I think, *He didn't call Daniel,* Daniel calls him.

To save his ass, I tell him, "Give me the phone." He hands over the phone, and I tell Daniel what I viewed.

"Thanks," Daniel says, and he hangs up. Joseph is looking out the window.

"You didn't have to turn around; I had to talk out loud in front of you."

"Daniel told me to turn around and not listen."

I fight to control every muscle in my face to keep from laughing out loud.

"Okay, let's eat. I'm hungry. What about you?"

"Sure," he says.

Looking in the fridge, I find a bunch of stuff to put together a quick meal. Wonder who keeps these houses stocked with food? I boil a few red potatoes, microwave a chicken breast, and put canned peas in a saucepan. All is ready in a few minutes—not too bad.

We're halfway through eating when the sedan pulls up with Chad and Angie inside. Neither of them looks very happy. They have nothing to say when they come into the house. Guess they lost their man again.

I invite them to share our meal, but they both decline. They look at Joseph and ask him to meet them in the living room when he's finished. They seem upset with him.

"Thanks, that was good," says Joseph. "I don't get home-cooked meals very often, especially when we're on a case." He stands and excuses himself.

I follow him; I feel I could stand to use the bathroom.

They gather in the living room, and I enter the bathroom. Even with the door closed, I can hear most of what is said. Joseph is being reprimanded for sharing information with me.

Let me guess: don't get close to the client, might have to kill her one day. Wait, that's not funny. After surveying the bathroom, I decide the one in the trailer is better and I exit through the kitchen.

I run a hot bath, fitting fairly well in the smaller tub. I enjoy a good twenty minutes of soaking. It's getting late, and I'm ready to go to bed. These guys have a bad habit of leaving at any moment. I get out of the tub, wrap myself in a towel, and lie down on the bed. Finally, I get to stretch out and begin thinking about Eric; I wonder why he hasn't called me again.

Closing my eyes, I let it all go.

There she is again. I open my eyes and don't move. It's better to have your eyes open if something like this occurs. I'm seeing that female face again very clearly; either she's watching me or I'm in her space. Then, just as quickly, it ends. I'm wondering who was in whose space? Who was being viewed, and who was the other viewer?

I rethink the episode; I'm here, relaxed, and my eyes are closed. She appeared to be awake with her eyes open. When I open my eyes, she is still there and blinks. I have been viewed.

I'm rattled to my core. She entered my space intentionally, even though I've used all the safety protocols I know to not allow anyone to do so.

I had always wondered if anyone had viewed me—purposely or accidentally, but viewed all the same. I did have one case where I had the constant feeling someone was watching, but I never saw the viewer. I've got to tell somebody.

I find a fresh set of clothes, dress quickly, and head back to the house, needing to find Chad. I call out to him as I knock on his bedroom door. "Chad, I need to talk to you."

"What do you need? We're leaving in the morning."

"I have to talk to Daniel."

He moves around, and I step away from the door, not knowing what to expect. He finally opens the door and hands me his cell phone.

"Go ahead," he says.

I dial out, and Daniel answers. I tell him something is up and I need to speak to him in private.

Chad doesn't move a muscle or change expression as I speak with Daniel.

"Chad is cleared for all information," Daniel tells me. "Continue."

"I'm positive I was viewed. It was an Asian woman."

"What is the protocol for that?"

"Try to camouflage yourself in the ethereal by having another viewer run interference, or just ignore the other viewer. When you're in the ethereal, it's safe; it's common to be seen, but there's nothing the other viewer can do about it."

"She is not to be ignored. Evidently it's a compatriot of the person we're looking for."

"Okay, I'll try the camouflage. I know of only two viewers that are trained to run interference for another viewer, and I'm one of them."

Daniel agrees and asks to speak to Chad. Chad takes the phone from me and returns to the bedroom, closing the door behind him. Funny—he can listen to my conversations, but I can't listen to his.

I venture back to the trailer with the hope of getting some sleep.

Once a viewer reaches upper-level training, she must learn to hide herself. One of the worst ways is to surround herself with white light. Why not just put a beacon on your head?

Camouflage is a must. Not to be seen is the goal—not to get caught up in some kind of ethereal battle. This is not fantasy. We don't use light sabers and unicorns, just pencil and paper with a disciplined mind.

It's late, and apparently we are leaving early. Back in bed I close my eyes and feel at ease. With one eye open, I look around. Tell me I'm not paranoid.

I feel nudging and pushing and hear my name. I open my eyes and see Chad. He's in a white T-shirt and slacks—not what I want to see early in the morning.

"Get up and let's go," he says.

Sitting up, I look out the window, it's still dark. I glance at the clock on my phone. 3:00 a.m.

I hear the others, and then Chad yells, "Ashlee, now!"

I hurry around gathering my papers and pencil and stuffing it all into my bag. I realize nobody is prepping the rig. Where is Joseph?

Angie steps out of the house and opens the door for me. "There's coffee in the kitchen. You've got ten minutes."

I hurry to the house and find the pot on the counter. Go figure, there's a to-go cup. I put together cream and coffee. I exit as Angie cranks the truck. As soon as I jump in, we're rolling. I look at her. "What is so important this time?"

She begins pulling out of the driveway. "We're compromised. We believe the terrorist viewer found us through you, or maybe we have a mole. Your information was confirmed. We got a report of someone picking up a hitchhiker on I-10, fifty miles west of San Antonio. The driver of the car was left for dead on the side of the road. Lucky for us, he was found still alive and gave a description. It seems you were followed."

More feedback. Even though this is all dangerous, the good thing is, I'm on target. The bad thing is, that woman who I saw viewing me is more skilled than I thought. Could she have notified the terrorist that I saw him board a bus?

We travel the same dirt road back to FM 1341, to I-10, and then under and up onto the highway westbound to El Paso.

"Why are we constantly taking the same path as the bad guy?"

"We're tracing his steps. The satellite topside is trying to find him, and we're boots on the ground."

I can't believe this. Boots on the ground? I'm no gun-toting fed looking for a gunfight.

"This is not in my contract with the agency. Take me someplace safe, now!"

"We are. With your info and our technology, we should be closing in. Buckle up, safety first." I wish she would stop grinning at me.

I try once more to convince her to let me out someplace other than where they are headed. I have no interest in meeting this fellow. None.

She doesn't answer, just drives at a steadfast pace of 70 mph. We're really in a hurry to be someplace.

My phone rings. My heart jumps; maybe I'll get to talk with Eric again. I'm ready to talk with somebody other than this posse.

It's Daniel. "Relax," he tells me, "agents are doing their jobs. I'm doing my job. An agent will always be at your side. That is why there are three."

"I take it you were listening."

"Always."

I remind him of my contract.

"It's been amended. Besides, you're in good hands."

He hangs up. I'm stuttering, trying to find the right words. Amended?

Six

We travel at a good pace for about two hours. Fort Stockton—now we really are in the middle of nowhere.

We take exit 261, on the east end of town, and ride the feeder until we reach a left turn leading onto Highway 385, go under I-10, and backtrack east. After about a mile on the right is a prison. The entrance sign reads, "Fort Stockton Unit." A chain-link fence about ten feet high with razor wire across the top surrounds many gray buildings, most with no windows. What a gloomy looking place.

We turn in at the entrance.

"Are you serious?" I look at Angie incredulously.

She looks at me and grins. "You asked me to take you someplace safe; here we are!"

They are full of surprises. A rest stop at Fort Stockton Unit; a men's minimum-security prison.

As we approach the gate, Angie shows her identification to the guard on duty, and he can't "Yes ma'am" her enough. I really have to get one of those badges; no door is an obstacle.

"You're already cleared," the guard says, not questioning her ID. "Pull in to loading bay two."

We pull forward and see four open bays that have electronic doors like my garage but are much bigger. We pull into number two.

Once the bay doors are closed, we exit the truck. Four gray walls with no windows. There is one doorway, and who knows where that goes. Eerie silence sets in as we stand around waiting. I really want to leave.

The door opens, and there stands Chad. Go figure.

He gestures for us to come toward the door. Angie goes to him without hesitation, leaving me with no choice but to follow. We go through and find ourselves in a Plexiglas room just big enough for the three of us. In fact, if it were any tighter, we would become really good friends.

We hear a buzzer and a loud click. The wall we're facing slides to the right. We step forward and are now in a hallway leading into the prison. We walk about fifty feet until we get to a metal door on the right. Chad looks into a small window on the door and pushes the handle, and it opens.

We walk down another hall. We pass a clinic, a laundry, a library, and a recreational room. The rooms are nice, except there are no windows and the doors are barred. At the end of this hallway is another metal door with a small window. Chad motions for us to continue.

We next enter an administrative area where civilian clerks work behind partitions. There are two offices on the right wall. One is labeled Warden and the other Assistant Warden. The upper half of the door is Plexiglas, allowing those in the offices to see anyone in the hallway.

Chad opens the assistant warden's door, we enter, and he closes and locks the door. The room has no windows but is well furnished and well lighted.

"Why here?" I had to ask.

"You; this is all about you," Chad answers.

"Me? You're joking. I would have settled for Motel 6."

"You were viewed. You're our most important asset in settling all this, and we were instructed to protect you."

It's true. The camouflage for a viewer is to blend in with lots of people and lots of the same colors—become a part of the immediate environment. Chad hands me a white inmate's jumpsuit.

"No way!"

I stand there holding the white suit, not wavering. I'm standing my ground.

He steps up to me with that deep, serious look. "If you don't, I will do it for you, and then I will know a whole lot about you."

That could be bad, or maybe not. I can't help but grin.

Having worked with him these past couple of days, I have no doubt that he would do just what he says.

"Nice offer, but I'm accustomed to dressing myself. I expect privacy and someone to watch that door."

"Relax. Just put it on over your clothes. But you need to take everything out of your pockets. Inmates don't carry anything."

I take a small pouch from my pocket. Inside is a stone attached to a string about nine inches long. Nothing fancy, plain and simple, a piece of crystal I picked up in the desert while in White Sands, New Mexico, on an outing with Teacher. It has no value but is priceless to me.

There is an announcement over the speakers: "Inmates to the mess hall for breakfast."

"Time to eat!" Chad says. He opens the door and points.

This is way out of hand. When this is over, I'm going to complain—to whom I don't know, but I'm going to bitch. We cross the administrative area and head down the hallways to a door marked Mess Hall. A guard comes to the door. Chad stops to talk to him for a second, and the door opens. We enter into the twilight zone.

All the characters from the Star Wars bar scene are inside. All of them.

Being with two well-dressed feds is good protection among these guys. But it does make me an easy target for an expert viewer, since they stick out.

It doesn't stop the stares. They may be first offenders, but they are criminals all the same. They know I'm not one of them. But what they don't know is that they are my camouflage. Most of us are all dressed alike. This should work; it may not so bad after all.

We have a light breakfast. Reminds me of elementary school days: pull a tray, stay in line, and a server places food on your tray. Scrambled eggs, two slices of toast, two slices of bacon, and one cup of coffee.

We sit at the table nearest the guards and eat our breakfast. It feels as though all eyes are on us. It's okay for them to see us, just as long as I remain undetected by the woman.

Once we finish, we sit waiting for the inmates to leave. A guard signals to us to come to the doorway; we do.

There is a red line eighteen inches away from the walls of the corridors. That is the path inmates must take. Guards walk down the middle. I look at Chad. He looks at me.

"No way!"

"Of course not; you're under our protection—today."

I never know if he is kidding or if he is just anal.

We head back to the assistant warden's office. Chad locks us in.

"If you feel up to it," he tells me, "there's a desk you can use. The guy who uses it is out for the day."

"Okay," I tell him, "I could use a Texas map."

I have to maintain the thread that if this guy is the target, I have to find him. I still can't say absolutely, because of the multiple locations I've seen so far. The target could involve him or not. I must not have trash on my mind.

We look through the desk but find no map. Guess nobody here has any hopes of traveling.

I set myself up to continue using a new tool—paper clip and string. Wish I had my dowser.

I sketch a rough outline of the state of Texas onto a blank sheet of paper. I find a paper clip and pull a piece of thread from my shirt sleeve—all the tools I need. I divide Texas into four parts and tie the paper clip to a nine-inch thread. I place my left hand over the top of the desk and my right hand on top of my left hand. The end of the string is between my thumb and index finger, with the paper clip dangling below. Beneath the dangling clip is the paper with the four sections of Texas.

The feds are watching me very closely. Earlier today they doubted my work, and now they are hovering in anticipation.

It's a pendulum—not like the pricey ones, but one all the same. The paper doesn't know the difference. I ask the device to show a no, and it slowly swings left to right; I ask for a yes, and it swings back and forth. Holding the pendulum over the right corner section of the paper, I ask myself, "Is the man viewed here?" It swings left to right. "No."

"Is the woman viewed here?" It swings left to right. "No."

I then hold the device over the section in the upper right corner and ask myself, "Is the man viewed here?" It swings left to right. "No."

"Is the woman viewed here?" The answer is no again.

Next, the bottom left corner. "Is the male here?" It swings back and forth. "Yes."

"The woman?" Left to right. "No."

Finally, the upper left corner of the drawing. Both answers there are no.

It would be much easier if I had a map of Texas. I would take the section with the yes and place it over the map. Then I could drill down to determine his general whereabouts.

I have used this method many times to locate missing persons, such as the pilot in Colorado. It's the pure way. A plain piece of paper has no misleading names or labels, just blankness. In previous assignments, I have quadrupled a clean sheet, dowsed each section, and then placed it over a USA map. I then dowsed that part of the map and repeated all this down to a street address. It's like a manual GPS.

Continuing with the present task, I and write "N" in the upper center of a blank sheet of paper. Under the letter *N*, I write "West Texas." I double-check the location of the male, repeating the previous steps and getting the same findings. No need to do so for the woman; she's not in Texas.

I mark "N" on another sheet. On the top of the paper I write "Pecos," at the bottom, "Rio Grande River," on the left, "New Mexico," and on the right, "Fort Stockton." I Repeat the procedures that determined the man was in Texas. I get a positive response on the left side of the paper. I repeat all, with labels representing closer boundaries; the left side reads "New Mexico," the bottom left corner, "Mexico," the right side, "Van Horn." The dowsing is beginning to indicate that the location is El Paso. I draw a circle on the last paper to the far left and write in it "El Paso." I then dowse a yes-or-no response to find out whether the man I viewed was there. The answer is yes.

Chad and Angie are watching closely. They may not have understood the method of the madness, but seeing it in action usually creates believers.

"One thing was different," I tell Chad. "There was no interference. Our camouflage worked."

I can't rule out the possibility of needing someone to run interference for me. There is almost a 100 percent chance the woman viewer will find me.

I gather up the papers and start making notes of what was involved: dates, times, results, and witnesses. I must document everything. If I don't, that analyst will be on my case.

While I was busy, I didn't notice Chad on the phone—no need to ask with whom. He hangs up and says, "Saddle up."

I remove the prison overalls, and we head back out of the prison. Once the bay doors open in front of us and we drive out, we are welcomed with sunshine. We'll all be glad to get away from here; too close of quarters for me.

Chad takes the lead with the sedan. Once through the gate and onto the main road, he turns left on the feeder and speeds out of sight.

We follow but instead head west to El Paso.

"Where did Chad go?" I ask.

"Backtrack a few miles to ensure we weren't followed."

During our stay at the state-sponsored hotel, I forgot about Joseph. I don't know whether to ask or not.

"What happened to Joseph?"

"He's ahead, El Paso."

Time to clear something up; bet she won't say.

"Why do you need me? It's evident you know the bad guy and his general whereabouts."

"We don't know who he is, but we suspect where he's from. You're the one finding him. We're trying to keep up with him using technology. We already told you this."

"Yes, I know, but you guys seem to be one step in front of me."

"No, three. There is someone farther ahead. Not the lead vehicle, but an advance unit; they are our eyes in the distance. In a sense, scouts."

Okay, there are three units with numerous agents and one far in the lead, plus satellites. Again, what do they need me for? Then it occurs to me. "I'm a witness. I'm the only one that can positively ID this guy, right?" I ask her.

Angie doesn't answer, just keeps driving west.

About two hours later we come to Van Horn. Angie is watching the exits closely. She is very nervous. Her nervousness has me scared and wondering. What is she looking for? We take an exit, ride the feeder for about a mile, and turn right on Highway 90. No station, store, or border patrol office anywhere in sight. Nothing.

We turn around in an abandoned parking lot and head back toward the freeway. She is watching closely, as if we're being followed. Are we?

"What are you looking for?" I ask.

She doesn't answer, just continues right onto a feeder road and reenters the freeway, continuing west.

"What are we looking for?" I repeat more firmly.

"Looking for an abandoned building or house, should we need to hide," she finally answers.

"Hide? Who from?"

"The bad guy. What if you're wrong and he's close by? Remember the first agents?"

How could I forget. Was it my suspect that killed them, or someone we have yet to discover? I leave it alone for now, I have another question.

"Everybody seems to have accepted my work as being accurate. What about you?"

"I'm skeptical. I believe in hard, hands-on facts."

"That's fair enough. Let me ask you, weren't my facts proven accurate by the feedback?" I continue to look at her, watching for any micro movement.

"Part of my job is to keep all options open. I have to keep you alive. If you're right, he's in El Paso. What if he knows about you and doubles back?"

She's right; he has a viewer also. He is doing the same thing we are, using all assets available to him. "You're right; we don't know if he backtracked looking for us, moved onto his next target, left the country, or is just hiding. There are no facts pointing to any of these possibilities."

It's been three hours since we left the prison, and I'm getting drowsy. I doze off and wake to the motion of the truck slowing down. I see an exit sign for Fabens. We take the exit and cross over to get to a gas station on the opposite side. The station has covered parking but appears closed. We pull under the awning.

"What's going on?" I want to know.

Angie tells me we're to sit tight until the teams approaching El Paso give us the all clear. So they're telling me no one knows the location of the suspect. Paranoia sets in. Where is this guy? Are we in a trap already, playing into his hands? I start to shiver.

Angie is watching me. She reaches over with one hand and touches my forearm. She has a very gentle touch for someone working with this outfit.

Angie looks at me and says calmly, "Relax, we've got you covered." She smiles, and I feel somewhat assured.

I gather my wits. "Thanks. I apologize for being such a wuss."

"Look, we train for years to do these jobs; sometimes it takes months to complete a particular mission."

"I trained for years too, but with books and paper. Not much good should this guy jump us. While I was in boot camp for the naval reserves, I fired the M4, but after that, I never saw a weapon. I wasn't assigned to combat-ready units."

We both relax and start to feel more comfortable with each other. Maybe Chad will come around too.

"What's Joseph's story?"

"He's the new guy, just completed dignitary training. He has been with the FBI for a few years as an analyst. He interviewed with us and later moved over to the unit."

"Figured he was new; he hasn't gotten that pissed-off look yet. But have faith."

She actually gives a light laugh. "Oh yeah, it's part of the training." She pauses briefly. "So what part of Texas are you from?" she asks, changing the subject.

"Come on, I know you read my file."

"I only had time to read the past ten years of your history. I've been a little busy, if you haven't noticed."

"Prior to this job I taught at the university in Lubbock. I went to UT, where I got my PhD in mathematics. While I was in college, I joined the navy reserves and became a member of naval intelligence. I was assigned to an electronic warfare and satellite imagery unit."

"How did you get involved with remote viewing?"

"After my discharge and a few years of teaching math, I felt a need for change. I went to a weekend job fair in Lubbock, and there sat a man at a booth. He was looking for students to learn the trade. At first I walked away thinking it was a bunch of hoodoo voodoo."

"Then?"

"I guess it was my curious mind. After one trip through the job fair, I found myself back at his booth. I took his card and went home. I called the next week and made an appointment for basic classes. Been at it ever since."

"Let me guess, the man at the booth was your Teacher?"

"You got it."

She asks no further questions and begins watching the overpass. Evidently we're about to leave.

It's been six years. I had actually never thought of that. I'd been on my own for four years and worked two with these guys. Now this, working the field—this was never discussed.

"Have you handled a handgun?" Angie asks.

"No, not even in the service."

"Open the glove box and look, but don't touch."

I look in the glove box. There sits a large revolver, stainless, with black rubber grips.

"If anything ever happens to your driver, grab that. It is a five-shot, shotgun loads. Just point and shoot."

Did she say point and shoot? Great, now they want an untrained person, me, to possibly be a pistoleer in time of need. I close the box.

Dad had showed me to use his .22 rifle for varmint hunting. I was never very good with it or shooting creatures. Now I wish I had paid closer attention.

We're finally moving back onto the freeway and on to El Paso. Twenty minutes to downtown.

Ten minutes later, I see the Rio Grande on my left and Mexico beyond. Two countries separated by only a river and a lot of fence. Looking across into Mexico, I can see the city of Ciudad Juarez, home to a million and a half people and more violence than one can imagine. I heard there was a curfew now, tightly enforced by the *federales*. Hard to believe; it looks peaceful, not much to the place. But death is common, and there's a civil war over who will control the drugs.

Entering El Paso, we pass the exit for Highway 54 to Alamogordo, New Mexico. Good time to bust through El Paso; traffic isn't too heavy now.

Every day, millions of people from El Paso and Ciudad Juarez intermingle. Most are citizens from Mexico crossing to go to work or school. To those living here, it's business as usual and has been going on since long before the river became the border. The Bridge of the Americas is the only toll-free bridge in the city allowing vehicle and pedestrian traffic.

Why hasn't our guy hit again? Where is he, and why El Paso? Fort Bliss or Mexico?

We're on the other side of the city, moving quickly. Once we clear the Guadalupe Mountain pass exit, the next stop is New Mexico. Goats, shrubs, and desert—we're out of El Paso, hurrah!

Angie's phone rings, and she answers. "Okay," she says, and she disconnects.

She tells me nothing. I'm not even going to ask.

We take exit 0 in Anthony and ride the feeder road. Left on Antonio Street in New Mexico, then south, and we go under the freeway. On the left is a truck stop. There must be fifty tractor-trailer rigs parked there, as well as RVs and regular vehicles fueling. Lots of people are wandering around. We pull in and park next to a pump. Angie exits and begins fueling the truck. I get out with my backpack in hand and walk around the trailer to her. "What's next?"

"Stand next to me."

"Okay, but why?"

I'm looking over my shoulder and to each side. What is going on?

She looks at me. "Just relax and blend in. Look around. Middle-aged people everywhere and lots of moving objects."

"I know how to camouflage, but why now? Who called you?"

"We need to utilize camouflage protocols whenever possible. You mentioned that at the prison."

She's right. Knowing I'm being watched, it's necessary to blend in as much as possible. Eventually I will be found. Nobody is exempt. With all that said, I look up at the sky. The bright, sunny, and endless Southwest sky—just looking at it helps me forget all that is going on.

She finishes fueling, and we park next to the building among other pickups and RVs and go inside. She was right; there are clusters of middle-aged people, truckers taking breaks, and people just traveling through West Texas. I blend rather well, being in a pullover and jeans.

There's a break room in the back. Upon entering, I find several small-framed recliners, a big-screen TV, and a counter along the wall with computers available. Angie and I go to the counter and pull up chairs. We're similar in age and color, but not appearance.

Angie says, "We're waiting for instructions."

"I take it nobody has found our guy yet?"

"No, even worse, we don't know which way he is traveling or how." She looks at me. "Time to go to work."

"Here? With all this noise, the smell of diesel, and all these people around?

"Now," she says firmly.

I reach into my backpack and pull everything out. This tops the moving vehicle; at least it was quiet and comfortable. A man sitting in a recliner turns and stares at us. Hope she doesn't shoot him. Oh well, I'll give it a try.

I scribble out "Break over" and retrace my fingers over all the ideograms and sketches.

Mental discipline is essential in this environment. There is a TV blaring, people on phones, and poor lighting, and now the guy in the recliner is snoring.

I write down "Distracter: noises within my immediate space." Then I write "Set Aside." I concentrate. The physical distractions around me cannot interfere with my objective—completing this session.

I take one long breath, and all becomes quiet. I hear nothing; my mind is totally obligated to the target, with all my senses aware—mostly the sixth. I'm writing descriptors, utilizing columns of the matrix. Multiple stray cats. It's time for a Mini P5. I label a new sheet "Mini P5" and begin putting stray cats in parentheses and sketching them. Again I view a large building with multiple entrances, a large, long, black surface, and possibly an aircraft. I document with the P5 and give myself a command. I place my hand on the facial sketch of the person we are pursuing and tell myself, "Locate and describe." There is confusion, clutter, loudness, busyness, darkness, dampness, and many people. The structure is single-floored and crowded. I tell myself, "Leave this structure and observe." I'm standing on asphalt, viewing a single-story, gray, concrete, double-door entrance facing south. I observe a sign near the entrance that reads "Annunciation House." I tell myself to move up from where I'm standing and describe.

I keep in mind "Write it down" and quickly jot notes as it's viewed.

The structure is triangular in shape, with the sharpest end facing two streets. I move to the intersection of the two streets: Olive and E. San

Antonio. The main entrance faces E. San Antonio. I return to the interior of the building I was last standing beside and describe it. I observe several manmade objects appearing to be beds. Many people are wandering around, but not the person I first observed.

"Break." I've got to tell Angie.

I describe the location and the address viewed. She calls in and relays the information.

"Relax," she tells me, "we'll know in a few minutes." These guys must be everywhere.

Five minutes later, her phone rings. "Yes, sir." She hangs up and tells me, "Time to move on."

"Tell me."

"Your location was exact, but no bad guy."

That was good feedback. One thing is for sure; I'm confident he was there. But did he know I was there?

When we get to the truck, I'm feeling dizzy. Must be stress. I can't breathe, and blackness is closing in. I climb in and lean back to catch my breath, and I begin struggling.

Angie sees my situation, and she grabs my arm and asks, "What's wrong?"

I can't answer. My throat is closing, and I'm going to pass out. I'm trying to relax and not panic, but what is this? I'm blacking out. Angie is trying to loosen my collar. I hear her voice, but she sounds far away. Then I remember that although you can't be physically harmed when in the etheric, you can be influenced by imagery. I feel like I'm strangling and I'm going to die.

Trying to relax, and pushing Angie aside, I take deep breaths. I begin to clear the thoughts of dizziness, losing vision, and struggling to breathe. Better. I do this for about thirty seconds, and the symptoms subside until I am almost normal. I have been influenced. In about a minute, I'm back to myself. This the first time I've had somebody use mind influence on me. Lots of people have seen me during a viewing, but never this. I know of only one person in the United States that can do it, and I'm glad he is my friend.

"Are you okay?" Angie asks.

I nod.

"Good, we need to get out of here now; we've been compromised. Get it together!"

We head west on the freeway. Angie calls in to tell Daniel of the incident.

I was once invited to learn the technique of influencing, but the responsibilities were a bit much—action and reaction. It requires actually entering the mind of another and, once there, being a part of her and her thoughts.

I have seen it done. Mental influence is commonly used to change documents, change driving directions, and so on. But to put a mental picture in someone's mind of strangling to death? Hope the other viewer is ready for "cause and effect."

Seven

I may not be influenced again immediately, but I have no doubt I will in the future. I really need another viewer trained in running interference, because next time I may not be so lucky.

New Mexico, the Land of Enchantment: fourth-largest state in the union, mountains, forest, lakes, deserts, endless stories of aliens and UFOs—you've got to love it.

I still can't help but think these agents know more than they are letting on. Why are we always physically close to this guy? It's not normal operating procedure.

We're on the south side of Las Cruces. Angie slows again and takes a right onto the exit leading to Highway 228, westbound.

It sure is flat here; farmland in every direction, with the exception of the slaughterhouse along the freeway. It was a close call back there, and I'd like to explain it to Angie, but it would take too long.

We turn down one dirt road and then another. There are three or four houses in a small cul-de-sac. We park in front of the largest house. Same setup: clear view in all directions. Once out of the cul-de-sac, there are two roads for a quick exit.

"Grab your gear," Angie tells me.

We leave the truck, and Angie stops at the door and turns, watching to make sure we weren't followed. I hurry into the house and find Chad and Joseph inside. Chad has that look again. He's too serious for me. Angie enters and stands by the doorway.

"You okay?" Chad asks. I'm surprised.

"Yes, for now."

Angie steps closer and tells us, "Perimeter team is in place and all clear."

"Listen up," Chad says. "This will be our main location till we find the bad guy. All communication has to be approved through me; one person will be on watch 24-7." He looks at me and smirks. "That means us, not you." Tell me he can't read minds. "Everyone stay inside and within sight." He turns to Angie. "Park the rig alongside the house, and then get back inside."

She leaves through the front door, and I hear the truck start.

I step over to the nearest window on the street side of the house. I watch her pull the rig around the circle of the cul-de-sac as if she's leaving. The trailer begins inching backward toward the north side of the house. She manages to push the trailer over a curb and onto the yard, continuing until it sits in the backyard. She gets no assistance, using only mirrors for direction. Impressive.

I step back to where Chad is standing, and a few minutes later, Angie enters through a doorway to the back of the house, probably the kitchen.

We are each assigned a room. Mine is a nice size and comfortable. I leave the bedroom and enter the kitchen. They all are there but very quiet. I ask a question to break the ice. "What's with that truck and trailer?"

"What, you don't like it?" Angie replies sarcastically.

"Sure, it's fine, a lot better than I was anticipating when I first saw it at the airfield. I admit the thought of becoming 'trailer trash' wasn't appealing."

I see Angie bristle as soon as the words leave my mouth. Uh-oh. I have stepped on some toes.

She grits her teeth and begins to speak. "I grew up in a trailer—of course it wasn't nearly as nice as this one—and we had a happy family. Dad traveled the country with a construction corporation."

"I'm sorry; I didn't mean to imply anything bad. Guess I was stereotyping. Now that I see what it's like, I wouldn't mind living in one. I can work from anywhere. I just don't see the point in us hauling it all over the Southwest. Sure seems like it would be a lot easier without dragging it behind us."

"We have our reasons," Angie says, smiling slyly.

I hear a short laugh behind me and look over my shoulder at Chad.

Somebody has made a platter of sandwiches. I take one and go back to my room. I realized that what I had told Angie was true. It would be great to go from park to park, staying a few weeks in each and seeing the country. The dogs would love it. I wonder if Eric could get a transfer to a job where he could come with me. As a matter of fact, I wish I could go back to the trailer now instead of being here in the house with the agents. I feel like a fifth wheel.

My phone rings in my pack, and I dig for it. Where is it? Who could be calling me when the team is in the next room?

It's Daniel. We have a lot to discuss, but I wonder why isn't he going through Chad this time. He asks about the second set of buildings viewed: Is it a second location or a stray cat? Even if it is a stray cat, could it apply? Who is the influencer? How is it that I was found even though I had used all my skills to not be seen? Who would this guy work for that uses remote viewing as a tool? Many parts of the puzzle have yet to be put into place. Normally an analyst would be deciphering my work by now. This job is unique; Daniel is having my facts analyzed, and feedback is obtained in very short periods of time. We both agree that more info is needed and that one or more of the terrorist's targets may still be struck. Also, where is the suspect? Did he go to El Paso and escape? Meet another operative crossing the border? Get more items to make explosives? Or is he just hiding for a time until the next target is available? Many questions still need to be answered.

We talk for an hour and agree not to presume too much from the information gathered so far. We will treat it as if it has little to do with this situation, and maybe the real facts will surface. Weeding out the old garden to allow vegetables to grow.

At the end of the conversation, I just have to ask "So, Uncle Ted, how are Eric and my dogs?" I hear him chuckle.

"All is well. Don't worry; there is a plan for their safety if the need arises."

"I was told no calls to you without Chad knowing, and all information is to be qualified before going to you."

"True, he knows I am calling. I am his boss and just wanted to check in and get the latest from you."

It is reassuring to hear that. We disconnect. It was nice to talk to someone other than Chad, Angie, or Joseph. I feel relaxed, and my mind is clear.

Back to work. I place my tools on the desk. I'll give it a try for a few minutes, but I really need to sleep. First I go over all the written information.

Pencil to paper, fingers across ideograms and sketches. Nothing. Maybe it's too much for one day? Sometimes I just need to stop, but not now; I must keep trying. I see an image. It's in the distance and appears to be a person. I begin sketching and writing descriptors. It's a female; again I feel that she is looking at me. I tell myself to get closer to the target, but not too close. I remember last time. I'm within twenty feet. It's her. She is stationary, sitting, staring at a desk or tabletop. Papers are everywhere, cluttered. She is not moving. I tell myself to close within five feet. Now I'm up close and see she is not asleep or meditating but appears fatigued. She is slumped forward but breathing. She raises and sits up straighter. She is looking right at me. Nothing is spookier than to be on target and have the target look right in your face. Too many times I have had them look right at me, knowing they see me but not sure if I'm real or not. Sometimes they run away, ignore me, or walk up to me and try to touch me. Not a concern; it's safe, or so I was trained to believe. We just look at each other, sort of sizing each other up. She sits square in her chair and stares at me. Retreat is not an option. I tell myself to leave that location; now I have a mental picture of the large structure from earlier. I, too, am exhausted.

I document "break" and leave the desk.

I need to stretch out and get some rest while it's quiet. I hear the others talking, and I get up to shut the door and then lie down on my bed. I reflect as to why my signature is being left in the etheric. Where have I made the mistake? I've used all the detailed and prescribed efforts to make sure I'm well protected, so as not to leave any trace of my origins—none.

You learn in basic class to guard yourself. We all have a distinct energy beacon, and when traversing the various plains of the realities within the universe, we leave a trail. It takes great skill not to leave a trail or, more importantly, indicate where you began. They might see you in the moment, but allowing them to follow you home is an invitation to danger.

My safeguard is simple but unique; I use all the particles of a desert as a mask. And it has worked, until now.

Then again, it could just be everyday espionage. Our physical records at the agency may have been compromised. One thing the agency taught me is that nothing is so safe it can't be found. I am living proof. They did say this mission was compromised in the beginning.

We're twenty years behind other nations in this work. It was initialized in the military and then carried on with intelligence groups in the government. Teacher was one of the first trained in the military. After retirement, he began a new career training remote viewers. A few of the original operatives retired from the military and filtered into government intelligence agencies. Others work for corporations as remote viewers, some have private practices, and yet others just disappeared, not wanting anything more to do with it. The level of skill the original viewers have is yet to be duplicated.

I realize they never did tell me why we have the trailer. Maybe I'll ask a little nicer tomorrow.

Putting all those thoughts aside, I close my eyes and fade off to sleep. I start dreaming. Lots of water, drowning, and a baby wrapped in white cloth. The baby looks old, maybe ninety. An open door, all is dark, then bright sunshine. I try to wake up, but it feels as though I'm passing through levels of consciousness.

Then I hear banging and someone yelling. I force myself awake. Someone's at my door. Chad.

"What?" I ask sluggishly.

"The door is locked, and I've knocked twice; open up, or the door is coming down."

I get up and open the door. I didn't know it had a lock. I must have palmed the lock when I closed it.

"Who cares if I locked the door?"

"I've been trying to wake you for five minutes."

"Okay, I'll be right out."

When I look out my bedroom window, it's still dark. I look at the clock on my phone: 5:00 a.m.

I enter the kitchen. Everyone's looking at me. What now?

Chad breaks the silence. "Workday begins in thirty minutes."

Soon breakfast is done and I have my pencil in hand. I'm just not accustomed to such a rush to start the day.

"Is it okay to use the trailer? The privacy would be nice. I'd like to grab my laptop and record my notes."

Chad says, "Already prepped for you."

I look out the back door, and there it sits, expanded and plugged in.

I gather up my things and head out to the trailer. Finally quiet—just my thoughts and my paper.

I lay out the necessary tools at the desk and pull up a chair. I sit still for a moment and let go of the morning.

Pencil at the ready, I pick up from my last break. Following the lines from all the sketches and ideograms, I see the large building again. The word "portal" comes to mind—stray cat. I see lots of sunshine, with nothing but the horizon for miles in every direction. Words: *desert* and *vastness*. I list all elements of the horizon, building, and desert that come to mind. My matrix and P6 tools are putting together a place. It's time to write a summary of some sort. I describe a small airport terminal, flat and dusty terrain, and a spacecraft. I'm trying not to have stray thoughts; keeping mental discipline intact is the key.

"Break."

I need to take a moment. Time has passed quickly, but I've been at it for an hour or so already. It's time to step away from the scenario and focus on the task at hand. I need to find the people creating so much death and devastation.

I decide to step outside, and there stands Angie. Smiling for once, she actually seems glad to see me.

"Do you have anything?"

I'm unsure whether to tell her; it might be too early. Besides, I haven't identified the location; it might not be the next target.

"I've got a location, but it needs more work. Just taking a break. I'll start again in few minutes."

"Your trailer is designed to be found from anywhere. The walls are laced with microfibers, making it like an antenna."

Microfibers, found from anywhere—what next? I have someone remote viewing me, a killer looking for me, and these guys watching my every move. I just want to look to the sky and scream. But I need to stay calm and not let on; these agents are well versed in body micro movements. I know; Teacher taught them.

"I sort of figured that. Daniel has made it I clear I'm never alone."

"That's only part of it. There is a coating within the walls to help block any radio frequency from penetrating."

I look at her closely, not sure what to say. She is leaving out one detail.

"Do you guys really think another viewer couldn't find me in there?"

"Yes. Our technical guys reviewed your type of work and thought they had come up with an electronic impulse. The impulse was tried by another viewer to see if he could find someone inside there."

"And it worked? He was blocked?"

"Yes, but apparently they didn't know there were others that can penetrate anything."

I remember reading many years ago of a European country that had experimented with remote viewing and come up with such a blocking technique, but over time viewers got through.

"Did you study the successful technique?" I ask her.

"Yes," she said, "but there have been scientific techniques created to stop them."

She is well informed. Bet she has experimented with my skill.

"Did you manage to do it?"

She grins. "No, but then again I'm only trained at the intermediate level. Not sure yet what I'm doing or if I want to practice to get better at it."

"Yes, it takes a lot of years of practice to reach the levels of Teacher, but basic skills are obtained immediately."

We end with that. She is becoming uncomfortable with the conversation, and I need an inside ally. Angie has learned an important fact about remote viewing. A little skill is fun, but great skill is needed to be considered a professional. Many have found out the same thing; it's intriguing at first, but there are many levels to learn, and it takes some a lifetime to master.

When hunting a person like our bad guy, death is a possibility.

I excuse myself and return to work. It's time to find this person before he leaves the country.

"Break over."

I begin. I follow the sketch of the face and maintain thoughts of him. It's not hard to view him immediately. But I'm too close; I'm looking right at him, and he is sensing me. I tell myself to back up ten paces. I'm standing in a small room with beige walls and ceiling. Appears to be adobe texture; it smells musty and is poorly lighted. He is moving his eyes—trying to see me? He moves around the room. Items are lying on a table in a corner. There is one door and two windows with daylight coming through. This is not a room, but a small structure. I command myself to stand on the roof. It's flat with adobe color and the texture of small pea gravel. I look at the sun and determine it hasn't reached high noon—still morning. A light breeze from the southeast feels good. The roof appears to be twenty by thirty with four corners—maybe a house? I reenter the room. He is at the table and appears to be assembling the items. I need to determine the location. I move fifty feet above the structure. Nothing. No other buildings, streets, or landmarks; only the open desert with fresh, dry air. I return to the interior. He is still assembling. He knows I see him but doesn't seem concerned. The hair on my neck rises, and goose bumps form on my body; I know I'm being watched. He is totally aware he is being watched and is too relaxed with it. He continues his work. I stand on his right side. I am looking at a small table covered with assorted electronic parts. Peculiar, there are no larger items to attach them to, such as an explosive device. It is important to determine where this is happening. I move one thousand feet above the target. To the southeast are multiple structures, a long distance from here. How did he get here? I close the distance to the house by eight hundred feet and go to each corner of the house. On the southeast corner is a four-wheeler—a common vehicle used to cross the desert floor, they are not usually registered, and many are stolen.

I move above the four-wheeler and look from the rear end. It is pointing east, and I can see structures in the distance. A common practice in the outback is to leave something pointing in the direction of something important, such as a landmark. This guy points with the rear end of the four-wheeler, while standard practice is to use the front end. He's good.

The wind has covered any tracks. I relocate to ground level and go inside. Now he is lying on a cot under one of the windows. It's nearing noon; he is resting. Is he readying for the next strike? It's time to view the structures in the distance to the east.

I ascend one thousand feet above the target and move to the last sighting of structures; distance and time don't matter when traversing the ethereal. There are many houses, railroad tracks, and a guarded gate. Standing in front of the guarded entrance is a sign that reads, in bold black lettering, Fort Bliss.

I can't assume that is the target. Viewing is not a guessing game, just a way to gather facts. Facts are from descriptors. If he traveled northeast from Fort Bliss into the desert, what is the distance to him from there? Using the entrance of the military base as a reference, I need to determine the distance to his location.

"Break; water and bathroom."

I step outside for some fresh air; I have been at it for an hour. There must have been a changing of the guard; Joseph is standing next to the trailer instead of Angie.

"Hello," I say, and Joseph walks over.

"So, are you getting anywhere with this?"

He knows better. Do I report him or just keep it under my hat for a while?

"I'm working on it. What are you up to today other than watching my door?"

He grins. "Just going over this case and others to determine if there's a connection."

Now he's dodging me. This team is tight, and his having been selected is a stepping stone for his career. It takes some agents years of interviews and time in the field even to be considered for an elite team. This guy got his shot after a few short years.

We chat for about twenty minutes, and then it's back to the grind. I'm feeling better after the break. It's a good way to release some of the info and make room for broader thoughts.

"Break over."

I begin. I again see the military base. I'm one thousand feet above the entrance and looking southeast. I will use another P6 tool—tapping. Holding the location in my mind, I put a ruler to a blank paper. I draw a straight line and make ten slashes, each representing ten miles. Pencil in hand, I begin. I tap the end of the pencil along the line, each tap asking the distance to the small house from the military base entrance. As I continue down the line, a thickness develops in the tapping at the thirty-mile mark. I draw the same line on another sheet, but the slashes represent fives, with final slash being thirty. I continue the tapping process until I feel the thickness of the mark; it forms at twenty-five.

From the military post entrance to where the suspect was last seen is twenty-five miles to the southeast.

One last view before reporting. The military entrance is Fort Bliss. I view the nearest highway marker: Highway 54 south. Standing over the highway marker, I look southeast; there is a sign: El Paso.

He is twenty five miles to the southeast of the Fort Bliss entrance on the south side of El Paso along Highway 54.

I document a break and step out.

Time to call Daniel.

He answers, and I relay the latest information. He says nothing and just hangs up.

I love this fresh, dry air of West Texas.

I turn toward the house to find some lunch. As I take a step, I experience vertigo again, I'm barely able to stand and am not sure of where I am. A headache sets in; there is so much pain that my skull feels as if it is exploding. As I go down, I try to call out for help but can't. I'm fighting to stay conscious; my head is throbbing as if deprived of blood, and my mind is losing direction.

I try denial technique; I deny whoever is doing this, deny this is happening, that it's only in my mind. It's not real. I regain consciousness, but the pain and vertigo remain. I'm wondering where help is.

I reach into my pocket and fumble for my phone. I manage to hit redial. Daniel answers, and I manage to say "Help" between gasps.

I drop the phone, leaving the line open. I'm getting better, but something or someone has me and will not let go. The next thing I know, Joseph is standing over me.

He grabs me under each arm and pulls forward, allowing me to use my legs. We're moving toward the trailer. With one hand he opens the door, and he then regains his hold and steps up, continuing to drag me. I do what little I can to help. Once inside, the effects slowly wear off. I'm on the floor of the kitchen, and Joseph is sitting in a chair next to me, both of us gasping for air.

Joseph is on the phone. I can't hear clearly, but there are lots of "yes sirs." He looks very worried.

I finally stand up and go to a chair in the living room, thinking, *The coating worked!*

Joseph hangs up and approaches me. "Are you okay?"

"Getting there; what about you?"

"Good, glad you're not heavy."

We both smile and sit quietly for about twenty minutes. My phone rings; it's Daniel.

He doesn't ask how I am; he gets right to the matter at hand. "He wasn't there."

I don't know what to say. I know it was correct. I've done this sort of viewing many, many times.

"Location is twenty-four point six miles to the southeast from the military base. The four-wheeler and all items in the house are gone. Crime scene team is there now, gathering prints and any other evidence."

He thanks me and tells me job well done, but this task is not over. I sit back wondering who or what found me.

"Will push on, but it'll be a bit," I say. "We both know that whoever attacked me tipped him off."

Daniel agrees and hangs up just as I am going to ask him what the trailer is coated with. I can view out, but they can't easily view in.

There's a knock at the door, and Joseph's on his feet. Chad opens the door without waiting for anyone to answer and sternly tells Joseph to come to the house. Joseph screwed up; he had left his post.

Eight

The day is going by quickly, its midafternoon, and the temperature outside is pleasant. I'm staying right here, I hope.

There's another knock at the door; this time they wait for me to answer. I find Chad standing there. He asks to come in. He looks pissed off.

We sit in the living room area. "Joseph dropped the ball by leaving his post."

"Don't worry. After all, he did save my life."

"You are not the only tool in this investigation, but you are the only eyewitness to the suspect."

"I understand."

"Someone will either be inside or right outside the door at all times." He sounds apologetic. This can't be the Chad I have come to know.

"I understand the situation and will continue on. I have the same interest in finding him, if not more. The person blocking for him needs to be found too."

He agrees and leaves. Now that is the Chad I know—don't excuse yourself; just leave.

My phone rings. Sure would be good to hear from Eric. It's Daniel. Before he can begin, I say, "I want to call Eric."

"No."

"Why? I believe I have earned it," I state sternly.

"This person has many resources. One you have seen firsthand. If you call and they find Eric, it wouldn't be good. I am sure that the person that attacked you can find him too."

He did study up on remote viewing. Daniel knows that when a person is viewed, his or her identity can be obtained. It comes from the subject's mind. It's kind of like someone hacking your computer and getting your address book.

"I've taken the necessary precautions. I don't have personal identification with me, and I'm using a technique to block my thoughts, even while sleeping."

"Good. When you're up to it, go back to work. I'm going to assign you one more task."

Task? Whatever could that be? The word *task* is serious in my business. We constantly task ourselves during a session. I listen to him closely; maybe his speech will give a clue.

"We don't know who this person is, but we need to know where he came from."

Now that is a tall order. Going back in time isn't the hard part. It's viewing the target on his home turf. The person blocking for him may very well be there. I hesitate.

He continues. "I understand the danger, but it's necessary. We have nothing on this person. We need background. This is not a request."

"Do you have anybody to run a block for me?"

"You know that only two exist, you and your Teacher."

With Teacher in retirement and having left no forwarding address, maybe I can do it for myself. There is a way.

"You know I won't say no, but I would like it noted that I'm doing it under protest."

"I'll note it, and we'll discuss it further when this is over."

He hangs up. I will have an opportunity to comment on the protest to his request after the mission, and then they will decide if it needs to be put in my personal jacket. There is a method: view the person running interference and disable her.

Find one person among six billion on a planet that's thirty thousand plus miles around. Not that I can't, but should it be done?

It's nearly dark, and my sugar is feeling a little low. I find a cup of soup and bag of chips in the cupboard next to the fridge. I unwrap the soup and slide it into the microwave. Two minutes later, soup and chips. Funny how I anticipate a microwave to manufacture a meal. Eating and looking out the window, I see Angie. I lean forward, tap on the window, and wave for her to come in; she does.

I offer her something to eat. She declines. We have a seat and talk.

"Was Joseph relieved?" I ask.

"No, severely reprimanded."

I hope it wasn't Chad doing the reprimanding; he probably ate his liver.

"We have four-hour shifts," she says. "He left early to go to the bathroom."

"A little stiff, considering the house is fifteen feet away."

"No excuse for leaving post."

And I thought my job was intense.

Since it's getting dark, I ask, "Would you prefer to be inside or stand in the dark?"

"Inside. I shoot better at close range."

Okay, that makes me feel better. Hope she's had a good day.

We leave the kitchen. Angie sits in the recliner in the living area, and I sit at the desk. It seems a little awkward, since I usually work at home alone. Honestly, though, the comfort of having someone here is good.

I thumb through a stack of papers to ensure they are in numerical order.

I need to repeat the past steps with an open mind. I don't know the whereabouts of the complex in the desert, the identity of the person being pursued by us, or who is running interference. Still just too much I don't know.

I document "Break over."

Ruler in hand, I draw a line on the paper. I mark each end with slashes and between the slashes write numbers zero through one hundred. Tapping with the pencil, I find a slash that feels correct—number fifty. I make another line on the paper. Beginning at 2011 and ending with 1961, I add slashes at twenty-year increments. I tap and stop at the mark for 1971. I make another paper with a line with slashes for 1971 to 1961. Each slash is a year. I tap and stop at mark seven, 1964. I make another line, this one with twelve slashes. I tap and stop at six. This person was born in June of 1964, age forty-seven.

I have his general description and have seen him up close. This age fits the description. Now where is he from?

There are numerous techniques for determining the past. I prefer using the tools I've been taught rather than viewing only. It gives physical proof to add to feedback. Like they said in the old late-night TV series *Dragnet*, "The facts, ma'am, nothing but the facts." Dad really liked watching that old detective show.

"Break."

I take a walk. This is the best method for me to release my mind. Angie is on my heels.

"I need about twenty minutes."

She says nothing. We walk around the yard and house. Should I continue or knock off for the night?

Angie turns to me before entering the trailer. "Time to change guards; Joseph is coming on."

"Okay, do I wait here or go inside?"

"It doesn't matter; just letting you know before you begin."

"I'll wait for Joseph inside then." We go on in.

Angie steps close to me. "Everything is good between us; no hard feelings."

I smile, feeling as though a burden has been lifted from my shoulders. Then she falls to the ground.

I grab for her, trying not to let her fall. I catch her under her arms and see blood oozing from her chest.

I fall to the ground with her. Fear has taken over, and I throw myself under the trailer.

I desperately try to drag her with me; she's not moving, just staring into my eyes. I'm sobbing and calling to her. I try hard not to scream, knowing that could lead to the wrong person finding me.

Someone is running toward us, a shadow of a figure. It's approaching fast, and my mind is going crazy. Is this the person who shot her? Is this person coming after me? Do I have to face the possibility of dying?

I hear a familiar voice. Chad is calling out to us. He has a rifle in one hand and small flashlight in the other.

Chad goes down to one knee, pointing the rifle in the direction opposite us. "Stay where you are!"

"Can I go inside, away from all this?"

"Stay there. You would be dead by now if the shooter knew your whereabouts."

Shooter? What shooter? I hadn't seen or heard rifle or pistol. What's going on?

Another person appears from the darkness. Chad glances up but doesn't react. He must know who it is; he isn't alarmed by the figure's approach.

I hear Joseph. He stops and drops to the ground in a prone position between us. Chad and Joseph are looking around in different directions; apparently no one sees anything out of the ordinary.

Fighting tears, I look at Chad. "Angie needs help!"

Chad leans over to us, holds Angie's wrist, and shakes his head. His expression doesn't change.

"She's gone, probably before she hit the ground."

I'm lying there with her in my arms, blood everywhere. Lifeless, she is still looking at me. They were right. This job is way above my pay grade.

I see Chad giving hand signals. Are there others out there?

He stands up and puts his rifle over his shoulder. With the flashlight, he begins to examine Angie's lifeless body. He handles her with the gentleness one would use with an infant. He reaches his hand up to close her lifeless eyes. There is a Chad I didn't expect—emotional and caring. His eyes show tears gathering, but he is not letting them roll.

He pulls her out from under the trailer. I crawl out next, trying hard not to cry. I am on the verge of becoming a wreck.

"There are two teams always within a short distance of us, just in case something like this happens."

I tell him what she had said—how she forgave me for the trailer comments and told me we would move on. I'm losing it.

Chad steps over to me and places an arm around my shoulders. I accept the embrace and step closer to him. I know that a killer lurks in the darkness, but Chad helps me feel safe.

"She was that fine of a person. We're going to miss her. She had that kind of impact on anyone."

I can't believe this is happening. Now Chad wants to be human. Who are these guys?

Joseph is up and standing close by. He stares at Angie. He knows that could have been him. Within minutes, a black SUV pulls up to the trailer. Two men approach and talk with Chad. One goes to the rear of the SUV and retrieves a fold-up gurney and body bag.

They handle her with care and place her in the bag and onto the gurney. She is taken to the SUV and loaded in the back. They leave without a further word. I'm speechless.

Chad looks at Joseph. "Don't leave her side until Angie's replacement gets here." He is being Chad again. He walks back to the house. Joseph tells me to go back in the trailer. He's now acting like the others—direct. He follows me inside the trailer, where he closes the blinds and curtains and turns off all but one light. We go back to the living room, and he points to a chair. "Let's sit," he says. I try to relax in one of the recliners, but my butt is so tight I can't feel the cushions.

"We have two roving teams of four trained in counterinsurgency and shooting. They are always within shouting distance. One of the teams spotted a shadow moving near the road in front of the house. Then a laser light was seen about five feet above the surface."

I'm lost. What two teams, and why have I not been told this before?

"Once the intruder was spotted, the team ran to intercede. The second team was moving back to the house to set up a perimeter while at the same time calling to alert us of a shooter."

I know she had an earpiece on, but I guess she didn't hear the call. Or had she intentionally moved in front of me?

Joseph continues. "The first team saw a muzzle flash; then the laser light stopped. They made it to the location within seconds, but the shooter was gone. A vehicle was heard starting and accelerating a block over. They escaped."

"Did Angie have her earpiece on?"

"Yes. Since both of you were in the open, she put herself between you and the shooter."

I stand and excuse myself, step into the bedroom, and close the door. I can't stop crying. A stranger, giving her life for me. They call it a matter of duty. I call it insane.

I'm not crying so much out of grief as out of anger. Anger is surfacing within me almost to the point of rage. I must find this evil bastard and his partner.

Teacher always told me to not get personal with the project. A project is to be conducted professionally and with protocol. It's only a project.

But this is different. It's not just a project. I'm the target.

I stand up and tell myself to get it together. Suck it up. Courage is in order.

I hear the trailer door open. I step out and find Chad and Joseph talking in the living room.

"Let's all have a seat," I say as I walk over to them.

Chad looks at me with a deeply concerned expression, like when someone's eyes are filled with grief or even agony. Angie's death is really tearing at him.

"Do you want to talk about Angie?" There he goes again, being human.

"I apologize for losing it, but this is something I wasn't prepared for, or even to be involved in."

"Your reaction is natural; don't be ashamed. We all have or will experience the same."

"I'm sorry about Angie, and hope I can do right by her memory."

Chad nods, saying nothing. We stand, and Chad exits the trailer. Joseph and I both sit back down.

"How did Chad know Angie was already dead when he reached us?"

"Microtechnology. It's attached to our belts, and our earpieces are hardwired to a module carrying the micro. It takes our vitals, lets us talk to each other, and tracks us by satellite."

Now, that would impress any spy. Even I am envious.

"Why don't I have one?" I ask.

"They are specifically programmed to our DNA," Joseph says.

"Guess the conspiracy folks were not too far off. They thought it would be a chip on our body."

He points to the top of his left shoulder. "Mine is right here."

I can't believe it. These guys are owned and operated by the agency. But it wasn't enough to help Angie.

"It's nearing midnight," Joseph says. "I've got to turn in for the night. Plan to be at it early tomorrow."

"I'm turning in," I tell Joseph.

"I'll be resting here on the couch."

We look at each other, not speaking. There is energy between us—not just grief from losing Angie, and not fear, but an uncertainty. I have a gut feeling that there will be more to come, and probably worse. We are the newbies on the team and really need the lead agents. We both turn away, and I head to the bedroom.

I strip down to a minimum, not knowing when I may have to jump and run. I lie down and make an effort to let go of the evening. I mentally draw a picture of Angie and put her in all the pastel colors I know of and surround her with them. I visualize her in a peaceful place, surrounded by all those that loved her. In my mind and heart, she is safe and forever in a blessed place.

I feel better for hopefully helping her on the other side. Viewers commonly see all sorts of planes of consciousness—levels of reality that parallel the now. I call it the other side. Not being theologians or scientists, we don't define these. We only record the facts; that line can't be crossed.

Putting all thoughts to rest and feeling better, I doze off.

I'm in a cave. The stone around me is dark brown and jagged, and the cave is lighted, though not artificially. I am holding an infant wrapped in a white blanket. The baby has dark brown skin that is weathered and wrinkled, appearing very old. It has the face of someone I know.

I try to hold on to the dream but I feel an intrusion; an alarm is sounding. I'm awake, and the surroundings appear the same, but the rock color is brighter. I go through nine levels of consciousness before truly waking. At each level, my surroundings change, with the exception of the infant. The infant has the same shape, color and features throughout. I feel it's someone I know. Evidently whoever it is, is attached to every level of my consciousness.

I sit up, open my eyes, and swivel around. I use an old technique to ground myself in the morning: stretch arms wide, take a deep breath, and put feet firmly to floor.

My first thought of the day is, *What are those levels of sleep about?*

I hear Joseph moving about, and I take a quick shower and get dressed.

I move toward the door and hear a faint voice in the distance say, "Thank you." I stop. I don't question it, just accept it. In some traditions it's considered a gift or a blessing. I do not know one from the other but respect it nonetheless.

I open the bedroom door and step out. Joseph is at the exit door.

We don't speak, just smile as if everything is okay. We exit and walk over to the house. We enter the kitchen to find someone new at the table—a man in a suit.

I stop one pace into the kitchen as we size each other up.

He's of medium height, clean cut, and well dressed. He has dark skin, darker than mine; his posture is erect. In a suit when others have gone to pullover shirts and jeans? Guess he didn't get the memo.

He stands and introduces himself as Ahmad Mkandla. I catch an accent—African, maybe?

I introduce myself, and we shake hands. He has a mean grip, but his hands are soft.

"Agent Mkandla," Chad tells him, "change clothes and relieve Joseph."

I pour myself a cup of coffee and sit down at the table.

Not much chatter this morning; everyone is still affected by the loss of Angie the day before. The atmosphere in the kitchen is somber, as when a pack loses one of their own. Sorrow and confusion dominate.

After finishing my coffee, I get up to leave. Chad motions for me to sit back down. What this time?

"Sit tight; Ahmad will be with you in a minute."

"I know the way; it's only fifteen feet out the door."

"I know the distance. Must I remind you that at no time are you to be alone?"

I'm not going to push him today. For someone that is a control freak, he seems on the edge.

Ahmad returns from changing and proceeds to escort me back to the trailer.

He is dressed down and appears more athletic than he did before. Even though he has a friendly face, there is a very serious person behind those eyes.

At the trailer, we go inside and sit in the recliners.

I begin to tell him who I am, but he stops me.

"I read your file. Not just the last fifty pages."

I'm really uncomfortable with so many people knowing my business. These guys are so secretive and don't seem to care about the privacy act, but I understand.

"I was attached to the CIA, five years ago I was recruited by this agency," Ahmad tells me.

"Your accent, is it South African?"

"Yes, I was with the South African Army serving as an intelligence officer after college. Then I worked with the South African national police. After I moved to the USA, I was recruited by the CIA."

"Let me guess, to spy on South Africa?"

"No, I have an MBA, and I speak five languages, including English. With my field experience, I was what they were looking for."

"This agency, I take it *they* found *you*? By the way, did the agency give you an office at the main building?"

"You know I'll not tell you the name of the agency or where any office is. But good try."

He grins at me. He has an air that says, "Yes, I'm smiling at you now, but I could just as easily pull your tongue out."

We ease up with each other. I let it go, really needing to get back on track and find this person causing so much sorrow and pain.

I head to my desk, fresh and ready for the day. First, I make sure all my paperwork is in the proper order. I go through each page by number. As I glance at my notes, I find that I have nearly a hundred pages, but I still am not on target.

I document today's date on a fresh page. I then sit upright and tell myself, "The answer is anywhere or anything within the universe." I write down a series of numbers. The pencil does its job, drawing an ideogram. It's a sketch of a person. I go through descriptors and list them as required, trying hard not to use too many stray cats. I can't let go of the word *woman* in my mind. I go into stage two.

"Break."

I don't get up, just clear my mind. I must not start castling.

"Break over."

More descriptors of a woman's face. Stage three; I sketch out a woman of Asian descent. I concentrate on this configuration and begin to draw facial features. It's the same as the one I viewed early on, the second person. Once I enter the details in the matrix, I put together her stature and possible clothing. Could she be resting or asleep? Terrain descriptors are flowing. I put together a target site, down to the building she may be in. If I keep going, will I be ready to face her?

"Break; water and bathroom."

There it is again, the need for courage. *Pull it together,* I tell myself, *you have viewed many a person before.* But am I ready to use influence to possibly destroy someone through her mind?

"Break over."

I begin with the last location—a small house among many similar houses. Wood frame and tile roof—possibly in a suburb. "Stop guessing," I tell myself. Some daylight remains; it's right at dusk. Dirt streets and paths lead in several directions; taller buildings stand to the east. It appears to be a city. I concentrate further; she's lying in bed but not asleep. I move closer. She doesn't stir, doesn't notice me. Time to apply influence. I use the mental image of being lost in a maze of signs leading nowhere. I project the thought into her mind. There is a barrier. She has made preparations for possible intrusions. I see a stone barrier with no markings. She is inside the barrier. This is a common way to protect oneself. Mine is much more complex and is modified daily. She did get to me, however, but only while I was viewing. I've got to work on not leaving a signature. I penetrate the barrier, and there she is. Again I project the thought of being lost. She stirs and looks at me momentarily. We look into each other's eyes, and I see hers dilate; she is thinking. I observe her more closely, and it hits me; she has the same cheekbones and eyes as the terrorist—or am I guessing?

No words are spoken. She stands, continuing to stare; her face seems to say, "Where am I going?" She sways as if dizzy and unsure. She falls back onto the bed holding her head in her palms. She turns pale and wants to call out. She is lost in her mind.

I watch, feeling sorry for her. I have gone where I have never gone before, and I have many emotions stirring inside of me. I monitor her further; she cannot shake it. She may have been taught how to influence, but not to ward off influence given to her. Her teacher was good but failed with that.

I hear others in the house, and I listen, trying to catch accents. Some are definitely Asian, but they are mixed. Is this a mixed household, or am I near borders?

I go to the doorway leading into her room. There are four men in the living room area. They are on their knees, chanting or praying. No women are in the room, even though I know I heard one. I need to wrap this up.

I view the woman in the bedroom for a moment. She is lying on the same bed, staring off into the distance. I move one hundred feet above the house. The view is the same as before, but it's now dark. I move east to the larger buildings. They are contemporary designs with cobblestone streets. I see modern vehicles, and there are people walking around wearing western-style clothing. I have to determine where this city is and use a landmark to determine where the suspect may have come from.

I move one hundred feet farther up and view a large sign. I move to the sign and see a city name as well as a speed limit sign with kilometers per hour posted.

The sign is in glyphs, Asian ones. I move five hundred feet farther up from the sign. I see a large city complex and what appears to be a city divided by a river. I move over the river. The city appears to be very modern on one side and less so on the other. There are fewer lights across the river, and I move over the darkened section. Nobody is about, and no vehicles are moving. I move to street level. Street and building signs seem to be in a different language from that used on the other side of the river. I make mental notes of the writing on both sides and take a break.

I tell Ahmad I need to speak with Daniel privately. He leaves the trailer and stands by the door. I make the call.

Daniel answers, and I get him up to date.

Calmly and methodically, he asks a number of questions: Is the other viewer out permanently? Do I think another one is trained, or will her teacher take over? Will I make examples of the printed language I observed and fax it to him? Will I listen to voices simulating the accents?

He knew not to go any further; it would pollute the target. I assured him that I had written down what I had viewed as required and would send it to him. It's not normal to move forward with your sessions before having completed all of the protocols. Once finished, the project goes to an analyst, project manager, and client. This is *so* not normal.

I told him I would dowse a map and locate the city and river. Dowsing is the most common means to locate such things. For as many years as anyone can remember, farmers have used a Y-shaped stick or fork-shaped piece of metal to feel for water underground, holding the tool in front of them as they walk around. They commonly feel a sensation like a light touch of electricity running through their hands and fingers when they find the water. Scientists refer to this as hypersensitivity.

I look through the fridge. I have to get some energy. Cereal and nonfat milk will work for now. No time for anything more complicated. I can't stop thinking of the female viewer. They say that even if you recover from a prolonged influence, you are never the same.

I was lucky; Teacher taught me that if a viewer is being influenced, you should just ignore it. By not accepting it into your mind, you eliminate its power over you, ensuring that you create a safe place for yourself every day.

After wrapping up my breakfast, I get back to work. It's time to find out where she is. I'm sure by now somebody in that house has found her. Since her mission was so important, they are sure to be after me again. I've got to stop leaving a trail.

I take the pouch with my dowsing stone in it from my pocket, and I remove the paper and world map from my backpack. I place a piece of paper over the world map and begin the process.

I practice by holding the string loosely in my fingers and asking for an indication of yes or no. I draw two lines, one across and one down, dividing the paper into four quadrants.

I dowse each while asking myself, "Is this where the woman viewed was?" One quadrant comes out positive. I remove the paper and find China and Korea under the quadrant. I draw an outline of China and Korea. I repeat the quadrant process on another piece of paper. I get a positive response in both countries. This indicates that maybe the city viewed is in both countries. Where is the river?

I dowse again with quadrants over the area of positive response. The border between the two countries is a river. I remove a pocket atlas from my backpack and find the border. The river system dividing the two countries has two names, Yalu and/or Amnok. One is in Chinese and the other in Korean. But what is the name of the city I observed?

I dowse the quadrants over the two countries again and get positive feedback in the left lower quadrant. The positive quadrant lies in the southeast part of China and northeast corner of North Korea. I sketch an outline of the two countries, laying the paper with quadrants on top, repeating the same procedure to narrow down her location.

Again the left lower quadrant is positive, but the pendulum begins swinging, leading me to the center of the quadrant. I remove the paper and mark the map. I need another resource—a pocket atlas. I usually have one to reference city locations and spellings. Glad I thought to put one in my backpack.

I have narrowed down the section of the two countries, noting that the Yalu River separates them. I begin writing descriptors. I see a modern city with a village neighborhood seen on the outskirts. It appears to be night. One city is well lighted; the other is in darkness, with no street or house lights. People and vehicles are moving about on one side, but the other side is still.

"Break."

Atlas time. I remember hearing that North Korea is known for a strictly enforced curfew. I must disregard these thoughts—stray cats, possibly castling. Viewers fight this all the time: stray thoughts vs. facts.

I place the atlas on the table. Definitely China and North Korea.

"Break over."

Using the atlas as a tool, I move my fingertips along the map. The map is now an ideogram. Searching for the energy or intensity of the location is a practice applied using the natural energies of your body to feel a target.

I get positive responses. The name of the city—or cities—is written in three languages. I remove a magnifying glass from my pack. After enlarging the print, I recognize the writing seen on the street sign as Chinese. I move the glass over the river and find the same in Korean and English—Dandong, China and Sinuiju, North Korea. That explains why I heard different accents.

"Break."

Ahmad had reentered the trailer after my earlier phone call. I ask him to step out again so I can call Daniel. He nods and exits.

I call Daniel and briefly explain my new findings. He sounds impressed. He says he will have the information analyzed and follow up with his resources. I remind him that if this is the location, I am still off target, as I didn't find the woman's house.

"Don't worry. Local agents can take over from there."

It's almost noon and I need to rest. I say as much to Daniel.

He agrees. "I'll get back with you soon."

I end the call and step outside for some fresh air. Ahmad is at the door, constantly scanning the horizon.

After viewing the men in the room praying and apparently facing east, it makes me wonder.

"Are you of Muslim descent?" I ask him. "I'm sorry; that's none of my business."

He looks at me with piercing eyes, and I wonder if I shouldn't have asked. Did I upset him? Have I gone too far?

Then he smiles and asks, "Why?"

I'm so relieved. "I viewed some men in a room on their knees facing east, chanting or praying. I'm no good at religion. I only know what I view."

He tells me he is a practicing Muslim.

"Were they wearing a small cap or head covering?" he asks. "Were they kneeling holding a string of beads? Kneeling before a statue?"

"I viewed nothing in their hands and no statues. Why?"

"One is the common practice of a Muslim in prayer, and the other would be Buddhist."

"One man was older; I believe he was leading the prayers."

"It's common that an elder leads the prayers."

"Is it common for Asians to be practicing Muslims?"

"Yes, the Muslim faith is everywhere."

"What about the borders of China and North Korea?"

"There is a sect of radicals along that border. They recruit those that have nothing to live for and for whom dying is not a concern."

"Hmm. Thanks for the info. Maybe we'll talk more later."

"Okay," Ahmad says, "not a problem."

What is the world coming to? I'm chasing a radical Asian Muslim and being guarded by a federal agent who is a practicing Muslim. If I went to an office every day, there would be lots to talk about around the water cooler.

Back inside I sit in the recliner to think. The past forty-eight hours or so have been a bit much. There is a technique to control the flood of thoughts. I must store them.

Nine

I mentally create a file cabinet five feet tall with five drawers. One is labeled with today's date and another with the previous two dates. I create a file folder and put today's events into that folder. I Place the folder into the drawer dated today. I repeat the same with the past two days. These are files I can go to anytime to put aside thoughts and to clear my mind.

Better. My mind is clearing, and my thoughts go to Eric and my dogs. Daniel assured me they would all be out of harm's way. I'm holding him to it.

I lean back and take in a deep breath, feeling much better. My mind is settled down, and I see Eric at a house, but it is not mine.

I see my house, but where are the dogs? I move to the backyard—what a mess! Having been a viewer for so many years, I thought I could handle anything. But not this! My dogs are lying in the backyard, dead! I view the inside of my house. Everything is turned inside out. I sit up. My heart is pounding, and I'm trying not to assume the worst. I grab the phone and begin dialing, my hands trembling.

"Daniel, what the hell is going on? Tell me Eric is okay." I am squeezing the phone, expecting to hear the worst.

"Calm down. Eric is at a safe location; he's with agents."

"You gave me your word." Tears fill my eyes. "When were you going to tell me about my dogs? Please tell me they're alive. When, Daniel? When were you going to tell me?" I'm losing control, and it's all I can do to keep from screaming.

"Soon. You weren't in the right mind-set and you know it."

"How would you know what state of mind I have been in?"

"I told you, we're watching and listening."

"What about my house? How did they find it?"

"We don't know how."

"I'll tell you how. When the other viewer was watching me, I had a fraction of a moment of a thought of home. She or her counterpart traced it, like I would. This is my fault."

My dogs are dead, Eric has been hidden, and the house is destroyed. What next? All their technology and assurances, and I feel totally helpless and vulnerable.

"Have your agents found the other viewer, the one I influenced earlier?"

"Not yet, but your information of the two border towns in China and North Korea was dead on."

"Thanks for the feedback," I tell him dryly, "but not for not telling me about Eric and my dogs!"

He doesn't apologize or give an explanation, just hangs up.

My dogs, why kill them? Who is this evil bastard?

I just sit there, thinking about Eric and my dogs. I break down; I can't stop crying. I just hold my hands in my lap and let it happen. Minutes go by. I stand and walk to the sink in the kitchen, pull a dry towel from a drawer, and run it under a faucet. I put it to my face. The cool water feels good as I try to pull myself together.

All the training hasn't prepared me for this.

Regaining my composure, I walk back to the desk. There sits pages of information; this will be my weapon of choice. Now it's payback time.

"Break over."

I'm well into the matrix when the phone rings. I note "Break for phone." There is a silence on the other end. Not again!

"Hello?"

I hear a familiar voice say, "Ashlee? Are you there?"

"Eric. Eric, is that you?" There is a lump in my throat, and I'm not sure what to say next.

"Yes, it's me, babe. Are you all right? Are you safe?"

Tears are streaming down my face. "Yes, an agent is with me 24-7."

I have to get him off the phone. If they have a viewer watching me, they may find him. It's no different from tracing a call with a computer. "I can't talk. I'll call you back when it's safe."

"What's going on? Who are these people? You said nothing like this could ever happen with your line of work."

We both are distraught. I want to run to him and leave all this insanity.

"I can't explain now. Please, please, just do as they say."

He wants to say more, but it's just too dangerous. I hang up. I'm not sure if that was the right thing to do, but at least I know he is all right, at least for now.

The phone rings again. I let it ring. *Please don't let it be him again, I think. They will surely find him.* I check the number; it's Daniel.

"He's okay; we have a detail with him day and night."

He hangs up. My thoughts are running wild. What have I done to put Eric, the team, and myself in such danger? I can't believe this is happening. There are no more tears; I'm not going to lose control. Now I'm angry.

I have viewed and witnessed a lot over the years—missing persons, lost aircraft, sunken ships—and I've always handled it. Teacher always reminded me, saying "It is only a target; do not get attached." But he never covered losing those you love the most while working a target. He owes me one hell of an explanation.

I step outside, and Ahmad is on my heels. I'm tiring of all this.

I can't even look around me without feeling frightened. It's as if the whole world wants me and those associated with me dead.

I walk around a bit trying to regain myself. After a few minutes, I go back inside. I return to my work. Again I take a minute to clear my mind. My mind is the instrument that can find an end to this mess.

I begin again.

"Break over."

My fingertips scan all ideograms and sketches. I feel the need to draw. I sketch a building: round top, multiple white bay door entrances. I try not to castle. On another piece of paper, I sketch manmade elements, including various sorts of aircraft, one of which appears to have an air-lift system familiar to space aeronautic engineers.

More paper. I sketch terrain: a flat, sandy color with brush on the perimeters. People are around moving equipment. I note a narrative and detail an area on flat terrain: blacktop roadways, one large hangar, two outbuildings, various type of craft (one different from the others in design) people working, and a small building with a person standing nearby as if guarding it. I'm viewing a small compound that is used as a possible runway for aircraft. It's well guarded and is preparing for something. I'm still not able to identify the location; where is this?

"Break."

After months working on viewing aircraft designs and production for a client, I realized that it's amazing how far aircraft have come since that first flight in Ohio. My sketches involved many hours of minutely detailed aircraft lift systems. I had the privilege of meeting with that client at an aeronautic seminar afterward. I have to clear my head and stop castling. I believe I have found the next target.

Ahmad is sitting, watching me work. I'm accustomed to Eric watching, always curious. I mentally picture that I am here alone, with no distractions; I'm ready to get back into it.

"Break over."

I review all my notes. It's apparent I'm looking for an airport of sorts, possibly in a desert. New Mexico comes to mind; I list it in the matrix as a stray cat. Maybe I will use it later. Using the same tool as before, I sketch an outline of New Mexico and begin another dowsing session, using the quadrant technique to determine that the target is in the southwest corner. Using my fingertips, I glide over the area, viewing a city. Many buildings and a highway. I move one thousand feet above the area viewed, and I see a highway and focus on signs: "Interstate 25," "Albuquerque 223 miles." I turn around, looking at Interstate 25, and see another sign: "Las Cruces, next 7 exits."

No area seems to match the location with a small airport. Where is this place?

Then the unthinkable: Ahmad interrupts, saying, "Take a break."

I note the break.

I turn to him. "What the hell are you doing?"

"Daniel is calling. Everyone stand down."

Please don't tell me we are going to another shoot-out.

We leave the trailer and enter the house. Everyone is silent and looking confused.

Chad tells me, "Daniel needs all your information, now."

I don't question him. I run back to the trailer and retrieve my notes. Maybe this is all over.

Chad tells me to take my phone into the other room and call Daniel. I do as he says.

Once I have Daniel on the phone, I tell him what I've found. He instructs me to get back with Chad.

I meet Chad again and ask, "What's going on?"

"We might have found the suspect."

"Where?"

"An Asian male matching your description was confronted; he resisted and was shot to death at a border crossing in El Paso."

"Can I see a photo?"

He holds up his phone, showing me a picture. I see a person meeting the description, except for a hole in the forehead where he had been shot. There was a lot of disfiguration.

"You know that might not be him. Yes, he's Asian, but he's disfigured."

"That is where you come in; you're the only witness."

He's right. I'm the only person to see him up close. I search through my notes and find a sketch of him.

"Something isn't right. The guy on the screen has a longer jawline, and the forehead is different."

"Are you sure?"

I hesitate. I really want this to be him, but I have no way to be positive. Chad is looking at me, wanting an answer. My palms are sweating from nervousness, but I am sure.

"No, this isn't him; I'm positive."

Chad grabs his phone and calls Daniel. They talk for a minute. Chad looks fatigued. All this is too much even for him.

After talking with Daniel, he turns to me and says, "You're right; this person's photo was circulated to all agencies immediately. The deceased is not Chinese or North Korean. An agent abroad looked at it and identified him. He was an informant for another agency. We have agents working to determine what he was doing in El Paso. He's not our concern."

I take a deep breath. As much as I wanted it to be him, I know more work needs to be done. I will push on; he has to be found at any cost.

Chad says, "Daniel told me about what you've been seeing. Do you know what is in that desert?"

I smirk. "Missile sites and amusement parks."

"I guess anything is possible in the New Mexico desert. This guy has both the resources and means to create death and destruction. The pressure is on."

"We already know his capabilities; why is there more pressure now?"

"Time. These guys hit, run, and usually find safe havens out of reach."

"What kind of reach? Don't you remember what I do?"

"Lots of people we're hunting today for similar crimes have fled to countries that even we can't enter."

That doesn't stop me, so why them? I think. *Aren't they the elite of the elite?*

"You're saying it's now or never to catch this guy?" I ask.

Chad looks at me grimly. "Yes, time is not on our side. In fact, he may be gone or planning his escape as we speak. For instance, the fellow floating in the river—is he another agent or a decoy? The only one that can tell us that is dead."

There's that word again. Death comes to us all. I never thought I would see it on the mass scale, as I have the last couple of days.

I begin racking my brain. I usually read four to six newspapers a day. In my line of work, one must be up to date with current events. But this time I'm living it.

What's happening currently in southern New Mexico? As Chad said, it's a desert. It's vast and has many possibilities. But I'm tasked with finding the right one.

Chad's phone rings, and he answers. He talks a few minutes and then turns to us. "The person shot at the river is Asian. Identity is being held by another agency. He had papers on him that were printed in a North India dialect common along the Chinese border. He probably was a messenger or planted decoy. We will never know for sure."

Curious, I ask, "You're saying someone hired this guy to be at that time and place, knowing he was to die there?"

"There's a good probability," Chad replies.

I'm still confused; these radical groups give so little concern to life or death. Life's cheap to them.

Ten

I excuse myself and walk outside to a warm and sunny day. I'm trying to absorb it all.

I was taught that life is precious, that you should live to the fullest and respect your fellow man, that one should always say thank you and speak a kind word—nobody turns that away. But now I have met the complete opposite, and thank goodness I am on this side of the fence.

I look over my shoulder. Yep, there's Ahmad. This guy is good, and I'm glad of it.

Chad calls out from the kitchen door. "Saddle up; let's take a drive."

I start to walk toward the trailer. Surely he doesn't mean me? Ahmad taps my shoulder and points a thumb toward the SUV. You've gotta be kidding.

"Do I need my tools?"

"Put everything in your backpack."

I enter the trailer, grab my backpack, and shove everything in. I'm really trying not to have an anxiety attack.

Once outside, I see two vehicles. Ahmad is in the SUV, and Chad and Joseph are in the sedan. All are glaring at me, wanting me to hurry. Guess I'm not quite the bolt of lightning they are.

"Where to?" I ask Ahmad once I'm in the vehicle.

Ahmad says nothing.

"Excuse me, but what is going on?"

He turns to look at me. "Be patient."

Be patient! They hurry me along, make me feel guilty, and now tell me to be patient.

Ahmad starts the SUV, and we leave.

We exit the neighborhood and work our way to Interstate 25.

Highway signs indicate we're not far from Las Cruces.

Ahmad finally speaks. "*Feedback*, I believe, is the term you use. What is it, exactly?"

"When we work up a target and receive information back. Sometimes it makes sense and sometimes, not so much."

Information may not mean much to the viewer, but once properly analyzed, the client finds it useful.

"Where are we going?"

"Into Las Cruces, want you to meet some people."

"What people?"

"There is a large contingency of Asians living in the area of Las Cruces, descendants from the railroad days."

"What area, like a neighborhood?"

"Mostly in concentrated neighborhoods; many are land and business owners."

"Today is a workday."

"Yes, but today at the city park there is a parade and festival."

"What kind of festival?" I ask.

"Once a year, the locals celebrate the founding of the city. It usually draws a large crowd."

"Why would the Asian population come out? Wasn't Las Cruces stumbled upon by the Spaniards? It already had been established by Native Americans living in the region. It was a crossroads of the Southwest, as determined by artifacts found belonging to people living hundreds of miles in the four directions from there."

"Asians have been here for well over a hundred years. They were imported to work railroad construction and mining jobs. Now they are locals, just making a living. There will be a couple of vendors there selling ethnic food."

This is bizarre. First I'm to stay low, and now they want me to walk out among a crowd.

"What if the terrorist is there?" I ask.

"There will be a van there loaded with video monitors. There are a lot of cameras around the event. You are to sit in the van and watch the screens. There will be an alert team on standby in the park."

I'm still not comfortable. This guy has proven to be more resourceful than expected. Surely we'll have agents in the area.

"Who is on the ground in the crowd?"

"Not your concern. Stay focused on the monitors in the van."

Shortly after entering Las Cruces city limits, we turn north on Interstate 25 and come to mile marker three.

We exit and travel on the feeder road until we stop at an intersection marked E. Lohman Avenue and turn left. We travel west about a mile and turn right onto South Reymond Street. A few blocks later, we come to the intersection of West Las Cruces Avenue; on the left is a sign reading "Pioneer Women's Park."

We turn into the park and follow a small two-lane road into the park. We pass hundreds of people. It is a typical southern New Mexico day— sunny and warm.

We roll toward a large parking area at the west end of the park. There is a blue one-ton van facing the crowd.

There go my nerves; field work is not for me. What if I see this guy or he finds out we're here?

We pull alongside the van. Ahmad stops the SUV and looks around, waiting.

We don't speak. He is being observant, and I'm scared. The park is filling fast. Seems people in New Mexico are like us Texans—never a bad day to have a party. I don't have a good view from where we sit, but there are several vendors. The monitors will be a big plus.

"Be ready to get out and step to the side of the van," Ahmad says. "Do it casually; try not to draw attention."

"Okay." I wonder if he can see the fear in my eyes or notice it in my voice.

"Get out now, and do as I said."

I open the door and step out. The weather is warm and pleasant. I move casually toward the rear of the SUV. Ahmad is already there and looking in all directions. He does so smoothly; even I barely notice. We step up to the van, and the side door slides open.

I get in first, then Ahmad. The doors close quickly. Two agents are sitting inside on swivel chairs. The wall opposite the doors is covered with monitors. There is one small chair, and an agent points to it. I sit, and Ahmad kneels down beside me.

An agent instructs me to watch the monitors. We hear everything going on in the park.

My armpits are sweating profusely. I can't help thinking our guy will find us.

There are many cameras scanning the crowd. Two cameras are focused on vendor booths operated by Asians. Nothing is being said; we are all watching vigilantly.

Ahmad speaks up. "If you see anyone that may be the person we're looking for, tell me."

"What if the guy we're looking for sees us first? He does seem to have some talent."

"We're prepared for that, too; just do your part."

I knew it. They expect him to do something. Sure hope this van is bomb proof.

I watch closely, and I have to admit this is pretty cool. I studied for years to do this with my mind, and these guys just throw up cameras to do the same thing.

I see four Asian adult males walking through the crowd in the center of the park. One closely resembles my guy.

I get Ahmad's attention. "See those four guys walking? Focus a camera on them."

The group comes into better view. "What do you think?" Ahmad asks.

"Not sure, but the one with the yellow shirt resembles him."

Ahmad tells one of the agents, "Close in on them. Zoom in on the one in the yellow shirt."

Ahmad grabs his handheld radio and relays the information.

When the camera zooms in, I move closer to the monitor for a better look. I really want to be right.

Ahmad breaks my concentration. "Well, what do you think?"

"Close enough, but still not one hundred percent sure."

I grab my backpack and start pulling papers from it, looking for sketches. I look at the sketch of his face and back at the monitor. They seem to match. I show Ahmad the sketch, and we both look at the man on the screen. Close enough. Ahmad calls over the radio. I see two guys step out of the crowd near the four men. The two agents closing in are Asians; now that is too cool.

We watch as they approach the older man in the yellow shirt. He is looking over his shoulder. On another monitor we watch plainclothes agents close in. Then the unexpected happens.

The man in the yellow shirt reaches in his belt and pulls a pistol. He grabs one of the men next to him and points the pistol at his head.

"Gun!" we hear from the speakers. The agents stop and draw weapons, causing mass chaos to break out around them.

The crowd sees all this and begins to scatter; people are screaming, shouting, and running in every direction.

Without looking at Ahmad, I ask, "What now?"

"Sit tight, watch, and listen."

The agents at the monitors turn up the volume on the camera focused on the incident.

It's like something out of a movie. The agents confront Yellow Shirt, them telling him to put down his gun and him telling them no way. This goes on for a few seconds, and then another shock occurs.

In a flash, Yellow Shirt points his weapon and fires twice. The two agents go down. He then shoots the hostage and runs south through the park, all within a few seconds. I am watching but can't grasp it all. I had no idea someone could be that good. I've seen it in the movies, but seeing it for real is frightening.

The agents are typing fast and furious on keyboards, trying to keep a visual on this guy. They turn down the volume; the screaming in the park is too much.

He runs through the park toward a crowd of picnicking Asians. The park has many trees, and the cameras lose him. Where are the agents on the ground?

I look at Ahmad. He can see the terror in my eyes.

"He's fleeing away from us, not to you; relax," he tells me.

"Doesn't mean he can't double back now that he knows we're here."

"You're right, but agents are on the ground and in pursuit."

That's not good enough for me. I just watched two agents on the ground get gunned down. I want to run away, but the door is locked and I think Ahmad would shoot me if I tried.

The agents manning the cameras are steadily talking to others in pursuit. The cameras have lost him, but an agent has visual. What a mess. I hear the agent in foot pursuit giving information as they run. He relays that the suspect is attempting to enter a jeep parked on the south perimeter. He is closing in. We hear a shot. This shot is much louder than the pistol shot. Then another agent broadcasts, "Agent down!"

"Suspect is in a green jeep with no top and is armed with a rifle," we hear over the radios. The jeep is last seen heading toward downtown. Ambulances are everywhere. Wounded agents, people running on top of each other—he had the upper hand all along.

I turn to Ahmad. He is fixated on the screens and talking with the agents.

"We will find him," he says, trying to assure me.

"No, I will," I tell him confidently, but I'm shaking all over.

He looks at me as though I slapped him. "We're in pursuit. We will have him shortly."

"I don't think so. You have underestimated this guy. Why do you think he has a jeep?"

"It's a common enough vehicle."

"No, he has already cleared the city limits and is out in the desert. You guys didn't factor that possibility in."

Ahmad looks pissed. He turns away and then back at me. He knows I'm telling the truth.

"Are you monitoring the chase?" I ask.

"Yes."

"Have they lost him?"

He looks at the floor and mutters through his clenched teeth. "Yes."

I would never tell this guy "I told you so," but I sure am thinking it. Ahmad stands and points to the door. Guess it's time to leave.

We exit the van and get back in the SUV and leave the park. The silence was thick enough to cut with a knife. "I understand his shooting the agents," I say softly, "but why the hostage?"

"Once the agents divert their attention to give verbal commands, lag time is involved. A moment is all it takes when you're susceptible. He took advantage and fired twice; you know the results."

"But why kill the hostage?"

"The hostage could identify him."

"The third agent, what happened there?"

"Open-top vehicle, allows you to pull a weapon more quickly. He used an M40."

We travel through the outskirts of the city and back to the safe house where the trailer is parked. This was an education from hell. We travel in silence. Ahmad probably doesn't need or want to explain. I'm not sure I want to know.

We rally in the kitchen. Chad looks exhausted. Joseph steps up and relieves Ahmad. He looks more confused than I am.

Joseph and I return to the trailer without further instructions. It's a given that more work is needed. Joseph sits close by. I can feel the urgency. He is vigilantly watching out the windows and makes sure the curtains are closed and the light is on at the doorway. There is tremendous tension.

"Are we in danger here?" I ask before beginning.

"We're in danger everywhere. The enemy is resourceful and walks side by side with death themselves."

"How did he get away?"

"He left in the jeep, traveled a few blocks, and was last seen on a four-wheeler heading for open country."

"How did he get through the crowd?" I ask nervously. I'm wondering what prevents him from doubling back to us.

"He made sure to blend in with the locals. Nobody could keep a constant visual, much less get a shot off."

"Did he know we were watching?"

"He knows we're always watching."

Over the years I have heard of such people, but to encounter one is beyond my experience.

Joseph looks at me as if he's trying to console me. "To ease your mind, we have posted another roaming alert team close to our location."

"Where were the local eyes in the sky?" I ask, not letting him change the subject.

"They weren't notified."

"Why not? Don't they have personnel and equipment to assist?"

"We're not in the business of trusting anyone from anywhere."

"Not anyone?" I ask in disbelief.

"Never. It's not uncommon for a suspect to know someone working for outside agencies; they infiltrate their intelligence, even work for them."

What a job. Trust nobody—none of the six billion folks on the planet. Note to self: don't apply for his job.

"Remember, this guy has proven he has resources and will use them at any cost."

"When does Chad take a break?" I ask Joseph.

He grins. "Seldom; such is the job of the lead agent. He is the direct link to the main office. He is required to see and know all. I mean *all*."

"I take it nobody really wants that job?"

"Wants it? No. There is no application for his job. One day you get a call and Daniel says, 'You're it,' no questions asked. We maintain the utmost secrecy. Until a mission is assigned, you don't know where, when, or who is lead."

Okay, I've got it. Thank goodness I have a job and work from home. I will never complain about that again.

I pull my work from the backpack and browse through it. Sure is a mess; I've got to number the pages. Oh hell, there is Teacher's voice in my head: "Write it down."

Teacher really liked telling me that. When one gets a site picture, it is like watching TV; it's difficult to stop and write it down. But with experience, one understands why it's necessary.

It's been a long day and much more than I bargained for; I need to eat and take a decent break. Fatigue is not a viewer's friend.

"I'm going to eat and take a long break," I tell Joseph.

He agrees but adds, "Not too long; we're still in the fight."

Still in the fight? Now that's new, me still in a fight. I can't remember ever having gotten in a fight with anyone, much less still being in one.

I raid the fridge. Seems cereal and milk are in order again. Light on the stomach but has some nourishment. Once I'm done eating, I will lie down and try bleeding all the actions of the day out of me so I can clear my mind. My mind is the weapon of choice for this fight. It has no boundaries. I sure hope that woman comes out of her confusion when this is all over. Better still, I hope they don't dispose of her. Seems that's the way with these guys once you're of no use to them. Like the guy in the river.

I would like to ask more questions. Who is this enemy? How was it so easy to just walk into our country? With all our resources, why did we not know about these people? Why do they hate us so much?

After some thought and then letting it go, I'm back at the desk, with Joseph still maintaining vigil.

I sort through papers to find the sketch we used earlier. Even though the man had been wearing a cap so nobody could see his face, the sketch was right on. Feedback—I now know his face. Now, do I attempt to find him, or do I find the next target? The target is still pure in nature. I don't know about this guy; is he a target, or is he trying to escape?

Commonly, when pencil and paper go to work, the answer comes into view. I must maintain an open mind; the universe is a large place.

I document "Break over" and begin with the matrix.

Descriptors come into view. A large structure. It's white, rounded. Entrances, exits, small, large, dirt. Site picture gained. I move five hundred feet above the structure and try to describe it. I look for markings but find none. It is dome shaped, but not entirely. Approximately one-third is covered with dirt. I face to the north. The end covered in dirt faces north. The structure is large enough to house many large items. Three entrances seem rounded. I move to the top of the structure. I tap on it—metal. It's painted white but has no markings. I move to ground level and tap on it—concrete, and possibly some blacktop, the difference being that the sound of concrete is a distinct, solid thump and blacktop is softer with no thump. I look around. It is a bright, sunny day, and light reflects strongly on these surfaces. The ground outside the structure is flat; it appears to be a long roadway running north and south away from the structure. Approximately a quarter mile to the west is a smaller building. I move to it.

It appears to be large enough to hold two people and has large windows facing all directions, allowing anyone to observe the oncoming roadway. It seems to be a checkpoint—stray cat, I add it to the column. I move back to the large structure. The doors are closed. I move inside and find aircraft of various sizes. No markings.

I begin gestalts with stray cats.

"Break."

I push away from the desk. Even though these were documented in the matrix, they are not good to have. Sometimes they lead to false images, but then again they may be useful eventually. I take out the manual Daniel gave me, thumb through it, and read over some sections. It's good to go back to basics when I'm working—gives me the reassurance that I am following protocols. This is a discipline that takes years of practice and is used professionally by very few. I put down the manual.

I document "break over" and begin.

Back onto the last target viewed.

It's the same location, and I'm inside the large structure. Standing on the floor, I look up. The ceiling is crisscrossed with steel beams. I view several doors along the walls. I move to the wall on the north. The doors are labeled as if they are entrances to individual offices. I enter the first door: desk, computers, and file cabinets. I look on a desk for possible clues to where I may be. There is a book on top of one desk. I pick it up and read the title. It is labeled *Space Flight* but not labeled NASA or any other government agency. "Space Flight Inc., Commercial Flight" is written inside. I put it down. I'm not here to read the book. My job is to find the location. I move to the center of the structure. People wearing work uniforms and hardhats are moving around; they have papers in their hands. I move next to them. One holds up a large, rolled-up paper. He begins to read it to the others. It is a schematic of the rooms behind the doors. He tells the others, "All looks good, just a little tweaking." They are not important at the moment. I need more descriptors of the location.

I move to one of the three aircraft in the center. Two are of the same size, and one is larger. They are all white with the same markings: "Space Flight Inc." I move inside the smaller one. There appears to be seats for passengers. There are closed envelopes lying on each seat. They are not labeled. I move to the center again. Time to get back to the original task—finding out where we are.

I move one thousand feet up and see desert in all directions. A two-lane road leads out across a railroad track and possibly a main road. I move to it. There are no markings, but the roadway runs north and then sharply turns west. I move ten miles to the west—still no markings. I move twenty miles west and begin to see structures. I move five miles toward them. A highway sign reads "Truth or Consequences." Is that a town? You never know in the desert. I move to the edge of the buildings. There it is, a city limit sign for Truth or Consequences.

"Break." Time to call Daniel.

I tell Joseph I'm making the call. He steps outside. Daniel answers, and I begin to relay my findings. He's silent, and I get the feeling that he is listening to me, but not really listening.

"Am I boring you with all this?" I ask.

"No, it makes sense. Can't tell you why now, but it does make sense."

"It's almost midnight. I need to get some rest. It's been a long day—a number of them, in fact."

He agrees and hangs up. He never says "Thanks" or "Good-bye" or "Talk later." But then again, why would he?

This is the part of the job where a viewer researches her findings. I'd normally use a computer, scanning the web for information, searching for locations meeting my descriptions. This is instant feedback for my own personal assurance, but even then what I find may not be the target.

The target may not be a structure or an aircraft. There are endless possibilities. Sometimes the findings are never known to the viewer. On many occasions, I have never been told one way or the other. The findings are the clients' to use as they please.

I go to the door and give Joseph the all clear. He comes in and sits on the edge of the chair. He is staring straight at me; his curiosity is killing him.

"Got a question?" I smile at him.

He doesn't answer. Per protocol, what I view is none of his business. Only Daniel or Chad can relay that to him.

"You can ask simple questions, but nothing that has to do with the target."

"Okay," he asks. "What is your accuracy with this stuff?"

I hesitate. "Believe it or not, I don't know. I'm not usually told the real target or even if the target applies. It's the nature of the job."

"Then how do you know if your work is of value?"

"I don't. Again, Daniel tells me if my information is useful or not. But a viewer never knows positively unless the client tells them so."

"Mostly I'm given target sites that have multiple uses. If it has value to your agency, I may receive feedback. I really don't concern myself with it."

He thinks for a moment. "Have they ever told you if your work was exactly on?"

"There is no 'exactly on.' Like I said, you guys have target sites that have multiple uses and can be played into multiple scenarios."

He does not understand. If I knew every target I worked, my mind would be full of details that could possibly pollute the current target. I am told of my accuracy in percentages.

"For instance, I know I'm on target today, and my feedback will come when Daniel calls back."

He is looking down at the floor. "I understand. Nothing appears as you may see it. In our line of business, nothing is ever exact. You must play out all the possibilities."

"Exactly. What I do is a science. It is always developing, and new applications are being discovered. Now I'm off to bed for a while."

I head to the bedroom, leaving Joseph to man his post. The look on his face tells me he's thinking hard about what I said.

Exhausted, I lie down and reflect on the dream. What is it with the infant wrapped in white? Were those my facial features? Someone is holding the child, but I never get a close look at that face. They say a repetitive dream is one that needs your attention. I'm paying attention.

I'm too tired to think anymore; I'm falling asleep. I will follow up on it later.

When I wake up, the clock on the phone reads 5:00 a.m. Time to work.

I get up and hit the shower, get dressed, and look for coffee. Joseph is awake, dressed in the same clothes he was wearing the night before, and looking tired. A little pale, he has baggy eyes and is moving a little slow.

"When is shift change?" I ask, trying not to state the obvious.

He speaks a little slowly. "When you got up, I just called in. Coffee's ready."

There is a knock at the door. Joseph stands and opens it; Ahmad's reporting in.

Joseph exits without a word, and Ahmad enters. He walks to the living room but remains standing.

"Want some breakfast?" I offer.

"No thanks."

I'm starving. Seems ages since I had a decent meal. I pull three eggs and butter from the fridge and then find a skillet in the cupboard and place it on the stove. I take a bowl from the same cupboard, put it on the counter, and break the eggs into it. In short order I have an omelet. I put it on a plate and grab a chair next to Ahmad.

"Any news of our guy?" I ask between bites.

He shakes his head. "Not yet."

"When you were in South Africa, did you work in the desert?"

"Yes, many times."

"Is it true that deserts are not all alike?"

"Yes. For example, this one is flatter."

I am trying to strike up a conversation, but he doesn't seem ready. I need to walk. I get up and wash up my breakfast dishes.

"I want to walk around outside; it's almost daylight."

"Okay, but stick close to the trailer or go back into the house; the others are there."

I walk back to the bedroom and find a pullover from my backpack. It's common to be chilly in the morning in the desert. I step outside, and the air smells and feels fresh. The sun is coming up. The desert always has nice mornings—crisp and clear.

There are several mountain ranges surrounding us. As the sun comes up, silhouettes of mountain peaks can be seen in all directions. I begin walking away from the trailer with Ahmad right on my heels. The way he moves speaks of experience. He really can make you feel either at ease or terrified. I prefer at ease.

I see the others moving around the kitchen. Chad is watching us through the window. Chad never makes me feel at ease. He's all business.

After a short walk around the trailer, watching the sun come up, I head back inside. I'm starting to really like this camping out. Nice-sized trailer, electricity, water, bathroom, satellite, and Internet. Now that is primo camping.

Once I'm inside, Ahmad gestures for me to wait. He is on the phone.

When he is done, he says, "Gather your things, we're going for a ride." I sigh and snatch my backpack and materials. I'm not ready for another day like yesterday.

We move quickly. Ahmad loads a large black bag. We are in the black four-door sedan, and there's so much gear I can't see the backseat.

I could guess, but I ask anyway: "Why so much artillery?" It's not like they're not always armed.

We leave the neighborhood and hit IH 25, northbound. We're clipping along at a serious pace. He must be close, but I have to know for sure.

"You brought more guns, and we're hauling ass. Is he close?"

"Don't know, but Daniel said saddle up and start traveling."

"We're obviously heading north; if the bad guy is trying to leave the country, wouldn't he try the Mexican border again?"

"You're not thinking of all the possibilities. What if he wants us to think he's trying to escape?"

I tell him, "That is what I think, especially after yesterday."

"Again, you're starting to become narrow-sighted. These radicals are well trained in deception."

"Where to now? Are we joining up with other agents?"

"My instructions are to follow the team with you in tow and keep you alive."

Well, that answers that. Keep me alive—I can appreciate that. But if I'm to stay alive, why are we running to an obvious encounter?

We ride for about an hour, I see exit signs for Socorro. We pass these exits and continue north. The next highway sign reads Truth or Consequences. Feedback. Seems they liked my work from yesterday.

"So we're going to Truth or Consequences?"

Ahmad fumbles with his earpiece. "I don't know. I haven't been given a location."

We travel onward. After about thirty minutes, we're seeing the numbers on the mile markers numbers getting lower. We exit at Truth or Consequences, follow the off-ramp, and travel side streets, still moving at a pace fast enough that I can't note street names. Finally, we stop in an old neighborhood where there is an adobe house with a large open yard. We pull in. It's nearing 10:00 a.m.

Ahmad exits the SUV, telling me to stay put. He walks up to the lead car. He speaks to Chad and returns.

"Get your backpack and come on," he says.

I exit and follow him inside the house.

The rest of the team follows. Everybody is tense and constantly looking out windows. They are really making me afraid. Chad tells the team to close the shades. He has Joseph go to the Suburban and get the communications equipment. "Don't let her out of your sight," he tells Ahmad.

"What's with the radio equipment? What about your implants?" I ask Ahmad.

"We are connected to a home base; not all agents involved with this mission have our technology."

I would like to pursue this further, but now isn't the time.

I'm told to take one of the bedrooms. I pick the one in the middle. I throw my backpack on an old table in the corner and walk back into the living room, where they are all in action.

They have begun setting up communication equipment and laptops on the kitchen table. Each has been issued an additional weapon, either a rifle or a shotgun. It seems we are preparing for a siege. With all these weapons, communication devices, lots of people here, and more agents on the perimeter, why don't I feel safe? The only weapon I can depend on is my mind. But that has proven to be accessible to the enemy—an enemy I have yet to identify.

Chad looks at me. "Stay close."

He looks at Ahmad, nods once, and points toward me. He doesn't speak, but his order is understood.

Chad's phone rings and I hear, "Yes, sir." He listens for a few moments, and when he's done, he looks confused.

I walk over to Ahmad and ask, "What do you think that was all about? This guy is never off his game."

"I don't know, but I think we'll know in a moment."

We both look at Chad. Chad appears to be looking for answers.

Chad stops and takes a deep breath. "Possible target has been identified."

We all freeze. Does this mean the target has been determined or, worse, has already hit?

He continues. "Daniel said we're to concentrate our efforts on White Sands Missile Range."

I'm racking my brain. I never mentioned a facility. Was I wrong, or were my descriptors leading factors? That's the nature of the job. There must be an analyst on this mission.

I stand close to Chad. "Is it okay to ask? What's the leading factor in determining the site?"

"Your information and ours led to a hard target."

Their information? Are we sharing information, and where did theirs come from? What is he doing? His words make no sense.

"Do you agree?" I ask.

"Not my call," he says, looking right through me. "We have instructions, and we will follow them."

Of that I have no doubt; he is so serious and stern, and I just let it go. Chad turns to his team. "We're to maintain here. If anything goes wrong, fall back to the last location."

Fall back? What is fall back? Are we preparing for a firefight or conducting an investigation?

I turn to Ahmad, knowing Chad won't answer another question. "What is this fall back business?"

"We always have positions to fall back to. He is making it clear should it be needed."

"Needed?"

"We're dealing with a cunning and dangerous person. We don't know positively if there are more, what they know of us, or if they know our position or positions. We just don't know."

"You're telling me that after these last few days, with so much death and destruction, we still don't know?"

"We have information, we have guesses, but as you well know, facts are all that count. We're short on facts."

"Why White Sands Missile Range? Why not a small city or a military base?"

"White Sands is still an active missile range and a testing ground for experimental aircraft. Fort Bliss and El Paso are nearby. Target makes sense."

I don't believe this. White Sands as a target doesn't make sense. It's too obvious. This guy has been anything but routine from the onset.

I look over at Chad. He hasn't heard us. He was busy instructing others. I would like to think he isn't buying into this.

My phone rings. Daniel starts by saying, "I take it Chad told you?"

"Yes," I say, "but I don't understand or agree."

"This has come mostly from your descriptors: desert, aircraft, facilities, and so on. We had agents on the ground in El Paso following up on these descriptions. The terrorist was last seen traveling across lower New Mexico, east, toward these facilities."

"What about the hangar, the aircraft, and the envelopes for possible passengers I viewed?"

"All were considered. Some were considered stray cats, castling, or stress."

"Except for one thing, Daniel. I'm a trained viewer. I know how to avoid those traps. As far as stress, hell, I thrive on stress."

"Okay," he states firmly, "your views have been heard and are noted."

He hangs up. I'm steamed. Who is this analyst? I wasn't told about having a monitor, analyst, or project manager.

Chad calls to me from the kitchen. I join him, leaning against a counter. He's holding a paper in his hand.

"I'm to ask you to dowse these."

He knows not to tell me or hint at a target. He looks like a child who wants something but won't ask permission. "Does Daniel know?" I ask. "I just got off the phone with him; he didn't say anything to me about this."

After hesitating for a moment, Chad says, "I have some liberties while in the field. I would like to double-check all the evidence gathered. Would you dowse some information? It could be important to this case."

"Why are you asking? Is this going to be added to my other paperwork?"

"No, this is like a sidebar. Once you're done, I'll hold on to your results. I'll compare them to the files when I feel it's necessary."

He looks as though it's a real burden for him to ask. But is the burden the question, or the reason he needs to ask?

"Yeah, it's no problem." Daniel did not ask me to continue with this task.

"This is for your and my eyes only." Chad looks into my eyes. "Understand?"

"Look, you guys scare me enough, but to do something behind Daniel's back? Get serious."

"Not behind his back. I will hold it, and once it's done, I'll pass it along to Daniel."

I'm still not sure. I have known Daniel for a few years but Chad only a few days. He looks truly compelled to do this, though.

Finally I say, "Okay, but Daniel will know of the findings."

"Of course, I wouldn't have it any other way."

"Don't let me see them," I tell him. "take them to my room and put them facedown on the table. Put a blank sheet of paper on top and let me know when you're done."

He walks toward my room.

I turn to find Ahmad is right there. He is looking at me; now I'm stressing.

"Something I need to know?" he asks.

"No, this is between me and Chad."

He doesn't say anything.

Chad returns and says, "Ready? I'll be with the others when you're done."

"Okay, don't know how long I'll be."

He turns and leaves the kitchen. I look at Ahmad. He doesn't flinch.

I head to my room, and there lay five sheets of paper, blank side up. Good, no clues exposed. I need to decide, hotspot or instrument? Hotspot it is.

Eleven

Approaching the table, I close my eyes and wonder what Chad's gain is in all of this. I grab a chair from across the room, and I sit upright and focus.

I gently pass my right hand over the first sheet. With a pen, I mark it number one. I do the same with the others, marking them two through five.

I begin with the paper labeled one. I hold my hand about two inches above the paper, pass it over, and focus on feeling. There is a sensation in the center of my hand. Over that spot on the paper I feel heat; that's the hotspot.

I repeat this three times, and the same spot shows hot each time; it must be the target. I mark that spot on the blank top sheet. I remove the blank page and find a terrain map underneath. No idea of the area it shows, though. It's a well-laid-out grid of ten-mile squares.

I mark the grid on the spot that corresponds with the mark on the blank paper. I'm feeling tension, maybe fear. I step away from the table. It's common to have feelings once a site picture is found. It's part of being there.

Back at the table, I stand over paper number two. I repeat the three passes and find the spot. I mark it and remove the top sheet. There is another terrain map of five-mile squares. Still no markings showing where the grid applies.

I repeat the same procedure with the remaining pages. They are a mixed bag of terrain maps. Number three and five are a no-go; I find nothing on them, but the maps are similar. Chad really must have something going. When I'm finished, I mark each accordingly and begin to document in my matrix.

I look over my shoulder. Chad is in the doorway. He dismisses Ahmad and closes the door. "Document that later," he tells me.

"Protocol," I say in protest. "Once something is found, write it down—too easy to forget or lose it."

"Document later," he tells me, stepping closer. "Tell me your findings."

You never know with these guys. He may just be all business, or else he's ready to blow. He steps up to the table. His body language is showing a need to know now.

I point to the five maps. "Two are no good; the other three hit."

"I have the maps that those grids apply to; just doing background on other evidence."

"Whatever, you're in charge. No explanation needed."

"Until I apply your findings to these maps, keep a lid on it."

"Okay, you tell me the findings."

"Of course, and leave Daniel to me."

Chad is being so serious; I wasn't going to tell him otherwise, even though we had stepped out of bounds.

He turns and walks out. Not another word about the maps. He will make a good Daniel.

I put my findings in the backpack, still needing to document. That was different, but then again, everything else has been different over these past few days.

I hear other voices. I walk toward the door, but Ahmad stops me with one hand, gesturing not to go farther.

"What now?" I ask.

"Meeting with the other two alert teams."

"After all this, I'm not allowed to sit in on briefings?"

"Chad's instructions. I'm to keep you here until I'm told otherwise."

"Told otherwise? Told what?" I'm beginning to tire of being out of the loop.

"You know better; letting you in the intelligence briefing could pollute your thoughts."

By the look on his face I can see I am pushing my luck. But what could be more important than the information I've given them?

They meet for about twenty minutes, and then I hear them leave. One team leaves through the kitchen and the other through the front door. Chad looks toward my room. He gives Ahmad the all clear. Our team, my protection detail, gathers in the living room.

Chad again states the location of the possible assault. Everyone is listening, but it seems not all of them are in agreement, especially me. He tells us, "The alert teams are splitting. One will be paralleling us at all times, and the other will go to White Sands to do a sweep. We will proceed to White Sands."

There is silence. The feeling in the room leaves no doubt.

"Are we on the right track?" I ask Chad. "Were those the teams attached to us all this time?"

"One is, yes; the other is newly assigned."

"With all the firepower in this room, what's the need for more?"

Chad looks me right in the eyes. "Keep you alive."

I'm shivering, and my neck is sweating. The possibility of being killed by this lunatic terrorist is haunting me again. For just a moment I wish I were back in my trailer in Las Cruces.

Crap! I can't believe I just did that! I mentally gave away that I am not there. I know better! Not just my thoughts, but all these people planning and openly discussing a mission. We need to move out, and fast.

Chad calls everyone to the living room. He gives the order to saddle up. I go back to my room, grab my gear, and meet Ahmad in the living room.

He is jingling a set of keys. "We'll use the sedan, and the others are gearing up the SUV."

"What exactly does 'gearing up' mean?"

He points out a window to a black Suburban. "We call it the war wagon. All sorts of self-defense and counterterrorism gear."

"What more do you guys need? I have seen enough today to stand down an army."

"The war wagon is designed to take on anything from small-arms fire to an RPG assault."

"Who came up with the term 'war wagon'?"

He smiles. "Cowboy movie, don't you remember?"

"I grew up with sitcoms and prime-time soaps, but I'll give it some thought."

"Load up," he tells me. We walk through the kitchen and out the door to the black four-door sedan with heavily tinted windows. Gee, nobody will see us.

We leave the neighborhood and head for I-25.

"If you're to keep me safe and out of harm's way, why am I going with you guys?" I ask.

"We told you, you're a witness. Besides, Daniel told Chad to bring you—something about feedback."

"We use it to confirm a target sighting."

"Evidently you're on to something."

"Yes, whether the viewer is dead on or it's a total miss, feedback will tell us."

He looks as though he's really not interested. Guess it beats talking to himself.

"Look, I can do this from a room anywhere on the planet; why travel with you guys?"

"Just following instructions. Besides, I don't really get into this job of yours. Boots on the ground is where real information is generated."

Okay, this guy doesn't really like this job. He is a professional. At least I know where he stands.

We travel for about thirty minutes and stop. The desert air is always brisk and clean. You can see for miles in every direction. Mountain ranges stand in the distance. I've always loved the desert.

Ahmad is on the phone. He looks confused and not sure of what to say. He puts the phone in his lap and turns to me.

"Chad wants to know if this seems familiar—this road, from where we came from to this point. Does it mean anything to you?"

I consider for a moment and say, "The town we came from, the road, and the horizon of the desert, maybe."

Surely they know it could be anywhere. Sometimes descriptors may apply to things other than what they appear to apply to. So many variable answers, and they want one now.

Ahmad relays my comment to Chad. They talk for a moment and disconnect. Ahmad looks frustrated.

"What's up?" I ask.

"I don't know. Chad says he's trying to confirm information of a possible attack site."

"Chad's lead agent; he has leeway to do his own thing."

"Yes, but we're to take you to White Sands Missile Range."

"Maybe he is on to something and wants to confirm it before telling Daniel."

"Maybe, but this is unusual."

We turn around and pass the SUV. It turns and follows after us. We travel for about thirty minutes and exit onto I-25, southbound.

"Why did we turn around?" I ask.

"Back to Highway 54 south of El Paso instead of cutting across to Alamogordo. The freeway system is faster than the two-lane road from Las Cruces."

We travel for about thirty minutes. I think it's nice to have someone drive me around out here; the scenery is great.

I gaze out the window for a moment, absorbing the scenery. The Guadalupe Mountain Range divides Texas and Mexico. No trees, brown soil, no desert tan color, no snow at the pass this time of year, wide-open skies.

"Are we making good time for White Sands?" I ask.

"Yes."

He is deep in thought. Something is really eating at him.

It's normally a good two-and-a-half-hour drive, but Ahmad has this sedan pushing 80 mph. We pass a trooper without being stopped. Sure wish I had one of those identifications; these guys must have serious connections.

We pass Las Cruces, heading east. Wonder if we have to go through El Paso?

As we approach El Paso city limits, there's a sign that reads "Mountain Road Pass." We make the exit and circumvent El Paso.

We come to Highway 54 on the south side of El Paso and turn south; I see entrance signs for Fort Bliss. We're in the danger zone. Where is this terrorist?

Traveling on this road is not a sweetheart ride. Once a busy roadway, now it's virtually abandoned. It's barren and dusty, lined with empty roadside rest stops, not at all attractive.

"Do you know what happened out here?" I ask Ahmad.

"No water; this area lost its water rights to El Paso."

How did he know that? Supposedly we didn't know which direction we would be traveling today.

"You read a National Geographic earlier about southern New Mexico?"

"My chip—I can have them monitor us." He grins. "Answers to your questions are passed to me through my earpiece. This technology has been around for years. We just improved on it."

Did he say they talk to him through an earpiece? I have looked many times and have yet to see one. These guys have some major big-boy toys.

"Are we getting close to White Sands?"

"Yes, it'll be coming up shortly."

Up ahead is a border patrol stop. What is he going to do? Stop? Roll through? Or did someone already call ahead?

We slow, follow the coned-off shoulder, and pull under a large awning. The young officer, dressed in green, signals for Ahmad to roll down the window. Ahmad reaches into his pocket and shows a black wallet with a silver badge. The officer smiles and instructs us to move along. I look in the side mirrors and watch the war wagon do the same. I've got to get one of those.

"I thought you don't trust anyone. Why did you show him your ID?"

Ahmad smiles and opens the wallet. There is a badge labeled US Marshall inside.

"You're not serious. What's wrong with your real badge and ID?"

"As I said, trust nobody. And we don't have badges."

I'm blown away by these guys and their ways.

In short order we're at the exit for White Sands Missile Range. We turn right onto a blacktop road and stop at a guard shack. Guess it's time to use the old badge trick again. As we pull up, the guard signals us through. Not even a hint of a stop.

"Okay then," I have to ask, "what was it this time?"

"VIP."

"So now I'm a VIP with a war wagon escort?"

"Yep." He leaves it at that.

We don't go far; several buildings are coming up. We pull to the right onto a service road. We approach a small hangar with the bay doors open, and as we get close, I can see that Daniel is there, along with four well-armed men.

We pull in and exit the vehicles. Daniel motions for us to meet him in the center of the hangar. I look over my shoulder as one of the other alert teams enters the hangar and closes the doors.

Daniel has huge black bags under his eyes. They are even turning a bit yellow. This one-man-terrorist act is getting to everybody. Daniel welcomes us all and begins a briefing. We're told of the possibility of our man being near, or even at, this facility. For what reason, it isn't known.

We all listen attentively to his words. Everybody here has been tasked to their utmost ability. This is one battle-driven outfit. Daniel goes over possible scenarios. All in all, no one has a clue as to what this guy will do next. Then again, that is the nature of intelligence gathering—always wondering if the right target is being followed.

Maybe he led us all to this place so he could escape out of the country. After all, he is on a four-wheeler. Crossing the desert or even the Rio Grande in places would put him out of the country quickly. Our diplomatic connections with Mexico are strained at best. Current events there are bleeding over into the USA. Nobody really has the time and resources to search the two-thousand-mile border for one man. Is he is trying to escape through Mexico?

Daniel completes the briefing and gives each team instructions. Chad is lead agent in the field. Daniel tells us he is leaving, returning to the command post.

What command post? I wonder to myself.

Before Daniel walks away, I ask to speak to him. He hesitates at first but gives in.

"You didn't tell me about my part of the operation. I need feedback."

"You've done your part. We're here."

"You know better," I tell him. "This might not be absolute. I need to work on it more."

"The analyst and operation manager reviewed your work. That is how this site was determined."

"Thanks for the faith in my work, but really, after seeing many locations, I didn't give you enough to point to just this one."

"I'm finished here." He looks at me with what seems to be disgust. "If you want to try, go ahead. The team is not to be out of your sight."

"Okay," I tell him, "I'm going to try, and I want these guys on my side."

Daniel walks away and gets into a tan sedan. The bay door opens, and he is off. Where is the command post?

Ahmad is right behind me. We both look around the hangar. I need a safe place to work. Where are we to stay?

"Are we planning to overnight here?" I ask.

Ahmad nods. "Pick an office upstairs."

I look around. Entrances run along two walls. Each entrance has a sign. It's the same upstairs. We walk over to the metal staircase and go up. I choose an office in the middle labeled Commander.

"Is this guy going to need his office?" I ask Ahmad.

"No, this hangar is abandoned. This is the old base commander's office."

I open the door and walk in. There is a gray metal desk and a wooden chair; the desk is sitting in front of one of two large windows. There is a good view of the airstrip and miles of white sand.

I am wondering who the operation manager and analyst are. My field is limited to but a handful. I must know them.

I spread my work out on the desk. By now I have lots of pages that need organizing. As I sort by page number, I try to scan them all. Seems this place could be it, but then again, that's why we stick to descriptors.

I find one sketch and a write-up that describes a place similar to our location. What about the hangar and aircraft? Everything I viewed there was new. I saw the construction guys and schematics. The place in the materials I found goes back to pre–WWII.

I lay out a fresh paper. Put myself in deep thought and place pencil to paper.

I hear sirens and people yelling—not in session, but real! Now!

I stand up, and as soon as I do, Ahmad grabs me and pulls me down. He has a pistol in his hand and is reaching for his phone.

"Never stand in front of a window or an open doorway when there's an alarm—never!" he yells at me.

I don't answer. He's right; I was just what someone may have been waiting for, a silhouette ripe for the shooting.

Ahmad is on the phone. "Yes, sir." He's looking intense.

"What do we do?" I ask.

"Nothing," he tells me. "Stay close."

I don't understand. Stay close? We're as close as I care to be. We are on our knees and practically under the desk together.

He puts away the phone and motions for me to follow. We duckwalk a short distance and then stand up near one of the windows.

"Look across the airfield." He gestures with a motion of his head.

I look with half my face, trying not to be a target. I'm petrified. Ahmad ducks and goes to the other side of the window.

"We're to watch this end of the complex."

"For what?" I ask.

"Not what. Who."

"Did someone see something, or has there been another incident?"

"A person was seen crossing the perimeter onto the airfield behind this hangar."

"Did security follow him?"

"No, they just watched him cross the airfield and walk toward this location."

"Why didn't they stop him?" I am trying not to sound afraid even though my stomach is in a knot.

"They were instructed not to. You have seen him at work; they would be no match."

I looked at him. "Would anyone?"

"Don't worry; with our alert teams out there and us inside, you're safe."

I can't believe my ears. They used me as bait. They knew he would come here. I know from experience this guy is capable of killing us all.

I'm shaking so hard sand fleas couldn't hold on. My sweat is pouring so hard they would drown anyway.

I lean away from the window. "Is he here for me?" I ask Ahmad.

"Yes." He looks away.

I knew it; they planned this. Daniel knew this was not the target. They have flushed him out, but at what cost?

"So what is your plan? This guy is known for stealth."

"You know all the protection that's around us. Relax."

Relax? What the hell is he thinking? He is trained to deal with all this death and destruction. I'm only a person that sketches and writes summaries. How can I possibly relax?

Hours seem to pass, but it's only been a few minutes. Feels like I'm a pressure cooker about to blow. I'm going to lose it at any minute.

"Get down," Ahmad finally says. "We need to move to the other side of the room. Just do as I do, and stay close."

We squat, begin a duckwalk, and stop in a corner across the room at an angle to the door. It feels like we're in a shadow. This is better, but then again, where is the terrorist?

Ahmad motions with one hand to stand. Our backs are to the corner. The day is ending, the sun is setting, and we are on the shaded side. Thankfully, the room is darkening.

We hear one shout, then another. Ahmad is talking over the earpiece.

"Squat down!" Ahmad whispers loudly.

"What now?" I ask.

"Lower your silhouette in case anyone comes through the door."

"Who was on the phone?" I want to know.

"Chad. They are chasing someone outside the building."

Outside the building? They let that guy get this close? Where are the alert teams?

Ahmad moves closer. He is squatting right in front of me. This is the second time an agent has placed himself in front of me.

There is noise outside the door. It's getting dark both inside and outside. I look toward the window and see that street lights are coming on. I hear the distinct sound of a helicopter, and suddenly the whole outside is lit up.

Ahmad whispers, pressing his fingers onto his earpiece. No "yes, sirs" just "okay." He stands and motions for me to stand up.

We stand and stretch. Squatting all that time was tough enough, and the tension in my muscles is numbing.

"Stay here." He turns, facing the door.

He walks across the room, opens the door, and steps out.

I hear voices. Please tell me the voices I hear are outside that door and not in my head.

He returns and motions for me to come to the door. I walk over and step out. Lots of people with guns are out there. Chad is standing there talking with other agents. He is giving instructions, as usual. He doesn't give me a glance.

"Change in plans," Ahmad says. "Joseph will take my place."

"Thanks for being there with me." I want to reach out and hug him, but I resist.

Ahmad looks at me and smiles. I'm surprised; these guys don't smile enough. It's a handsome smile, fitting for him.

He walks away, and I turn toward Chad and Joseph. Chad looks stressed and somewhat fatigued. "Back inside the office," he tells me.

I step back through the door, followed by Joseph. He looks around the room and then closes the door. What did he think, that the bad guy was in here?

"Well, did you catch him?" I ask.

"No. He was last seen at this hangar, but he disappeared."

"Disappeared? What's next, wait for him to find us?"

"Relax, this hangar is well protected."

"I have seen this guy at work. Excuse me if I don't relax."

"You're fine; he made it to the hangar, skirted it, but found no way in."

"So did he just go for an afternoon stroll afterward?"

"He walked around the building and slipped away on the shaded side."

"Does *slipped away* mean *escaped*?"

"If you want to call it that. We were waiting to determine if he was going to enter here or if he had another objective."

"By the other objective, you mean me as bait?"

"We have to stay positive; let's just get through the night," he tells me.

"I'm not waiting here through the night knowing that guy is on the hunt."

"Yes, you are." Joseph is a very serious young man with determination in his voice who makes himself very clear. He shuffles his feet to show he is standing sturdy. His body and voice make his point. I don't think I will play this bluff any further. Besides, if I get past him, there is still Chad to contend with—no thanks.

"Fine, I'll try to make the best of it. What about food? I'm starving."

"Food and sleeping arrangements are being taken care of." What appears to be a look of a fear comes into his eyes. "Bring that chair from the desk to the corner of the room." He points to the same corner Ahmad had me in earlier. I go quickly to the desk, grab the chair, and push it to the corner.

I sit down, not knowing what to say or do with an agent standing next to me. This time is different. Why am I sitting here?

For a place with so many people both inside and out, there is an ominous quiet. This is an active airfield and missile range; where did this silence come from? It's like the world is watching and waiting for this one person.

When I get a chance, I'll have a couple of questions for Daniel. What was he thinking, making me the bait? Why are we not at the most obvious location viewed? This is close, but maybe I missed the target. Did I go back to a time before this was constructed? Are we in the right place at a different time?

Viewers have used time to find locations for many years. But there is the rule of change. Change occurs by the millisecond, and what may be viewed at a certain time can change—not always, but it must not be ruled out. The universe is known to do whatever it deems necessary.

It's not unusual for a target to be viewed before the current date and time. The viewer must document what is seen at that moment. If you have a site picture and have documented properly, your time line should be accurate. That is what a well-disciplined viewer can do. My favorite are nautical events; unfortunately, most noteworthy nautical events are tragedies. To go back and look for a lost ship is good detective work.

Joseph is on the phone. He is approving someone to come through the door. He has his weapon in hand just in case.

The door opens, and two people bring in food and folding army cots for us to sleep on. One is pulling two cots, and the other has small bags. Nothing is said. The cots are left near the door, and the bags placed on the desk. They leave.

Joseph walks to the desk, looking out the windows as he goes. He turns to face me with an odd expression on his face; it seems almost sorrowful. The look says he is about to do something he will regret. He draws his pistol and points it in my direction.

He takes a deep breath. "Get down on your knees. If you scream, I'll shoot."

"What are you doing? Please point that gun somewhere else."

Slowly, he steps closer, looking me directly in the eyes.

"On your knees, now!" Sweat is pouring down his face.

I can't breathe. My head is swaying; I'm about to pass out. He has the barrel of the pistol inches from my skull. The room suddenly erupts with the sound of breaking glass, and Joseph falls to the floor.

My eyes follow him as he falls. I kneel next to him. I look into his eyes as they begin to lose life. A pool of blood forms under him.

He grabs my hand. Blood is oozing from his mouth, and his skin is turning pale. He manages to say in a whisper, "Ashlee, please forgive me."

I squeeze his hand as it goes limp. He is staring at me, but I can tell he is gone. Tears are so thick in my eyes I can barely see the door.

I crawl to the door and attempt to open it. Two agents burst through and are on me almost immediately.

One grabs me under my right arm and drags me into the hallway. The other rushes over to Joseph and kneels beside him.

The agent pins me to the floor. I'm having a hard time catching my breath.

A helicopter lights up the exterior. What just happened?

I hear yelling outside; loud at first, and then fading away.

The agent on top of me finally gets up. Whew, I can breathe again. He helps me to my feet.

We're on the catwalk that runs in front of the offices. We walk two doors down and enter. The room has no windows and only one door. Chad is in the room. He looks weary and a bit shaken.

"Are you okay?" he asks.

"No! What the hell is going on here?"

"Let's get you someplace safe first. Then I'll explain."

"Joseph! He was going to kill me!"

"Yes. Our investigative team is on it."

I'm trying not to go radical and start screaming, but if I don't get a straight answer, I'll lose it.

"Did he say anything to you before he went down?" Chad asks. He has changed his tone; it is now a bit demanding.

"Why?" I scream. "What the hell is going on? Tell me!"

"Control yourself. It is important we note everything to pass along to the investigation team; you know this. What did he say to you?" He steps toward me, looking into my eyes. I can see that he is pissed.

I look away, not giving him the chance to see whether or not I'm lying. The eyes can be a dead giveaway.

I give in. "He asked me to forgive him." Tears are flowing down my face.

Chad steps next to me, reaches into his pants pocket, and hands me a handkerchief. I take it. There is a logo on one corner; it's faded and worn, but "USMC" is still legible.

"Thank you. It's important we make note of everything." He actually sounds sympathetic about the ordeal.

I wipe the tears from my face and the corners of my eyes. "Thanks. I'm done with this." The emblem can be seen once the handkerchief is flipped over; it's from the United States Marine Corps.

"He knew better than to let himself be detected. Why would he expose himself like that?" I must know more.

"He didn't."

"What?"

"We knew the terrorist had to have an inside informant. The terrorist was close to us at every moment."

"You knew someone was a plant, and you allowed me to be in danger?"

"We found out yesterday. Only two of us knew; me and Daniel."

"One more time—did you set this up just to catch the insider?" Rage is flowing through my veins. I'm clenching my fists so hard I think I might draw blood.

He continues with his explanation, still not answering me directly. "It was either Ahmad or Joseph. The intrusion onto this facility confirmed our facts."

I move even closer to him, and we stand nose-to-nose.

"Did you bother to ask if I wanted to participate? No! You put me at death's door to what? Catch one of your own?"

He points his finger in my face. "When I need your permission, I will ask for it. Until then you do *as* I say *when* I say. No exception." His eyes are blood red, and he is near exploding. He lowers his hand and steps one pace back. "We don't have time to ask permission or forgiveness. If you haven't noticed, what we deal with is beyond the norm. Hell, over time you don't even know what the norm is. We are the last line of defense against an enemy with no rules or morals."

I turn away and take a deep breath. He's right, but I'm not going to admit it. We are engaged with an enemy beyond most people's imaginations. Nobody wants to be in this situation.

I think for a moment and ask, "Do you think he was waiting for the perfect moment?"

"Perfect, no. Just a good chance to execute you." His voice is calmer, sounding more like himself.

"How did he know when to shoot?"

"He didn't shoot; we did. The room was monitored; Daniel and I were watching. Once we realized it wasn't Ahmad, I replaced him with Joseph. An old communication tower is just opposite of that office window. We had a sniper positioned. When Joseph pointed his gun at you, we had him shot. The shot wasn't lethal. He's still alive. He was unconscious when you left."

"I really don't care if he's dead or alive." I don't know whether to be grateful or pissed. I understand that these people are dangerous. But I still think I should have been clued in.

"Like it or not, that was the plan, and you are safe. My job is to keep you alive, and that's what I did. You will get no apology."

"Okay, then I guess thanks are in order. Sorry to question you. But if you should want to use me again as bait, please tell me first."

"So noted."

I begin to turn away. "I need fresh air. Is it okay if I go outside for a walk?"

"Take Ahmad, but don't go far."

I leave the room and find Ahmad. Silently, we walk down the catwalk past the commander's door and take the stairs to the hangar floor. We walk across the hangar to a doorway. Ahmad opens it, and we step out.

Being outside never felt so good. A light breeze hits my skin as I look at the stars above. I say to myself, "It's so good to be alive." We walk along the side of the hangar for about ten minutes.

"You ready to go in?" I ask Ahmad. "I'm good."

"Yes, time to get some sleep."

We enter the same door and find the hangar dimly lighted. We climb the same stairs and walk the catwalk, stopping short of the commander's room.

"Gear from the other room has been moved. We're to bunk here," Ahmad tells me.

Nothing more is said. We unfold cots and bags. I lie down, afraid to close my eyes. I keep thinking what hell these past days have been. Sleep comes, but only because I'm exhausted from the adrenaline rush and then coming back down.

Twelve

There it is again—nudging. Ahmad is hovering over me.

"Ashlee, wake up." He shakes me.

"What now?"

"I know it's early, but we're bugging out of here. Get ready."

I slowly sit up. I struggle to comprehend what he's saying.

"Ashlee, come on, we're leaving."

What he's saying finally sinks in. I get off the cot, stand up, and look for my backpack. Where is it?

"Your bag and computer have been compromised. They are being sent to a lab to find out how."

"I need my bag; all my work is there! No way was it compromised; it was with me the whole time."

"No time for discussion. Let's go; they're waiting."

We leave the room, step onto the catwalk, and head down to the hangar floor. I look out the bay door windows. It's still dark.

"Wait for one minute. I'm going to take a bathroom break first," I say, glaring at Ahmad.

"Okay, use the one near our ride. Five minutes." He points to the toilet facility along the wall. He can make things clear with that stern voice.

Inside the bathroom I clean up as best I can. When I step out into the hangar, I notice that something is different. All the agents and military personnel that were here earlier are gone. There are just the three of us and two vehicles; Chad is standing next to the war wagon.

"What happened to my backpack?" I ask when I get close to him.

"Where were your bag and computer while you were asleep and Joseph was on watch?" Chad asks.

"I usually left them on the desk."

"Exactly. We're not taking any chances. Now let's go."

"I need my notes."

"Improvise," he tells me. "Now load up."

Ahmad and I enter a black sedan, and Chad gets into the war wagon. The big bay doors open, and both vehicles exit.

We pass through the main gate of White Sands Missile Range.

No one says a word during the first part of the ride. Ahmad looks tense and fatigued, yet I feel I'm in good hands.

A few miles farther on I ask, "Was the terrorist even there? If he was, what direction did he go?"

"We think he got away somewhere out in the desert, to the north."

"How is Joseph?" I ask, not that I really care after what he did. But then again, I am being the better person for asking.

"Alive and having surgery at the Fort Bliss army hospital."

"Did anyone actually see the terrorist?"

"A team member saw a shadow east of the hangar. When the sniper shot, he was seen running to a small truck."

"I thought he walked onto the facility? Where did he get a truck?"

"He stole one and planted it to be used for his escape."

"What about weapons? Was he seen carrying one?"

"Yes."

"With all your experience, what do you think of the way we flushed Joseph out?" I watch him closely, looking for any sign.

"Sometimes we put ourselves at risk of death. You just gotta do what you gotta do to catch someone."

We travel for about five miles and then turn north into the desert, following Chad in the SUV. There is nothing out here—flat and miles of sand, not even a trace of a road.

We stop, and Chad exits the SUV. Ahmad tells me to get out but to stay near the vehicle. I do as I am told.

Ahmad and Chad huddle together. I can hear bits and pieces. Seems we are spending the rest of the night here. Just what I want—camping out with these guys.

"You and I will rest in the SUV," Ahmad says as he walks back to me. "We will continue at first light."

"Okay, where did everyone from earlier go?"

"The alert teams are doing the same thing we are—finding a safe spot to rest. Remember, this is the war wagon."

I had forgotten about that. This SUV is the one with all the latest and greatest in human destruction. A single person could take out a whole town with it. I really would rather sleep in the sedan.

It's quiet here in the desert. All the chaos and death from earlier didn't affect a thing out here. I gaze out the window and see the endless night sky. There are stars, and lots of them. They make one wonder—all this going on, and yet it's still so peaceful out here.

With one more glance, I find Ahmad awake and alert. After what seems like mere moments, I feel a nudge and hear a voice. I open my eyes, and there he sits, smiling at me.

I sit up and ask, "Where to now?"

"Nowhere for a few minutes; you have a while to wake up. We may have a full day ahead of us."

"Are we chasing this guy farther, or are we assuming he has finally left the country?"

"Don't know." Speaking softly, he says, "These guys are clever and resourceful. We must expect the unexpected."

Unexpected. This terrorist, assassin, or evil bastard—however one perceives him—he wrote the book on the art of the unexpected.

I'm feeling very uncomfortable, slightly nauseated, as though an illness is coming on.

I hold on to my stomach. I'm queasy, dizzy, and losing my bearings. *Not again,* I think.

I look at Ahmad and let out a moan.

He looks alarmed.

"What is it?"

"I don't know; something is hitting me hard ... I'm not sure what."

"What can I do?"

"Nothing, just sit still and watch."

It's getting worse. I'm having problems focusing. I feel a presence just like before, but stronger. They are trying again.

"I've got to get outside," I tell Ahmad. "I need air."

He exits quickly and runs to my side of the SUV, where he opens the door and helps me out.

I can barely stand, but I plant my feet firmly and concentrate. I must not give in; I need to hold my ground.

I begin concentrating on the last known place the other viewer was seen—in the house—but she is gone. Another building stands close by. Holding on to my thoughts, I view inside that building. There is a man. He has features similar to the woman's but is stockier. He sees me. I feel a brief lull in the ailment. He actually looks startled. I adjust my thoughts to interfere with his concentration. I feel him wavering. I keep constant eye contact with him. I then change my thoughts. *Reverse the illness.* It gets better, but I still may lose it. My legs are wobbly.

I look at him intently, and he looks just as intently back at me. I maintain and begin trying to influence him. We're locked in a fight of thoughts. I feel the intensity between us; we are like two people engaged in a physical fight, but with no blows being exchanged.

I dig deeper into my mind and maintain my posture. I have to change the imagery in his mind. With one last mental image of myself entering his mind, I feel him physically stagger. It's working. He stands up. He appears to be struggling to keep his balance. His face is pale, and there is moisture around his eyes. I command myself to stand in front of him. I do so, looking directly into his eyes. He begins to fall but catches himself on the chair.

I look further into his mind and find darkness, with a feeling of gloom and mystery. He turns slowly and manages to remain upright. He walks toward a door and enters another room. He closes the door. I do not follow.

I mentally tell myself, *End; break off.*

I must regain myself. He may be waiting on the other side. I'm too weak. This has taken a lot out of me. I collapse. Ahmad catches me before I hit the ground. I no longer see the man or the location. I'm looking at the sky again, and the sun is rising. Taking deep breaths, I try to relax. I look around and try to focus. I'm still not sure if everything around me is real or not.

I hear voices and look around. There's Chad. I'm still staring blankly, but the sickness has left.

"You all right?" Ahmad asks.

"Yes," I say, "for the moment."

"I thought we lost you there. Thought you might be flying away. You definitely were not here."

Still feeling weak, I say, "Yeah, they tried again. That was my first time viewing in a self-defense mode. Don't know what to make of it."

They stare at me. I don't believe they know what to say or think, but neither do I.

"I'm fine," I assure them.

Chad steps in, saying, "Mount up; get ready to move out."

We walk to our vehicle; Chad walks away with his phone in his ear. He must be getting our marching orders.

We head back out to the road and proceed west. We're either going back to El Paso or maybe even back to my trailer. I sort of miss that thing. Everything was at my fingertips, and I had the opportunity to change neighborhoods quickly.

We come to NM 54 and turn right. The highway sign ahead reads "Alamogordo." *Why there?* I wonder. *A town in the middle of the desert?*

In about thirty minutes we come to the city limit signs. Ahmad hasn't said a word. His phone hasn't rung; we're flying blind.

Uh oh, I spoke to soon; I hear a phone ringing. It's mine. Daniel.

"Hello," I answer.

"Are you all right?"

"I wasn't too sure there for a moment, but I'm fine now."

"Do you now understand how serious these guys are?"

"Got it. How is Joseph?" I try to change the topic.

"Critical, but alive. Don't worry about him; stay focused on the objective."

"What exactly is that?"

He takes his time and then says, "To capture this terrorist before more life and property is lost or he escapes the country."

"Okay, that will be my only objective. What about the other viewer in China?"

"He will be dealt with along the way, either by you or us. We'll locate him and deal with it." His voice sounds very assuring.

"Good, he's a very dangerous person. He's well trained or maybe even the trainer. Either way, he is lethal."

Daniel, true to form, hangs up. Now I know the main objective. The viewer on the other side of the world will most likely know it too.

After a few miles, we enter the city limits of Alamogordo.

Now why would we even consider such a place? Home to an air force base, a small town, and lots of desert known as the Tularosa Basin.

There is one unique statistic, though. With White Sands Missile Range, Los Alamos, and Holloman Air Force Base all in close proximity, there are more PhDs per capita in a few square miles than in any other location in the United States, possibly the world.

We travel about two miles and come to the intersection of Highways 54 and 70. Left on 70 takes you to Las Cruces. Straight ahead leads to Holloman AFB, training ground for the Raptor jet. Germany sends pilots there to train. They even have their own complex with German flags and insignias displayed.

A right turn becomes the main drag of Alamogordo. Turning left or going forward leads to long drives across lots of desert. A right turn leads to chain restaurants, Tularosa, or up the mountain to Cloudcroft.

I look at Ahmad; he is concentrating on the intersection. He appears to be listening, but to what? There is no audible radio, so it must be the implant. I know they use them to track, but for communications?

He stops listening to say to me, "We're going to take a break. Just giving you a heads-up."

"I sure could use one."

I look to the right and see many restaurant and hotel signs. All the hotels seem to have their No Vacancy light on.

"Looks like there aren't any rooms available; should we go to a safe house?" he asks.

Are they asking me if I have any ideas, or am I imagining things? I guess they did do their homework on me. I haunted this area for years while I was training. Why am I surprised? Daniel knows all. The light changes, and we go straight. Now we're really heading to nowhere.

"Why ask me? You're the one with the GPS implanted in your skull," I ask, trying to see just how much he knows about me.

He doesn't flinch, but his eyes dilate a little. He's thinking, or listening, hard. Hope it's all good.

"I was instructed to ask that question. I really don't care what you know."

"Look, I'm aware you guys know I was trained around here. But I only came out here for short stays."

He doesn't answer.

It has been a tough week or so, and we could use a break from each other. Considering the situation, though, we probably won't get one soon.

"I've been here many times in the past," I tell him to ease the tension a little. "A lot of my remote viewing classes were out here. I really liked Cloudcroft; the hostel there was cheap and usually empty. *Cheap* being the key word; in those days, I was struggling financially."

He smiles then. "I understand. While attending basic agent school, we were not paid for a month. I used up every penny I had waiting for payday. They were testing us to determine how bad we wanted to be there."

That helped. Different training, but you had to prove yourself.

We're cruising past Alamogordo, heading north rapidly on I-70. After passing the front entrance to Holloman AFB, there will be many roads leading off in every direction to who knows where.

If I wanted to see foreign places, I could do it out here and never leave home.

We don't travel long before we begin to slow. We take a hard left onto an old paved road that runs straight across the desert. About two miles down on the left is an old stone house.

We park in the rear with some other vehicles. Apparently the alert teams are joining us. We pull up alongside the other cars and enter the house. From the outside it looks as though it's about to fall down. I'm surprised to find it to be fairly modern, though not very big; inside is one large room and a small bathroom.

Chad looks around, making sure all are accounted for. "Okay, find a space and get your gear set up."

Agents leave for a few minutes and return with sleeping bags and folding chairs. Great, camping again. Jeez, I sure miss my trailer.

I am happy to see that there's electricity and a small air unit running. This is an unexpected surprise.

"Where are we? Who owns this place?"

Chad says, "In the middle of the desert, and we do."

Somebody is getting a little edgy. *"We own it" he says.* It must be on BLM ground. Bet this old house is a layover for federal workers.

We each find a spot in the large room. After putting all the gear against a wall, we meet in the middle, where a table and some chairs are set up. For a moment no one speaks; we just look at one another. For the first time I see the people that have been working so hard to keep me alive. I am moved that so many would give so much just for me. I want to thank them all, but now isn't the time.

All eyes turn to Chad, looking for direction. He looks exhausted, but his posture shows he still commands respect. We wait. He begins to explain our situation. I listen but don't quite follow.

"We will stand down for the remainder of the day and possibly into the evening. Find a spot where you can make yourself comfortable. We will rotate the watch, starting with myself. I want everybody to eat and sleep."

"What about my work?" I ask him. "Daniel gave me instructions. Didn't he tell you?"

"Yes, he told me, but now I am telling you. Stand down."

"What about the outside perimeter?" Ahmad asks.

Chad turns to him. "We've brought in fresh teams, and they are working about a mile out. There's satellite surveillance."

So we are being babysat. People plus satellites; it doesn't get any better than that. Then again, there is a single individual on the other side of the globe that can still get to me. I can't forget that.

"What about the terrorist?" I ask.

"We know he is working this area of New Mexico and either has a hard target in mind or is playing us to allow him to escape."

"What's your guess on that?"

"You are part of the hard target. If he succeeds, we will be occupied, allowing him time to escape."

He has that long look again, the one that makes me want to pee my pants—the look he gives when he is usually right. I'm sweating so hard I'm beginning to chill from the coolness of the air unit.

Needing a minute alone, I stand, excuse myself, and head to the bathroom. There I find a small room with amenities closely plumbed in. The toilet is unique—a large box-shaped object with a two-inch pipe exiting through the ceiling. It reminds me of an outhouse at an old ranch house where plumbing was a luxury. It does not smell; that's surprising. There is no flushing device, but it does have a foot pedal. I kneel down to read the label on the lower front. Suremaid. So this is an indoor chemical toilet. I've heard they're big in countries where water is scarce or water tables are too close to ground level. We are in a remote desert area. Makes sense to me.

I rinse my face in the sink and tell myself, "Get it together. Clear your mind."

I go back to the main room. Ahmad goes into the bathroom next and closes the door. These close quarters are going to be a bit much if anyone gets an attitude.

"Does anybody know how this place gets its water?" I ask, just trying to start a conversation.

"Did you notice the enclosed bin on the east side of the building when we arrived?" Chad says.

"Yes. Thought it might be storage. It's high enough to not allow critters to take food items stored there."

"Yes, but also it has a five-hundred-gallon water container filled by employees working out here and also by the rain catcher on top of the building."

"Thanks. You know I'm curious by nature. That is why I really get into my job."

He glances at me and then turns away. These guys are being pushed to their limit, and I'm beginning to feel it too. Time for this to end.

An agent places a couple of paper bags on the table. "Chow," he tells us.

We take turns going through them. There are small plastic containers marked either "stew" or "rice and beans." I take the rice and beans container.

I look at it for a moment. The instructions on the package read "shake well and eat."

"Add a cup of water and shake it for a minute," Chad tells me. "It is instant. Once shaken, it will heat the ingredients. You can pick them up at any outdoor or camping outlet. Take a spoon from the table and eat."

"Thanks." I follow his advice and open the package. He was right; it's a warm meal. I grab a spoon and chair, and I sit at the table with a few of the others. No one speaks.

I devour the meal. I'm hungrier than I thought, and other than needing a good shot of hot sauce, it's not too bad.

I walk over to the gear along the wall and grab a sleeping bag. I make my spot in the room opposite the stack of gear and sit.

Ahmad is sitting close by. I ask for a pencil and paper. He hands me a pen and tablet from his shirt pocket.

"Thanks." I turn my back from the others. I need my space, even if it's only one square foot.

I mentally recall notes of the past few days. I use a technique to visualize the file cabinet. There are files inside, dated the last few days. I go through them all, recalling events. Suddenly I am overwhelmed with emotions; I'm shaking, and my eyes are filling with tears I'm trying to hold back. I pray: "Please don't let me break down. Please don't let me disappoint the guys, not after what all they have done for me."

I tremble all over, my tears flowing like a West Texas flash flood. I'm trying hard to hide them. Too late; I burst out crying. There is a hand on each of my shoulders.

I look up; Chad and Ahmad are standing on either side of me. They kneel down and look at me with compassion.

"It's okay to shed tears and show our fear; we all do it," Ahmad assures me.

Chad adds, "Let it go. What goes on in this room stays in this room."

"I'm no hero," I say with a sob. "I am just a person with a particular skill that is a little different. I'm not trained like you guys, but I want to be a team player."

"You are," Ahmad tells me. "We all have different skills, and each part is what makes this team work."

Tears roll down my cheeks, and body tremors are reaching deep into my bones.

Chad says softly, "You are facing your inner fears now. Don't be ashamed; every person here has done it, never at a convenient time."

I finally get a grip, and the tears slow to a stop. I sit for a moment, telling myself, "Get it together and make your mind right."

I sit up straight and wipe my face with a hand towel that someone handed me. I begin to get my shakes under control and start to focus.

The team is standing around me. They remind me of gathering pack animals; when one is injured or ill, the pack surrounds it and stays with it no matter the consequences.

I look up at all of them and say, "Thanks, all of you. Daniel gave me instructions to find my true goal. But now I know a big part is not to let you guys down."

Chad and Ahmad stand, and the team members all smile at me. There are no words for these moments. Thoughts and feelings make the bond. I'm now a part of the team.

Thirteen

Everybody returns to their respective spot and sits, waiting. I continue with my notes, looking for any clue as to who this other viewer may be.

There are few on this planet that can view. View and interact with the target—even fewer.

Though Chad had told us all to stand down, my work allows me to do the opposite. While everybody begins to sack out, I stretch out and concentrate.

I close my eyes and hold the image of the target site where the Asian female viewer was. I return to the room with the file cabinets. Each cabinet has a date and target numbers on it. I find the file cabinet with the target numbers used for this assignment. I open it, and there are my notes. I sort through the matrix and look for locations. I return to the target site I want, but the woman is gone. I push aside my feeling of remorse for her to allow for better viewing.

Standing in her room, I look around for possible written evidence. I hear voices in the other room. I move to that room and see a man and a different woman. They are in the kitchen, sitting at a table, talking. They are dressed casually. The man reaches across the table and holds the woman's hand. She is crying, and he is comforting her. She pulls a picture from her shirt pocket. I move to the table and see that the picture is of the female viewer. The older woman at the table is gazing at the photo. She is crying, mourning. The photo shows the female viewer prepped for a funeral. I don't know what to think next. Did I kill her?

Evidently these are relatives, maybe even parents. The photo of the female viewer shows a single gunshot wound to the forehead. That would rule out suicide. Women seldom commit suicide with gunshots to the face. She didn't die from my actions, but apparently someone did not want her telling where she'd been or what she had seen. I step back, leaving them to their grief.

I look around the room for something in writing. Nothing. Someone had to have gone to great measures to ensure no evidence of her being a viewer was found. I move five hundred feet above the house and look in each direction. It's crowded with small houses, narrow walkways, and an unpaved street. I can smell open sewers, probably under the walkways. The walkways all lead to the river, meaning that they are gravity fed. It's a common practice in some countries to direct grey and black water to the nearest tributaries. There are a couple of multistory buildings to the northeast of my location. I move to the top of one.

I see flat, smooth, gray concrete and multiple a/c units. I move to the front of the structure and find an entrance with a metal door. No name or numbers are evident. The front entrance has a double glass door; I move toward it. Inside, two people in uniform are sitting at a desk. I move next to them and read their patches, making a mental note of the lettering. I sure could use the language reference books back at my house.

I can feel intense energy around me. This place is being protected by someone or something. It doesn't feel like another viewer. It's more like a high energy output. While viewing, it's common to sense what you normally would not. I move to various points in the large room. It measures roughly fifty by fifty. I see two elevators with different floor numbers at each set of doors. One set is for basement to tenth; the other, eleventh to thirtieth. Each elevator has an electronic card reader for security. The energy pulse is getting stronger and becoming annoying.

I need to take a break.

I lie still. I mentally go to the file cabinet for this target. I open the drawer and take out a paper and pencil. I note my findings in the matrix and add a side note to have the writing on the patches deciphered. I note the break time, date, and reason.

I need to get some rest. It's still early in the evening, but everybody appears to be sleeping. I doze off; feeling better thinking I have found the home base of the other viewer. I say a prayer for the female and her family.

Then I have that dream again. I mentally task myself to hold on to it and remember all parts of it. I commonly dream of what is about to happen or of multipart puzzles that are a message for someone. I believe I am that someone.

I hear noises, people talking; am I dreaming, or is this real? Struggling to awaken, I go through one level. I have to awaken from seven to ten levels of sleep. At each level, I feel awake, but there is always one particular different part of my surroundings that is not real. I feel a hand on my shoulder and hear a voice. I'm startled to the point that I open my eyes and have to take a deep breath; it's Ahmad.

"On your feet; we're moving."

I try to wake fully, but I'm still struggling. I push up with my arms, trying to stand. These are all symptoms of a deep sleep. Waking suddenly is difficult at best.

I'm finally sitting upright; others are hurriedly packing without much chatter. Chad is on the phone; I'd bet money it's Daniel. He ends the call and instructs everyone to the vehicles. I take a quick glance at my watch. Midnight.

We rush out into the night. It's dark but with a sky full of stars. One thing about being in a remote area of the desert—the sky is limitless. If you want to see infinity, just look up.

We load the vehicles and leave, with Chad in the SUV and me and Ahmad in the sedan. We travel back toward the highway. Everyone is still silent. Ahmad has determination in his eyes. What have they learned?

"Okay, where are we going? Why? I thought a down day was in order."

"We're going to Truth or Consequences, New Mexico, or thereabouts."

"Again? We were just there."

"I'm just following instructions; once we're at the next location, we'll be updated."

"Why are we traveling by land? Wouldn't a helicopter be faster and easier to relocate to these remote areas?"

"A chopper would be fine, except there are a lot of us and lots of equipment. This way we're low profile and mobile. That can't be done with a chopper. I know from experience that once you are in the air, you become a singular target."

Good point. Us in an aircraft with all the team members—not good. But what if you use decoys?

"Why use just one craft? Couldn't you use a few, with some as decoys?" I ask.

"That would be fine if you could control the airways. Once anyone uses a radio, phone, GPS—anything electronic—you can be identified," he tells me.

"We do that—use multiple communication devices."

"Yes, but we can use blocking devices in each vehicle. That is difficult, if not impossible, with multiple aircraft. We can change vehicles rapidly, where you can't with aircraft. And don't forget the expense."

"I understand the need for a variety of weapons, but why so many of each?" I ask.

"We're all trained on each weapon. If need be, we can become a formidable force with only two to four of us."

"These past few days you looked as though you would use one of those weapons on me. Would you really?"

"Maybe," he says, looking at me with a slight glint in his eye.

I return the look. "Really?"

He looks out the windshield, gets a big smile, and says, "No, I would not. But let's not test each other again. We work under enough stress. It's not good to pressure each other."

I sit quietly and consider. He's right. This is a pressure-cooker style of life. When someone is rubbing you the wrong way, let it go.

It's time to reflect on the latest view. I saw a good deal of where the female was from and pinpointed the location on the globe. That building was not marked, and the use of armed guards is not necessarily uncommon. We use them at building entrances all the time. But that energy pulse was different.

Note to self: do gestalts of the building. I don't know if it was being created by something or someone. If something, what would be the need? If someone, why leave such a signature? Did I leave my signature?

"What was with the get-up-and-go gig in the middle of the night?" I ask.

"Our location was found."

"By whom? We couldn't have been in a better place."

"We were found somehow. The perimeter teams, using handheld thermal tracking devices, picked up a thermal image nearing the house. The helicopter found thermal prints as well. The satellite confirmed a solo intruder."

"What helicopter?"

He says, "The one always with us. It has the latest rotor technology. When it's at fifteen hundred feet, it's as quiet as a mouse."

Just when I am beginning to trust these guys, they surprise me. What else are they hiding out there? I think back to my last viewing. Surely I didn't give our position away. I know every trick to not leave a signature. What have I done? I can't tell the others that I was viewing while at the safe house. Now the terrorist is on to us again.

I'll keep it to myself. If they find out, there goes any trust. Besides, if I'm being followed by another viewer, it's more important to find a means to stop her.

Looking out the window, I see those endless stars again. I can't stop thinking about that helicopter that's so quiet you can't hear it. I look to the sky; there is a bright yellow full moon. The helicopter goes unnoticed on a night with a full moon. Hmm.

These desert roads are long and lonely. I try to make out the nearby mountain ranges to determine our true direction, but I can't. Then it hits me.

"Where are the response teams?"

"Out there." Ahmad points out the window.

"Out where?" I glance out the window, seeing nothing.

He says, "There are several teams poised near us. Once we determine the next location, they are notified and intercept us. When we get to the next location, they set up."

"Are they close by?" I ask.

"Sometimes, but not usually."

So we're solo for now. When we are near a major roadway, they close in. I can only stare out the car window, wondering if he's out there.

This terrorist has played cat and mouse with us for days. What is his next move?

"What do you think his next move will be?"

Ahmad wrinkles his forehead. "Don't know. Have to leave all possibilities open."

Good answer. We could lose focus by trying to second-guess this guy. I just can't let go of the mental picture of those that have been killed so far.

We're changing altitude. The roadway is inclining, and it appears we're heading northwest. We're slowing down. The road narrows and changes to gravel.

"I take it these vehicles are four-wheel drive?"

"No, all-wheel drive. With the weight that's being carried, it's enough for any terrain except heavy rock action. The sedan is all-wheel drive too."

We reach a high point crossing this range. The sky is in full view, beyond endless. I can't help but wonder if there are other places like earth with civilized life as self-destructive as we are.

We're at the top of the ridge for a few minutes. The road changes slightly, and we start the decline. We are traveling west, and for a moment I can see across the desert floor. Even though it's dark, the stars light up the sand and rocks. These basins remind me of the size of the sea that they were a long time ago.

Not quite on the flat yet, we take a left onto another gravel road. About a mile on, we take a left into a tree line and approach a shack.

We pull up behind it and stop. Chad exits the SUV and enters the house. A minute or so later, he comes out and signals the all clear.

Ahmad nudges me. "Inside."

I don't hesitate. I exit the sedan and follow him into the house. It's tiny with no windows. I look at my watch. Almost 2:00 a.m.

We stand huddled inside. It's very crowded. "What is this place?" I ask.

"Line shack for tick inspectors and range officers," Ahmad says.

Once our gear is brought in, we lack enough room to stretch out and rest. The alert teams arrive, and are all instructed to make the best of it.

I take a spot near the door. I can't really lie down, so I sit on the sleeping bag and stretch out my legs. It's been a two-hour rush, and relaxing isn't easy. I manage to doze off. As I fall asleep, I wonder who is watching the flock.

I begin dreaming. I see lots of people, aircraft, an airport, and much death. Not really sleeping, I open my eyes. Chad is up, and Ahmad is gone.

"Everyone, on your feet."

I jump up and leave the shack without hesitation. Moving toward the sedan, I see that the sun is just coming up over the mountain range. Where is Ahmad?

"Ahmad?" I ask Chad.

"Surveying the vehicles."

Before he finishes the sentence, Ahmad appears. This time Ahmad and I enter the SUV and Chad gets in the sedan.

We head around the house and onto a dirt road; then we turn left onto a gravel one. With all this hurry-up business, I suddenly realize I'm starving.

"Some breakfast?" I ask hopefully.

"Check the bag in the backseat." Ahmad points with a thumb.

I rummage through a black bag on the seat and find water, soft drinks, and granola bars. This will do for now. "Thanks, how about you?"

Ahmad declines by saying nothing.

We're not traveling as quickly as we were last night since the road is narrow and gravel. After about an hour, we come to a major roadway, NM 525. We turn left and, about twenty minutes later, intersect another, NM 380. We turn left, and I see a sign that reads "San Antonio, 20 miles."

After this many days on the road, I sure wish it were San Antonio, Texas. I could use a stroll down the River Walk with a margarita in my hand.

Fifteen minutes later, we come to a small town. We follow the signs directing us to I-25, and we take it south. We're heading back to Truth or Consequences. I can't help but wonder why.

I ask, "Is our roving team back there?"

"Nervous?" Ahmad asks, smiling.

"Of course, aren't you?" I tell him.

"Not really; we're well protected."

We're driving at a serious pace, but it's okay, he's a competent driver. Besides, he's young and healthy and has good reflexes. Then, suddenly, a change occurs.

I feel the same presence as before. Strong, it seems to be searching.

I look at Ahmad. His face is flushed, his eyes glassy. He doesn't look well.

"Ahmad!" I shout. "Ahmad! Pull over, now!"

He doesn't respond. We're increasing speed, and his body is locked up.

I feel helpless. I must quickly decide whether to try to block the viewer or try to wake Ahmad. Precious seconds slip by as I make up my mind. I've got to do something now!

I kick at his right knee to try to dislodge it from the gas pedal. It works! The car slows, but only for a moment. Ahmad looks at me; there is fear in his eyes.

I grab his right arm and tell him, "Think of something other than the thought being placed in your head."

He is muttering. "What? What? Help me!"

I pull on his right arm and dislodge his hand from the wheel. I have a hold on the steering wheel with my left hand and am trying to stay on the road. Chad sees us swerving and begins to brake. My phone is ringing; no time to answer.

"Ahmad, you've got to concentrate! Think about the team or anything worth living for. Just try to let go of the terrible thought in your mind."

He still doesn't respond and slams down on the gas pedal. We jolt forward.

I pull violently to the right, making the vehicle exit the road. At least out here there's not much difference between being on the road or off of it.

As we begin to leave the road, I turn off the ignition with my other hand. The engine stops. We're still going, but we are finally slowing. After about fifty yards, we roll over several large rocks and slow to a rough stop.

I look at Ahmad and can see that I'm losing him. I begin softly talking to him.

"Talk to me. Listen to my words; concentrate. Change your thoughts. Try not to listen to alien thoughts; they are trying to influence your mind."

One more time, his lips barely moving, he whispers, "Help me, please."

I have him by the shoulders, trying to get him to relax.

His door opens, and Chad is there, looking him over.

I yell at Chad, "Wait! I've got it; I know what is happening to him."

I sit close to Ahmad and tell him, "Try to let go."

He is alive but motionless. He stares into the distance without seeing.

Chad is on the phone, and moments later we're surrounded by an armed team. What good are they in this situation?

While all that is going on, I'm looking directly into Ahmad's eyes, talking to him quietly. "Think of the past couple of days. Think of the mission. Remember how upset you were with me."

He flinches and tries to move his lips.

"Remember, you just wanted to take hold of me and shake me," I say. "Push that thought above the pressure in your head."

He moves his arms and legs, still shaking. Slowly he loses the lost look, and a smile appears.

"Put forward the most blessed event in your life. Turn the negative in your mind to the most positive."

It is working; he is coming around. He shifts his eyes left to right and then looks directly at me.

"That's it," I say. "Look into my eyes. Not just on the surface; all the way through them. You see a calm and tranquil place. Now, with a mighty shove, release the hold on your mind."

He awakens. He sits erect, regaining his posture. Shaking his head, he shifts to open the door. He lurches out, taking small steps.

I exit the car and walk up to Chad. "He'll be all right. He may need a second to find himself, but he'll be functional."

"Good job," he tells me. "We're running short on good agents."

"He didn't stand a chance."

"I know. Influence has no recovery."

Guess he is better informed about my trade than I thought.

"What would you have done with him?" I ask Chad.

"He would have been flown to Bethesda."

"He may have lived but probably would never have recovered."

"It's better than what the other guys do with theirs," he says with a somber tone.

I just look at him. How did he know that? I told nobody. When will all this come together to make any sense?

Fourteen

Onlookers from the freeway begin to gather. Chad tells Ahmad and me to ride with him. We get back onto I-25 southbound. We started out as many, and now we're down to three. The terrorist is only one, but he seems to have the upper hand.

My phone rings. It's Daniel, of course. He asks if I'm okay and thanks me for saving Ahmad. Without anything else being discussed, we hang up.

We pass a sign that reads "Elephant Butte State Park and Truth or Consequences exits 15 miles." The vehicle slows, and Chad looks at a small gas station on the right. We turn in and pull up behind the building, out of view from the road.

He tells us to get out, stretch, and take a break. Now this is different—breaking protocols.

"What next?" I ask Chad as I open the door and step outside.

"The other vehicle may have been compromised. We don't know if the other viewer can find it again, or it may even have been bugged. Joseph may have done it before he was shot. It's being gone over. Grab some water and stretch your legs."

I head into the gas station. There's a small convenience store inside. A few other people are there buying snacks and sodas from the man behind the counter. I get a bottle of water and head back outside.

I wander around, sipping the water; Ahmad is constantly scanning the horizon, and Chad is on the phone. I can't stop wondering if the terrorist is a trained viewer. How did he get to Joseph?

Chad finishes his call, turns, and says, "The terrorist is in the area. Ground intelligence teams have spotted someone matching his physical description and a jeep nearby. Ahmad, is the Alert team in place?"

"Affirmative on the team; got them confirming via the comm."

I look all around us. It is slightly hilly, but I can still see for miles. What team?

"Daniel has instructions for you," Chad informs me.

My phone rings.

"Time to go to work," Daniel tells me before I can say a word.

"Sure," I say, "but where and with what? I left my bag in the sedan."

"No games, Ashlee. I know you have the ability to work without pen and paper. I have faith; so does your Teacher."

"I'll try. I'm not very good at that level." My thoughts stray; when did Teacher come into play with all this?

"Just do it. It's time for this to end; the target is hot." He ends the call.

I look at my cell phone.

"You have your orders," Chad says.

The pressure I'm feeling is immense. This day is starting out badly and is only going to get worse. I'll need to find some space to work, someplace quiet enough to concentrate.

I'm wondering again how Daniel knows so much about my level of training; could it be Teacher? Surely not.

Previously viewed target sites. There are so many, and most of them are in this area. We have spent days chasing them, but to what end? It's possible we've gone full circle and this has all been a wild goose chase. But I have my orders; time to begin.

I search the SUV for a stray pen or pencil, anything I can use as a tool. I don't find what I'm looking for, but I come up with a weapon—a pistol. Just holding it gives me a small measure of comfort and a sense of security. They did teach me to handle small arms, mostly pistols and carbines. I've never used one outside of training, though.

I sit in the backseat; it's almost dark inside because of the tinted windows.

I sit up straight and take a deep breath.

I mentally tell myself to let go of the day. I visualize my file cabinet and open the drawer with the date of the start of this ordeal. I hold the completed paperwork and scan the matrix. At the end of the last page, I begin again as if the target is new. I'm using today's date to try to narrow down the location of the terrorist. I'm sure the true target will come to mind. When the target and the location of the terrorist are confirmed, I will have a true view.

A true view occurs when a viewer uses only herself as the tool. It's pure—no pencils, paper, monitor, computer, maps, nothing—just mental capabilities. I visualize sketching landmarks. I see a small mountain range.

I instruct myself to move five thousand feet above the range. I look in all directions again. To the west, in the near distance, there are small structures. I give a command to move over the tallest structure. Once there I observe a stone building about four stories high. I look in all four directions. There is a major roadway with exit signs. I move to an exit sign and read it: I-25. I look north and south. Nothing of note comes to mind, just compass directions.

I move one thousand feet above the roadway. I see a man walking across a hilltop to the north. He is carrying a cylindrical device on his back. I move to him and hover above him. The device is a long green cylinder with caps on each end. The device might be a tube about five inches around. A short distance from him sits a four-wheeler. He is looking to the east, toward the freeway. I move to the front of the person. He is Asian and is wearing a ball cap, white T-shirt, jeans, and lace-up boots. I feel anxious; is this him? I pause. Could be a local. I need more facts.

I watch him as he walks about fifty yards to the north and up another hill. I follow and see a gas station sitting along the freeway; it's where we are parked. Ahmad and Chad are standing next to the SUV at the station. I'm trying to maintain visual long enough to confirm his intention. He removes the caps from the device and settles it on his right shoulder and begins adjusting a control on the top. I move next to him. I verify his target intention and that the device is a handheld missile-launch weapon. I close in next to him as if I'm standing right there beside him. I reach for the weapon, hoping to deflect his attention long enough for me to help the others.

I see English writing on the weapon. I notice he has a small tablet in his pocket. I grab it and immediately feel the presence again.

Many a viewer has touched a target and sometimes brought back an artifact, one that can fit in the palm of the viewer's hand. There are many such artifacts stored across the world that have been retrieved by viewers. I once retrieved a leaf from a tree in the Amazon. I never got any feedback on it, but it was a job for a medical research team. I have never been allowed to visit the location where the retrieved artifacts are stored. If I survive this mission, I will ask to.

As I begin to move away, I feel as though I'm being slammed to the ground. I feel I'm going to hit the large rocks around me. I sense that a major injury with a grim outcome is in my immediate future. I keep reminding myself that these are only thoughts, images. I know reality and refuse the impression. Not this time, mister. I'll reverse the thoughts and give him a dose of his own medicine.

I'm looking at the gas station where my team is standing. The man with the weapon is poised to fire. What to do first? Warn the team or stop the shooter? I'm still in the SUV; can I get to them in time?

Suddenly, I am overwhelmed by another presence. It hits me like a freight train. The person applying negative influence has disappeared and been replaced by one stronger and more dominant. There is no longer fear or the need to continue the confrontation with the terrorist. I have no time to wonder who or what the new influence is.

I close out the viewing and grab the door handle.

As I jump out of the sedan, I scream, "Incoming! Missile! Run!"

Ahmad is closest to me; he grabs my arm and runs. We run as fast as possible, putting distance between us and the war wagon. Chad runs toward the station. We all have the same goal in mind—survival.

In seconds there's a noise like a train slamming into something, followed by a deafening boom.

Ahmad and I jump behind a large rock near the entrance to the station. Metal parts are flying everywhere. Ahmad is on top of me, trying his best to shield me. We missed the initial blast, but the explosion sent up a large amount of debris.

He yells above the noise. "Stay down! There is more!"

There is a second boom, and even more debris rains down around us. The gas station explodes.

Ahmad looks above the rock and keeps me pushed to the ground.

"Be ready to run in case he has another one. The response team is at his location."

"He only had one device and a four-wheeler."

Ahmad looks at me like he has so many times before; he still can't grasp that I can retrieve so many details. He listens for a moment and then says, "All clear. Suspect has retreated across the desert to the south. He's on a four-wheeler."

We stand up and see Chad walking toward us. He is wounded, holding his left arm; blood is spreading across his shirt.

"You guys okay?"

"Yes," Ahmad says, "we're fine."

"Chad, you're hurt!"

"Yeah, took a hit when I left my vehicle trying to get to you guys. The debris from the second explosion got me."

"We need to get you some help. Is there a first aid kit in the car?" I ask.

"Later; no time now. The terrorist is still loose, and the intended target is still not confirmed."

He's right. The bad guy is being bold with a daylight hit and is quite possibly near his objective. But maybe that is what this was all about. No real target, just harassment to let us know we can be had.

Nevertheless, it's time to get it together. Ahmad is okay; Chad is injured, but not out of action; and I'm still not sure what the hell is going on.

We walk to the road as a black SUV pulls in. Chad walks up to the vehicle and opens the passenger door. A middle-aged man is driving.

Chad tells us to load. We enter the backseat and head south on I-25. On the opposite side of the freeway, fire emergency vehicles and an ambulance are heading northbound. I forgot about people at the station.

"How many people were in the station?" I ask Ahmad.

"Six total, four adults and two children."

"Didn't the SUV block some of the blast?"

"Could have, but there was a propane tank in the back of the building."

There it is again; death and destruction, more than I would have believed possible before now. The hows and whys don't matter anymore, just the capture or death of this guy.

I reflect on my experience on the ridge. I got so close to him but had no control. He was definitely being guarded by someone, and I had been challenged again. But there was more—another person, on my side this time. The list is so short. Teacher, my counterpart that trained with me, and a few others I know of but have never met. Teacher retired, and my counterpart got out of the program. We never meet the newly trained viewers; it keeps the work pool clean. It's better not to know each other's work.

So who could it be? Who has such a level of ability? Who is the other person with the terrorist? Who trained her to be this good? Even worldwide, there are very few of us.

Chad turns toward me and says, "Thanks for saving our hides. When we get to the edge of town, we'll be given another vehicle."

I looked at him closely. Pale skin, deep-set eyes—he looks as though he's aged years over the past few days.

The alert team arrives in two SUVs. The driver-side window opens, and inside is a white male in his midthirties. He's clean-cut and stocky; he looks out of place in all this chaos. Chad signals to us to load. We keep going south.

Chad is sitting in the front. He reaches over with his right hand, and I notice blood and what appears to be a deep cut on his forearm. They shake hands. I will press Chad to have his arm bandaged.

"Hey, Jake, long time no see," Chad says to him. They smile and greet each other as old friends.

We reach the city limits of Truth or Consequences. We take the first exit and then an immediate left, pulling into a parking lot next to an old warehouse. We look around for a moment and pull up to double doors. They open, and we drive in.

This time the alert team is in full view. They are all facing outbound, looking through windows and doors. Ahmad and I exit our vehicle and stand next to a silver sedan. They must have had to dig deep for this one, black being their favorite color.

Chad is talking with Daniel and another person who is well dressed and looks very much in charge.

One of the alert team members approaches Chad. Chad holds out his right arm, and the man displays a first aid kit. Chad doesn't flinch as his wound is treated.

"Take it Chad knows Jake?" I ask Ahmad.

"They met In the marines as young lieutenants working intelligence in Iraq. Became partners with this agency. Chad moved up, Jake went to the alert teams. Both have a hell of a record protecting this country."

"Did anybody follow the four-wheeler?" I ask.

"No. Both the bird in the sky and the satellite spotted the launch, but this guy is good. Once it was fired, he dropped it and escaped."

Ahmad looks at me and grins. "You knew the missile launched was from the terrorist."

"Yes, I can describe it down to the lettering on the tube."

He doesn't say any more, even though his look is full of questions.

I couldn't help but think of the new viewer. Did they see the escape? Did they stop the foreign viewer? I have so many questions, but I have to stay focused; it's time to complete this and get back to my new home on wheels. Too funny—get back to my trailer. Trailer, truck, and the open road; I wasn't laughing. Leave my house and hit the road? Am I really considering that?

"Thanks for pulling me through the ordeal earlier today," Ahmad says. "I can't believe they got into my head."

"Not a problem; you would have done the same for me. If you could, of course."

"When I looked in the back of your eyes, how did you create the perception of tranquility?" he asked.

"Many years of practice, a place I go to quiet my mind."

"Okay, for one moment you had me wanting to break your neck, and then I was in a peaceful place."

"Yes, first I had to get you mad enough to fight. Then I had to calm you down."

"Whatever you did ... Maybe someday we can have a longer talk."

"Sure, just as soon as all this ends."

Chad and Jake walk over to us. Chad gives instructions to get the gear ready and load. Readying for more action?

"Do you need me to begin another session; do you still need an ID on the terrorist?"

"You tell me," he says, cocking his head to one side.

Now I feel like I'm in a pressure cooker. This team has done more in a lifetime than most people conceive of.

"I'll do my best."

"Good answer. We will be confronting him, and probably soon. You have had a sample of his skill; the sooner we find him, the sooner we can end this."

I'm still sweeping dirt and smoke off my clothes. I feel something in the pocket of my jeans. I pull it out and find that it is a piece of paper I got from the terrorist. I must have instinctively put it there during the blast.

I look at it. Blank. I remember grabbing the whole tablet, so I search my pockets.

"I have evidence," I tell Chad.

He looks at me as though I'm bluffing and says, "Don't mess with me." He is giving me that look again. This guy sure needs a vacation, and soon.

"This piece of paper came from his pocket. It's blank, but he had to have touched it."

"Stand still and don't lose that," he says, pointing to the paper.

"I won't."

He gets on the phone with Daniel. I hear him say, "You're kidding!" He is getting a crash course in what I'm capable of. He hangs up and returns to me. Holding out his hand, he says, "I need that."

I hand the paper to him. "I really hope this helps. There must be retribution for what he has done."

"I'll get this to the right people. Remember, we don't get revenge; we gather the info necessary to do our job. Sometimes they are captured or killed."

He walks away and calls for one of the alert team members, and he places the note in a small plastic bag. The agent walks over to the SUV and opens the back door. He pulls out a small black box and removes the paper from the plastic bag. He runs a handheld scanner over the note.

I return to our vehicle, but Ahmad is standing in my way. He wants to say something but is holding back. "Go ahead," I tell him. "I have probably heard it before."

"Chad's right; we're not mercenaries. We take on challenges that others can't or won't. Don't forget we wear the white hats. Keep it professional, no matter what your personal desires are."

"Okay, got it. I thought you were going to comment on my ability to retrieve from the ethereal."

"Don't worry; when this is over, you and I will be having a long discussion."

I don't know where to go with that. Neither good, bad, nor indifferent. He is absolute in keeping me alive and is definitely good at it.

As we reach our sedan, someone calls to us. We turn and find Chad holding the baggie with the note in it. "Good job. We found DNA. We will have results in about an hour."

"I feel like I let you down," I say. "I was going for the whole tablet but failed; I thought I could get it."

"You did fine. You are the only one here that has found and engaged the enemy. You brought forward the only evidence giving us any chance to identify this guy. Don't apologize."

He walks away, taking the bag to his SUV. I stand there and realize he is right. Maybe he will want me to be a team member after all. Ahmad and I get in the sedan. I'm try to relax and clear my mind so I have a clear path of thought. Centering is difficult at times, more so under these circumstances, with someone mercilessly trying to do me in. That is the reason that what I do is considered a discipline equivalent to mastering a martial art. Many struggle to be a master, but few make it.

One way to center is to deflect your thoughts from the target. I think of a proud moment, the day I was accepted as a Mensa member. I had to complete some of the most rigid testing I had ever taken, and then I needed endorsements from other members. It was a true accomplishment.

Fifteen

I'm feeling good, and my mind is clearing. I have many visuals floating about—mostly locations, some not previously viewed. No castling or stray cats; it's time to be exact.

I mentally find my file cabinet in a safe room. I open and retrieve the paperwork from earlier and go straight to the matrix. I run my fingers along all lines and letters. Nothing. Trying to find some clue as to where the terrorist might be, I take the virtual pen and paper from earlier and begin to sketch. I begin outlining a four-wheeler and then a small building, apparently in a remote place.

I give a command to move next to the four-wheeler. It's sitting next to a doorway at the small building. I move five hundred feet above the location, where I look in all four directions and see desert. I've got to find out where I'm at. I move inside the building. There is only one room; it contains a table, two chairs, a bed, topographical maps on the walls, and a wood stove. It's similar to the shacks we have been at. I move to the maps; maybe they will give the location. There are two mountain ranges and a desert displayed. I look for labels and find "USGS New Mexico." I note that it's a government map marked "Elephant Butte," "Ash Canyon," "Mascol Canyon," and "Caballo Mountains." Colored pins have been stuck in these areas. An old road from Truth or Consequences leads through some of these locations.

I'm trying to make a note in the matrix when hear a noise. Somebody walked in as I was reading. I turn and look; it's the terrorist. He is wearing tan camouflage clothing and looks exhausted. He goes to the old bed and lies down. I step next to him and observe. I don't try anything, since his counterpart shows up every time I do. I treat it like a fact-finding mission. I make note of all parts of him and the room.

I move outside, looking for something to tell me the location. I see tracks leading to and away from the doorway. I follow them for about fifty yards. There is a mound of fresh dirt, possibly a gravesite. I move closer; it is a shallow grave. I look inside. There is a male, fifty or so, wearing a tan shirt and jeans. I see a name tag on a pocket of the shirt: Ted Perkins. I look closer at him. No forehead wound. I touch him and determine that his death was recent. There is no deterioration of the skin, and the body still feels firm.

I turn and face the building. It's an adobe shack with no utility hookups. I move to the four-wheeler and look closely for markings. A small placard on the left side reads "US Government." Next to it is a green Ford pickup with "USGS" written on the door. I command myself to return to the interior of the shack and stand next to the terrorist again. I so want to end this now, but I put aside personal feelings and remind myself of what Ahmad said. If I fail, he will move to another location.

I make notes on the matrix and break.

Ahmad is staring at me.

I look at him and smile. "Welcome to my world."

"You were just sitting there. Your eyes were open, and you seemed to be resting."

"I have his location."

We exit the sedan and walk to the SUV, where Chad and Jake are waiting. "I may know where he is," I say to Chad.

He hands me a pen and paper. Why didn't I ask him earlier for these tools? I should have known. I tell him what I saw and he grabs his phone.

While Chad is on the phone, I turn to Ahmad. "Where do we find food?" I ask.

"Ever been on a date and been a little short on cash?"

"Maybe."

We walk to one of the other war wagons being used by the alert teams. He opens the back door. Sodas and water are in one box; fruit bars and chips in another.

"You call this dinner?" I look puzzled.

"Sorry, honey!"

I grab a water and a fruit bar. He really knows how to entertain. Maybe I'll ask him if he ever gets dates.

We walk back to the sedan and get in. Once there, we sit for a moment. He is thinking.

"If your eyes are wide open, how is it you see the target?"

"Simple. Closing your eyes is extra effort. Closed eyes require concentration and muscle movement, whereas open eyes don't. Besides, seeing with your eyes closed and then opening them requires more memory. There's a good possibility you'll lose sight of the target."

He looks out the windshield. I can almost see the thoughts running through his mind. He shakes his head and starts the engine. We drive out of the old warehouse and turn onto a single-lane road. We're moving rather slowly; I'm not really sure he knows where we're going.

"We're stalling for just a few minutes. Teams are behind us and in other locations. It's best we leave just in case you were followed."

"So was the information good?"

"Need time to determine the DNA and positive identity of the person in the grave."

"Didn't I give them the name that was on the shirt?"

"The body found at the shack was possibly a geological survey person. We learned one was going to the shack for a thirty-day stay to monitor underground water tables. A witness in town saw a geological agent leave a local grocery store in a green government truck and stop at a nearby gas station. He met a person there needing a lift. We're thinking it was our man."

"I told you where your man may be."

"Yes, but nobody was there."

"That makes no sense. He was sleeping when I reported back."

"You're being watched and hunted," he reminds me.

I feel sick to my stomach. Had I been so clumsy that those deaths were due to my being followed? I can't bear the thought. I just want to vomit. I'm trying hard to maintain, but I don't think I'm going make it.

"It's not you that erred. We did too. Every time one of the team errs, we all pay the price."

"How did you guys make a mistake?"

"We have had opportunities to take him out but opted not to. We need to learn his target."

I sit still, thinking about mistakes—theirs and mine. I have tried every known means to not be seen. My foe is better than I thought.

"Where did he get that handheld missile?" I ask.

"Fort Bliss."

"From our military?"

"There is a black market for everything. The FBI has arrested one soldier for removing one from the armory. He isn't talking."

"Do they have numbers and letters on the side of the tubing?"

"Yes," he says, "there are control and inventory markings."

"Give me five minutes."

He drives slowly, still waiting for instructions.

I sit up and begin another session.

Immediately I see my cabinet. I open the drawer with today's date. I sort through the papers and find my matrix from earlier. I make a mental note of the numbers and letters from the missile. I then take a moment to gather myself and my thoughts.

I turn to Ahmad. He is staring again. Wish he would stop that.

I write down the information. "This was written on the missile."

Ahmad takes my note and calls it in. Not sure whether he talks with Chad or Daniel.

"They match the inventory list from Fort Bliss. I will be keeping this to log as evidence."

"What else do you have to look at?" I ask.

"The soldier being interrogated works only in the armory. We haven't found the person taking possession or making the deals."

"So all these locations have served a purpose. What do you guys think is the target?"

"There is a team of analysts going through all the scenarios."

Once they have analyzed all the information, they may learn he possibly escaped or even finished his mission. One thing is sure; the Southwest is a smorgasbord of possible sites to create terror in.

I give up. I should have done something to him while he was asleep, possibly smothered him. Instead, fearing that my foe would find me, I did nothing.

My phone rings; it's Daniel. "Are you ready to go back to work? We believe we're close to ending this," he says. "Your information is being analyzed as we speak."

"Who is the analyst on this job?"

"Keep working; more information is better. Our ground and air elements are gathering for possible capture of the suspect."

I start to ask again, but he ends the call. More surprises—someone intervened on my behalf at the ambush site, and now I'm positive there is an analyst. Who could it be? No time to dwell on something I can't answer now. It's time to look for more information on the bad guy. It's now a must that I obtain a true view of the person and target.

I look at Ahmad. "Work time," I tell him. "I'll be a minute."

He doesn't reply.

I sit upright and attempt to stop all the clutter in my mind.

I'm slammed right away with a large white object. I land directly at the target site. Too close. I command myself to step back fifty paces. I'm looking at a large aircraft. The skin of the aircraft is white, and the inscription "Space Flight, Inc." is in black letters on the side of the fuselage.

I close out that site picture and go to my notes in my filing cabinet. Thumbing through them, I find the ones I made previously of such an aircraft. I remind myself not to begin castling. It's easy after viewing targets with similar descriptors, for thoughts to go astray.

I make a note in my matrix, using the correct column. I make a side note that the location has been visited before and that this appears to be the same one. By making written notes, I have instructed my mind to not stray and to stay on target.

I begin the session again, back on target. I am standing on concrete that appears to be very wide and leads to the desert. I walk to each side of the pathway and determine it to be two hundred feet wide. Measuring from the point I am standing at to the other end is ten thousand feet.

I return to the first spot and view another concrete area. Standing over it, I see that it appears to be connected to the first concrete road. I make note of all the various concrete paths and their connections. One of the concrete paths leads to a large structure. There is an entrance with three large bay doors.

I move five hundred feet up and determine that the location is the same one I had viewed earlier. I look around and try to determine if any people are on the premises.

I follow a two-lane road from the bay doors. At about a quarter of a mile, there's a small structure, again the same as previously seen. Above the doorway to the structure is a sign reading Security.

I command myself to move to the interior of the larger structure. The same aircraft I saw in the past session is there. I make notes in my matrix columns.

I notice several people moving about inside the hangar, and I move among them and listen. Lots of technical talk with a suggestion of running out of time. Something is different; where are the security personnel? I move to the bay doors and look in each direction. There is a man in uniform walking along the north wall. He stops at each door and shakes it.

Another man appears from a doorway labeled Restroom. They walk to a small truck parked near the smallest craft. I move next to them and listen. One tells the other that the checklist is complete. The other says, "Time to get back to the guard shack." I follow them to the shack, and one of them exits the truck. Once inside, he places a microphone up to his mouth. They are talking, going through radio checks.

Listening closely, the one in the truck says, "Bosses and passengers will be arriving soon."

The one in the shack smiles with a slight smirk. "How could I forget?"

I close the view and write all descriptors.

I mentally draw a straight line on paper and make three slash marks along its length. A time line tool will help determine if the people meeting here are in present time or another date. This becomes positive feedback if it's in the present. Above the time line, I make note of today's date and time.

I run my fingers over the line, looking for some feeling as an indicator. There's warmth from my index finger, which is hovering over today's date. I repeat the procedure with the same result. I make a note and return to the target site.

Entering the larger craft, I see envelopes lying on each seat. Each is labeled with a name. After reading them, I realize three are names of heads of state. Four others are well-known corporate names.

I note all and break. Got to tell someone, now!

We're still idling, barely moving, Ahmad is waiting for instructions. I instinctively call Daniel. There's a huge noise. I hang up before making a connection.

The windshield of the sedan is shattering. The sound is like a severe hail storm. Looking outside, I see the sky is clear. Ahmad slams on the accelerator. He yells for me to get down on the floorboard. I hesitate for just a second and then do as he says.

I hear him giving out coordinates. We're on a feeder road just outside some town along I-25. Suddenly what is happening becomes all too real. I feel that fear again—absolute terror to the bone. We are being ambushed.

Ahmad is trying hard to see out the windshield, but it has been splintered on the driver side. I try to get a visual of anything useful, but my side is also cracking. We're flying along and entering the freeway. Then there's a loud thud and we're off the roadway. The noise is deafening; it's actually painful.

All this happens within seconds. Our vehicle is on its side and sliding. We hit something solid and come to a stop. I'm flung forward, slam into the windshield, and then whip backward into my seat. My whole body is in pain. I glance to the left before blacking out. I'm sinking into endless darkness leading nowhere. I'm not afraid but still don't want to go there. I feeling as though I'm moving along an automated walkway. I begin to see images of the past and try to stop them.

I have no control; my feelings are running rampant. I'm beginning to see recent images and feel as though there is an end coming, maybe forever. The images stop, and there is a bright light.

I feel my feet dragging. In a moment I realize I'm still alive, and I open one eye. There are men in black uniforms pulling me away from the sedan. I can't open one eye; it feels warm and wet. My head is beginning to throb. My whole body is in intense pain, and I can't hear. Where is Ahmad?

I see two other agents pulling a body. He is not moving.

The sedan is lying on its passenger side. The front of the vehicle is smashed.

I try to sit up, but someone pushes me down, saying, "Lie still; you're bleeding."

They begin to patch me up. I can't stop staring at Ahmad; he's so still. *Please be alive,* I pray.

It seems hours go by before an SUV pulls up and Chad heads toward me.

"You have anything to report?" he asks as he approaches.

I am startled at first. What? He's not asking about our condition? Oh well. I sit up and report. Even with all that is going on with my body, I believe I have remembered all my notes. I tell him about the airfield and all the particulars of the aircraft.

"Is there more?" Chad asks.

"No. What happened?"

"Ambush. Used an automatic weapon, probably a forty caliber."

I don't know weapons, only that they commonly are in the wrong hands. That is why I'm glad there are those who believe in bearing arms to protect us.

He starts to walk away, and almost yelling, I ask, "What about Ahmad?"

"Coming around; ate the steering wheel. He'll definitely need dental surgery."

I can't believe this is happening. I just can't come to terms with it. My phone rings, and I answer.

"You pass everything on to Chad?" Daniel asks.

"Yes."

"We have a second viewer; they are trying to run interference. You're not leaving a signature. Hard to find you before the others do. Think of what you're doing so they can follow."

I lie there racking my brain. I'm no rookie and have been in many other hot situations, always making sure I'm not seen.

"It's not unusual for target sites to put barriers up for protection against viewers. Some are etheric, such as a visual perception as a false image leading the viewer to think he is off target. Then there are physical barriers, commonly electrical. Electricity is sometimes known to disrupt the viewer's metabolism, breaking their concentration. It makes it very difficult to penetrate the target without being noticed. Commonly the viewer will be so involved in getting through they will drop their guard and leave their signature."

"Good point. Do you know how to penetrate a target without being noticed?" Daniel asks.

"During the eighties and nineties, teams would take extra time to ensure it. Sometimes it takes days, even months. I didn't work with them but was taught by those who did. Of course, you already know that."

"Can you do this? Do you have that skill level? I'm well aware of your instructors, but I need to hear it from you. We're out of time. Action is needed."

"I'll never make a promise or guarantee, but it would be my best effort to date. I also have Chad's information he had me do as a sidebar."

He hangs up, and I can't help but wonder who the other viewer is. There are few of us, and we seldom communicate.

I look to my right and see Ahmad. His lips are swollen, and his shirt is covered in blood. I stand; we would have hugged, but we just didn't have it in us. We both look at the car.

"Where did the ambush come from?" I ask.

"As we passed the edge of town, there was an old, abandoned two-story clothing store." Struggling with words, he takes a deep breath. "Eyes in the sky spotted a heat signature from one of the windows. When they radioed me, the firing had already begun."

"Let me guess, a stolen automatic weapon?"

"Yes, last night from a local national guard armory."

"He get away again?"

"Yes, but this time he is leaving fingerprints and DNA everywhere. At least we should be able to determine who he is."

"How did he get away? And don't tell me on a four-wheeler."

"A man was seen running out the back of the store and entering a government vehicle."

"The USGS truck—a good disguise to blend with traffic on local streets."

"Yes, no need for a high-speed vehicle when you can just blend. He has used this consistently. Take a break. You need to get some ice on that face, let that swelling settle."

We look at each other, battered, bloody, frustrated, and fatigued. Makes one wonder when all this will end.

Sixteen

Chad waves a hand over his head, mustering us around him to receive further instructions.

Chad points to Ahmad and me, saying, "You two come with us. Alert teams reposition."

The three of us load into the SUV with Jake at the wheel and head south on I-25.

I'm trying to get my mind right. I watch the desert town we are leaving. Funny how all of them look so similar but each has its own personality. Maybe when this is over I will take my RV and travel to as many as I can to experience each one.

We go a short distance and head into town. We turn left and then right. What are we doing? We've already broken a protocol by using only one vehicle. The other vehicles all scattered in different directions earlier.

"What's with the detours?" I ask Ahmad.

"Simple tactic—confuse a shooter setting up an ambush."

"What about the eyes in the sky and the alert teams?"

"All in place. We are safe in this vehicle. Ones built like this one don't grow on trees. We're having one flown in through Holloman AFB, along with more help. We are to maintain evasive action pending further notice. Information is being communicated to us now."

I've got to get one of those comm units someday. But then again, do I want them in my head 24-7? I've got enough going on in there as it is.

"Has the terrorist's identity been determined yet?"

"No, it's common to be recruited at an early age from provinces that don't document newborns. They begin training almost at birth and create the monster we're chasing and who is chasing us."

Finally he elaborates on something. Maybe this partnership is growing.

"We have an information network that gives us information on most known terrorist training camps. They train these people to enter this country by whatever means they can, with nothing more than the clothes on their back. They're known as OTMs: 'other than Mexican.' They come through our borders constantly, and we usually end it quickly. This is the exception."

"Him being the exception is only due to his viewer, isn't it?"

"We believe so. He was trained for this mission, but an edge like that has proven deadly."

"Don't forget Joseph. Do we know why he went over?"

"They have his mother and sister. The FBI is on it; we think they are being held outside Baltimore."

"What do you mean they have his mother and sister?"

"It's a quick way to create an insider—kidnap his family and tell them to agree or else."

Again, I'm at a loss for words. You hear about such things in countries under government suppression. But this is the USA, and the terrorist is not homegrown, but foreign.

"Has it been determined that our bad guy killed the first two agents?"

"Yes, he stole a vehicle out of Laredo and was told of your possible whereabouts. Joseph was part of your original alert team. He set the bug in your trailer."

I need no further explanation. The first two dropped their guard but didn't give me away. When I see them in the hereafter, I will apologize for thinking poorly of them.

"I have worked for Daniel many times and never once faced the situation I am in now," I tell him.

"Same here."

"Why doesn't this guy just escape? He knows we're onto him."

"Apparently he wants you dead, the only witness to his physical identity. That would destroy any future missions."

"What is his mission?"

"Hard to tell; there is so much happening out here. But we believe we will know soon."

We turn onto a roadway leading east. It is unmarked, but the two lanes are well paved. The sun has reached high noon; it's good to have it to your back this time of day, but it was, unfortunately for us, blazing through the passenger side windows. We go a few miles and come to a road leading south. I miss the sign, but I think it is an entrance. I have become confused at this point.

Underground control rooms, unmarked missile sites, military bases, and mysterious airports in the middle of the desert. When this ends, I'll not read a mystery novel for some time. When I get home, I'm going to grab Eric, load him into my new RV, and go anyplace he desires.

I'm noticing small signs posted along the road reading "Property of Bureau of Land Management." We have been on government property for a while.

"So what's with so much government property?" I ask Ahmad.

"New Mexico has nearly nine million acres under federal and state management. Mostly desert. It's open to the public for assorted reasons, mostly hunting."

I should have known he would be an encyclopedia. These guys have just got to know it all, and thank goodness they do.

We go another two miles. There is absolutely nothing. I don't know why they call this high desert; it should be called nothing desert. One thing I do know: prior to the expansion to the West and pre–Civil War, only Indians, Spaniards, and Mexicans lived out here. The thing they all had in common? Gold.

I learned that from an archaeological remote viewing session for the New Mexico Institute of Indigenous Studies a few years ago. As usual, I wasn't given any feedback. Sometimes the information gathered by the viewer is not what they are looking for, but it has some hidden meaning that is known only to the client.

We pull off about one hundred yards into the desert, and we park and sit. I had been so involved in thought and conversation with Ahmad that I had forgotten Chad and Jake were in the front seat.

Chad turns in his seat and looks at us grimly. "We're alone. The alert teams are not prepared to follow us through this terrain. The helicopter has been ordered to stand down. They're entering private air space and waiting for approval. The satellite has been diverted for another ongoing investigation."

I look at Chad and Ahmad; I just can't believe this—winging it, with me being the least prepared.

Chad says, "Get out and go to the back of the SUV." We exit and do as we're told. He opens the rear hatch; there are four black cases inside. He opens one and begins rustling through it.

Ahmad is keeping a vigil, and Jake is sorting out water bottles. I stand there wondering what is going on. Each case has weapons of various sizes and calibers, definitely personal choices. One of the boxes is missing the person it was packed for. I know it wasn't put together for me.

Chad opens one and removes the weapons and ammo. After he places them on his person, Ahmad and Jake do the same. They are well armed and look ready for a fight.

Nothing is said; they interact as one. I definitely feel like the squeaky wheel. What do I do, ask for a gun?

I step next to Chad. "There is another case; do I arm up?"

"No."

"Why not? I may need to defend myself."

"That is our job; you stick to yours. By the way, the next time you have information and don't pass it along, I will deal with you personally."

How did he find out I did that session and didn't tell him about it? Daniel and the other viewer?

"I didn't mention it sooner because the information wasn't solid and I wasn't sure if it applied."

"That was the only mistake I'll allow regarding information. All information, no matter how big or small, is to be passed along. Do we have an understanding?"

"Understood. It won't happen again."

He didn't say another word, just walked to the front of the truck and stared out across the horizon.

How did he know that? Out of fear I did not tell him I was seen by the other viewer. I had worked up a viewing and didn't relay the facts, leaving the team in jeopardy. I think he knows.

Ahmad steps close and tells me, "You're in a bad light with him right now. We share all information."

"It wasn't that I wouldn't report it; it just looked bad that I had led the terrorist to us."

"You forget, sometimes we lead them to us so we know where they are. Don't ever withhold information; it appears like you're hiding something—or worse, using us."

I thanked him for the advice and support. They were right; a team must know what each member is thinking at all times, and trust must be absolute. I have worked alone for so long I have lost any teamwork skills I had.

"So is the target close by? I have viewed so much I've gotten a little confused which desert we're in."

"We're unsure at the moment; gearing up for the possibility of a hostile contact. All information leads us here, but we lack one element: where is the terrorist?"

So they do it too. For a target to be a solid lead, the terrorist and location have to be linked together. I have not done that either. I've viewed all these locations, but I've never put the terrorist at any one of them.

Chad tells us to get into the SUV. Once in, the AC is welcoming. Nothing like the desert to heat up the skin.

He pulls out a map and begins to tell us where to head next. "We're approximately two miles from the entrance to the newly constructed SpacePort. There is going to be a launch later today with three heads of state onboard. Four of the other passengers are heavy hitters in the financing of global industries. We don't have a schematic of the location, but we do have an eyewitness."

All eyes are on me, looking for answers. I take a moment and then begin.

Pointing to the map, I say, "This road leads to a security shack manned by one guard. There is another guard on the move, mostly by small truck. The road from the shack leads to what looks like a huge earth home. There is a main entrance on the north and hangar bay doors on the east and west. The south side has glass walls. The structure was well thought out to conserve energy."

"What's the distance from the shack to the curve in the road, and to the structure?" Chad asks.

"A quarter mile from the shack to the curve; same distance from curve to the structure."

"The width of the road and the terrain along the road?"

"Two-lane black top with small rock, sand, and loose dirt. Similar to what we are parked on." I add, "There is an adjacent runway leading north and south, two hundred by ten thousand feet."

They are absorbing every word. I finally feel part of the team, more than a paper-pushing information gatherer.

"The satellite was diverted earlier to scan the location. Forward teams for the heads of state are there and searching the premises," Chad says. "At present, all seems clear. We're not sure this is the target, but all evidence indicates it will be."

"Our alert teams are being diverted to parallel the dignitary convoy from Fort Bliss. We're alone, and the terrorist, as far as we know, is still in country. With all this going on, resources are stretched to the max. What we have in this war wagon is all that is available."

He makes eye contact with each member. "Communication is still good, but we're short on backup."

No one flinches; they are well trained and ready. I feel like a fifth wheel again.

Chad looks at the team members. "Trojan horse," he says. "See if we can flush him out."

They nod their heads in acknowledgment. I hope it's a code name for a special weapon hidden away under the SUV.

"Ashlee, we need you to be found," Chad tells me. "You will be the beacon to our location. You will be in the rear of the war wagon. Ahmad will drive; Jake and I will be paralleling. Once he attacks the SUV, we respond."

I'm looking at him and want so badly to interrupt, but my lips will not move. I have a lump in my throat, and I want to run away. Does he not see me shaking? No words can explain what is going on with my mind.

I manage to swallow and gasp. "Wait, I'm to be inside this vehicle?"

"Yes, you're the Trojan horse."

"Really, leaving me in the rear of the SUV? You know he will pounce on it. Then I wait while you guys try to find him?"

"You've got the big picture. I'll call in the plan and alert the agencies at the terminal."

"This is our turn to distribute payback." Chad again exchanges glances with the team. "Instead of waiting to confirm his target, we will create one."

We exit the SUV. Chad turns, steps a few paces away, and calls in. Ahmad and Jake are double-checking gear and supplies. They stand facing each other, looking over each other's gear.

I would speak up, but my mouth is so dry I can't swallow. I would run away, but my legs will not move. They cannot be serious.

"Do you agree with this?" I ask Ahmad.

"It's a solid tactical plan. If we don't take him out, we will have time to divert the dignitaries traveling there. If it all goes bad, the last man standing will give a signal to the convoy to stand down."

"I am going to point out one fact—me in the SUV. What if he has another missile?"

"This vehicle can take an IED, small-arms fire, and most handheld missile launches. You will be fine."

"You'll be driving, Ahmad; aren't you concerned?"

"Not like you'd think. We have a remote control that is tuned in to this vehicle. It was designed to allow the vehicle to be used as mobile cover in a fire fight. You'll be fine."

Chad stands next to us and begins telling us the final plan. "Daniel is in agreement. We are to move ahead. We have a few hours; the agencies at the SpacePort, Washington, DC, foreign security forces, and private security for the corporations will be put into defensive posture at the SpacePort. Civilians are to be put into lockdown at the facility.

"We have an extra case of ammo; don't be stingy. And double-check your water. Communication up; use your implants.

"We're gambling that this is his target. As I have repeatedly said, nothing is absolute. Most likely he is doing just what we are—planning and preparing. Remember, he has the upper hand—surprise. He has a four-wheel-drive vehicle, topographical maps leading to the location, and is well armed, not to mention his skill level is backed with a viewer."

Chad hands me a small black radio that fits in my palm. "This is voice activated and satellite monitored. Both the team and the communication center will be listening and will respond as necessary."

He tells the others, "Step outside, grab clothing in the back, and dress for the terrain."

They do as they're told, going to their boxes and retrieving tan camouflage clothing. Ahmad opens the spare box and sorts through it. They close the hatch; time for me to do my part.

I try to clear my mind but just can't. I've got to divert my thoughts; I have only one weapon for this fight: my mind.

If I survive the day, I will travel with the truck and fifth wheel. Cruise through southern Colorado; the weather is cooler in the summer. Eric will be sitting next to me, not a care in the world. I think about my dogs being gone. Maybe we'll get a puppy.

Before me is a file cabinet. I remove a file with today's date, sort through the papers, and review the matrix. I find the location information of a foreign business building. I go there and pass around it and through it, being as reckless as possible. There it is—the feeling of being watched. I do not like it. I'm being viewed. I feel the presence of my anonymous viewer running interference for me. I almost see an image standing off to my left, but not quite. The person that is trying to find me should have it by now. I lit myself up like a lighthouse on the coast of Maine.

I retreat from the building, and the other presences leave as well. I organize my file and put it in the cabinet, allowing a few extra minutes to let myself be found.

I step out of the truck for a breath of air and to tell Chad what I had done. The team is standing at different points, watching. They are in tan camouflage gear and well armed. The real danger now is that we don't know where or how well the enemy is armed.

I look at the team; they know I'm scared. They never show any concern—cool and collected. If they have fear, it's well hidden under a mask of confidence.

"Why do I have to be inside? Why not out here, or be run back into town?" I ask Chad. "Not that I don't want to be an active team member, but I'm just a viewer."

"Your part is most important. You have let them know our location and you must stay here as the beacon. We don't know where he is. You are needed to draw the enemy to the fight. We've got to end this or he will win."

Why does he always have to be right?

"I do have another choice," I tell Chad. "Bio locates inside the truck."

"Already been discussed. Your signature is attached to you, and it requires your presence."

Who is he talking to? I hope we can meet when this over. I ask no further questions, just mentally prepare to be riding in a remote-controlled target. That is not covered in any manual I am aware of.

Then I remember that if I leave my signature to be followed, it will be seen here, where these guys are preparing. I approach Chad. "Wait a second; I made sure to be found, and remember, they have viewers also."

"Yes, I'm aware of that. A viewer trained in interference is being used to protect us all from other viewers. You were immediately found and our location determined by them."

"Are you serious? All that in a few minutes?"

"Yes, we have a team of analysts deciphering the information being gathered. We have a silent team member, another viewer tasked with protecting us ethereally, running interference."

I'm blown. Is there anything these guys cannot do? They better not plan on letting me go after this.

"What is that weapon on a sling?" I ask Chad.

"M4."

"Looks capable of a long shot. Probably good in all this open country?"

"Effective up to five hundred yards; any farther than that is the alert team's concern."

"But they are away."

"Guess I better let this guy get up close to use this effectively." Chad taps his rifle, grinning at me.

He is smiling, but I'm not. These guys are able to find humor in the worst of times. Guess it's a natural escape when you're afraid.

"Say this guy shows. Where will his weapon supply come from?"

"He bartered with a soldier at Fort Bliss and burglarized a national guard armory in Truth or Consequences. Since we haven't gotten word of similar offenses, he would probably acquire weapons from the airfield after neutralizing a couple of agents on the ground there." Chad points in the direction of the SpacePort. "There are agencies doing a sweep of the airfield and hangar. They will have weapons."

"Are you guys deliberately letting this guy know where to find weapons for this setup?"

"We're only making it look like you're on your way to the airfield. We intercept too soon and he'll escape. We would never know who or what was his mission."

I can't believe this—letting a terrorist with skills none of us has ever seen before steal weapons. Ones that will be used against a vehicle I'm sitting in. Can anyone say "fast and furious." Sounds like the gun running operation that's been all over the news lately.

I walk away and approach Ahmad. "I understand this guy will have a chance to steal weapons?"

"We cannot allow him to think otherwise. You have been briefed; no more questions."

"I'm in that vehicle and will be taking fire from him. Did anyone think to ask if I agreed to this plan?"

"One more time, you're what he wants. You know him on sight, you have seen his country of origin; you disabled one of their viewers, located a possible terrorist safe haven on foreign ground, flushed out their remote viewer network, and in general fouled up his plan. If we fail, there is no other chance to make up for the deaths and he could possibly complete his mission. All of our current intelligence points to this location."

He's right. In the world of remote viewing, I had a continuous site picture here. He made extensive effort to travel here, and the location viewed has high-profile targets. There were multiple viewing sessions without aid of a computer, pen, or paper. A true view.

I walk back to the SUV wishing I had my notes. I sit inside and take a deep breath. As I look out across the horizon, I see endless blue skies and tan, flat, rocky desert. A satisfying sight.

I tell myself to open the file cabinet.

I remove the file dated today. There are many papers, matrices, drawings, and summaries. So much information, and all led to the SpacePort. I have a visual of a man: tan ball cap, fair skinned, clean-shaven, five feet nine, stocky, tan shirt and shorts, tan lace-up boots. I move closer and see that it is the terrorist. I move back fifty feet. He is looking down. I look down and see a body. A police officer. Blood is oozing from his throat. I watch as he makes a final gurgle of breath. I look at the terrorist. He removes the officer's gun belt and throws it into a patrol car parked behind them. He gets into the car, removes the keys from the gun belt, and starts the engine.

He drives south on a two-lane blacktop road. I look around for markers and see none. I move five hundred feet above and follow. I recognize the road; it's the one we traveled on to the airfield. I move one mile in front of him. I see a black SUV parked on the side of the road. It's us.

"Break."

I must tell the team. I get out of the vehicle and run to the others and relay my facts in person rather than using the radio, in case we're monitored. They hang on my every word. Chad tells me to get back into the SUV and lock it. He instructs the others to scatter and get ready.

"What if you guys need in? Will I have control of the doors?"

Chad is walking away quickly and yells over his shoulder, "Yes, we all have electronic keys."

He blends into the terrain, and I run to the SUV. Once inside, I do as I was told. I wait.

My quick thoughts tell me that this was the target all along. So this *was* a true viewing. All of the other locations where either logistical or diversionary. I just happen to be an added feature for him.

It's so quiet that I can hear my heart pounding. My breaths are short, and sweat is dripping from all pores of my body. I'm not trained for this, and I do not care to be.

I watch out the rear window in the direction the police car will come from. It comes into view, moving slowly. If an officer is driving, he will slow to ensure we belong there, since this road is closed due to the high-profile people coming to make the flight.

It's closing in, and it moves close enough so I can see inside. I feel absolute fear run through me. The car moves up and is soon beside the SUV. There is a person in a uniform at the wheel. Looking closer as it creeps past, I see the slain deputy sitting upright behind the wheel. That means the terrorist is still out here and is aware that we are here too.

There is no gun fire, no yelling or talking over the radio. Where is everybody? I never knew silence could be so disturbing.

Chad went off to the west, Ahmad to the east, and Jake to the north. The agencies at the airfield have the south covered. Gunfire erupts behind me. There is no telling who or how many.

The shooting stops, and I look out the windows, trying to make out silhouettes. There are none. Surely these guys have binoculars in here. Just as I reach over the seat to grab a black bag, the locks pop open and the engine starts. My heart slams so hard I think it will bulge out of my chest. I swivel in my seat and see a person outside the driver-side door. I let out a scream. Please let it be one of ours!

The door opens. Ahmad jumps in. Sweating fiercely, he grabs the steering wheel. His hands are bloody.

He looks at me, a deep, drawn look on his face. I'm afraid to think of the others.

"Chad and Jake?" I ask him.

"Jake got it. The terrorist wounded him and overpowered him. Now he is better armed than before."

"Chad?"

"We closed in on him when he struggled with Jake; Chad got a shot off. He wounded him, but not before the terrorist got a shot off in return. He got me in the shoulder with Jake's M4. When Chad shot, the terrorist didn't go down.

"I went down and rolled off to a ravine," Ahmad explains hurriedly. "Chad radioed to secure the SUV. So here I am. I didn't answer so I didn't give away my position. Then I crawled here. The terrorist turned his attention to Chad."

The cool air from the air conditioner is helping to calm us down.

"Is there a medical kit in here?" I ask Ahmad while I fumble through a bag.

"Yes, but no time. We have to move you. Chad is giving us a window to escape."

We both look out the windows, scouring the area for Chad. Ahmad is shifting gears and looking over his right shoulder as if to back up. I hear a noise so loud I don't notice Ahmad grunt and push air out of his lungs. He falls onto the steering wheel.

I can't hear, can barely see. Ahmad is slumped over the wheel. I can't stop the loud shrill in my ears. It's all too familiar.

I look around and realize the SUV is slanted to the left. I can't think clearly, but I'm fighting the urge to get out. I smell smoke and look frantically around but can't see anything. My vision is still blurred, but

I can see well enough to determine that there are no flames around the dash or inside the car. The flames must be in the engine compartment. What happened?

Slam! This time the noise comes from the rear of the vehicle. I pitch forward, and my head hits the windshield. I'm barely conscious. Trying hard not pass out, I manage to sit up and look around. Nobody. But something is still pounding us. My face is wet, warm, and oozing blood.

Ahmad is slumped onto the seat, not moving. I'm not sure of anything; still fighting the urge to get away. Then I hear gunfire. If I didn't know better I'd swear it's coming from underneath the SUV. Chad must have made it there. Good! When I get a chance I'll let him in, and we can get the hell out of here!

I force myself into the backseat, looking out in the direction of the gunfire. I don't see anyone in the distance, but continuous gunfire is hitting the SUV and all around us. Another round of gunfire is coming from underneath. It's got to be Chad.

Voices are coming from Ahmad's radio, but between him lying on it and the ringing in my ears, I can't make out what is being said. I grab mine, and it's the same—just a loud echo.

I unlock the SUV and crack the door opposite the gunfire. I stick my head out and look underneath, where I see the bottom of a pair of desert camo boots. I ease the door shut and take a deep breath. He is just under the passenger-side door. If I can just give a signal, I can open the door on the opposite side. The only way is to jump out and make physical contact.

Bullets are flying everywhere now. I look over the seat at Ahmad; he's still out. I see his holster, and I remove the pistol. My training with firearms is minimal, but I want a chance to defend myself and the team if necessary. It's not complicated: point and pull the trigger.

I tuck the weapon into the waistband of my jeans. I move to the door opposite the onslaught of gunfire, crack the door open, ease out, and fall to the ground, rolling toward the engine.

I'm still not seeing clearly; the glare of the sun on the asphalt isn't helping. I reach under the vehicle with my left hand and tap on the bottom of the boots, yelling, "The door is open; roll toward me!"

I roll back toward the door and try to get up on one knee. I can't get up; my knee is racked with pain. I instantly grab it, and my hand comes away wet with blood. I feel the boots underneath the car pushing, wanting to come my way.

I open the door and throw myself in. Ahmad is wounded, I'm wounded, and no doubt, with all those bullets flying, Chad is wounded. Where is he? Let's get the hell out of here!

More rounds are slamming into the side of the passenger door. This guy is really pissed off.

I feel a push. Someone enters the vehicle, and the door closes. I wipe the sweat and blood from my eyes and scream. It's not Chad but the terrorist! I'm frantic! What do I do now?

He is pale, glassy-eyed, and shaking; his face and shirt are covered with blood. But he's alive and armed. He moves his lips; I can't understand what he is saying.

"You just could not leave this alone," he says, glaring at me with hatred.

I am shaking, waiting for him to shoot me. I manage to choke out, "Leave this alone and let you complete your mission, wiping out the SpacePort?"

"You killed my daughter. You have killed my family. You're no better than me."

I don't understand what he is talking about, and we don't have time for a long dialogue at the moment. I know only that he is looking at me with one intention.

He reaches down to his side, and his hand comes out holding a pistol. He points it at my forehead. His hands are shaking. I've got to do something fast.

I ease my hand into the waistband of my pants and grip the pistol. Even though I know it's my only means of defense, I hesitate. His grip on his pistol tightens, and I remember the faces of all the people he has killed.

With no more hesitation, I pull my pistol and point it at him. He looks at it and grins as if to laugh. "Go ahead," he says. "Finish this; you will be a big hero."

I look him in the eyes, seeing all the people who are dead or suffering. I squeeze the trigger. I squeeze again, and again. Nothing happens—no bang, no recoil, nothing.

The terrorist is laughing lightly now. "You aren't even smart enough to check to see if it is loaded. How did you get this far?"

I lay my back head against the door and close my eyes, whispering a prayer my mother taught me: "Spirit, when I leave this world, may those loved in this life welcome me to the other side." I visualize my grandparents and my dogs greeting me and being happy together.

I feel warm air over my head with a trickle of light in my eyes. *This is what you feel at the end,* I think. I hear a loud, sharp ringing noise. I wait for the pain.

Then I hear screaming; I open my eyes. The terrorist is falling backward against the door, fresh bullet holes in his face. I look up and see Chad outside; his weapon is at his side. But he must have opened the door to shoot him.

Next Ahmad sits up, grinning, with a pistol in hand. It's too much to comprehend; what just happened?

"Always carry a spare," Ahmad says with a chuckle.

I sit up and grope my knee; it's still bleeding and extremely painful. Looking at Chad, I see he is bleeding too. Guess we all got it.

"What were you going to do without your weapon drawn when you opened that door?" I ask.

"Earpiece," Chad says. "Communications said that Ahmad was down but his vitals were stable and he was awake. I knew he was in the SUV, so I had comm tell him that when I opened the door it would be his chance to take out the terrorist. They relayed the message. When I walked up and saw the terrorist, I had them tell Ahmad his location in the vehicle. Simple."

"What if Ahmad hadn't gotten the message?"

"Don't know; didn't work out that way."

"How long were you conscious?" I ask Ahmad.

"Most of the time; it all worked out as planned."

"As planned? I don't remember any plan that allowed him to nearly kill me."

"No, that was planned as the scenario changed. You still have much to learn," Chad tells me.

Chad steps away from the SUV and calls Daniel. Ahmad gets out and walks to the other side, opens the door, and pulls the terrorist out. He drags him to the driver side and leaves him on the ground, and then he gets back into the SUV.

I am rummaging again for the first-aid kit.

"What did he mean when he said I killed his family?"

"We're still not sure who he is. Like I told you, to motivate these guys to do the job, or to not defect while on the job, they hold their families hostage. Evidently you found his daughter, the viewer; and you can figure out the rest."

I'm sick to my stomach. Even though there are people on the planet like that, to have to deal with them one-on-one is a bit overwhelming.

"There's a good possibility that they held his family hostage pending the outcome of his mission. We will probably never know the full extent of the family situation," Ahmad explains as we both look for that first-aid kit. "There was a fire at the office building you viewed at the Korea and China border. The fires consumed it, and it was lost."

"Was there an impulse machine there?"

"Seems so. Supposedly it was strong enough to disrupt a human body. But then again, we'll never know; it wasn't found after the fire was extinguished."

Chad puts away his phone and gets back into the SUV. He and Ahmad both look like they want to say something, but they remain silent.

There we three sit, wounded and battered. We can't find the first-aid kit. Chad asks if I need a tourniquet for my knee. It's not that bad compared to the other guys.

"No, I think I'll be okay. What's next?" I ask him.

"Agencies at the SpacePort have been notified; it's a green light for the arrivals. In fact, they will be passing by in about thirty seconds. We will appear to be just another checkpoint for the convoy on the way to the airfield."

"What about the bodies? Jake and the terrorist?"

"A recovery unit that handles crime scenes will be here shortly to retrieve them. We'll have to keep them out of sight for a while; don't want the big shots getting upset by seeing a dead body. Wouldn't want to mess up the in-flight meal."

"I'm so sorry about Jake; I know he was your friend."

"Yes, he was; we went back a long way. But we both knew the risks of the job. He'll be missed, just like Angie."

We all sit quietly for a few minutes, reflecting on those we lost. All three of us are in pain, both physically and emotionally.

I finally find a first-aid kit in one of the bags.

We divvy up parts and begin to treat our wounds.

As Chad predicted, a convoy of six or so black limos passes by. Minutes behind them, the crime scene unit arrives to retrieve the bodies. A wrecker pulls up, and the gear inside the overturned SUV is transferred to the crime scene vehicle.

Hard to believe it's finally over. Once we have gathered everything together, the desert sand blows lightly, covering up any evidence of our being there.

"Load up!" Chad says one last time.

EPILOGUE

"What was that noise?" Eric asks me. "Why'd we stop?"

"It's nothing, just a trick of the trade to ensure that the kingpin is set in the hitch," I tell him. "Something I learned from Angie." I smile, thinking back to the days when I was first introduced to living in an RV. "Did you remember to close and latch all the doors? Don't want them banging around while we're driving."

"Yes, Ashlee; you taught me well." He's smiling too.

We're leaving Post RV Park, where I've been living since my last job ended. I drove the RV here myself, stopping at parks between New Mexico and Post, staying a day or so at each location. It was a great opportunity to recover from my injuries and settle my mind.

Eric managed to get a position with USDA that lets him travel to different areas in the Southwest. We're heading to Colorado for his first assignment.

I still miss my dogs. We're thinking about a puppy, but we'll wait until we get used to living together in the RV before we add another member to our adventure.

I drive slowly through the park. As we approach the exit, I see Jim walk out of the office.

"Looks like you're a pro at drivin' that rig now," he says with a grin.

"Yep, had a lot of practice lately. Thanks for all you help, Jim. Maybe we'll see you again sometime."

He winks. "I'd almost count on it," he tells me.